...SON, a former teacher, has published ...ty novels, twenty of which feature her series ...tive Inspector Jack Finch and his sergeant, Tom ...yce. She has also written six pastiche collections of ...herlock Holmes short stories. Her books have been translated into many languages. June Thomson lives in St Albans, Hertfordshire.

By June Thomson

The Secret Archives
of Sherlock Holmes

JUNE THOMSON

Allison & Busby Limited
12 Fitzroy Mews
London W1T 6DW
www.allisonandbusby.com

First published in Great Britain by Allison & Busby in 2012.
This paperback edition published by Allison & Busby in 2013.

A CIP catalogue record for this book is available from
the British Library.

10 9 8 7 6 5 4 3 2 1

ISBN 978-0-7490-1243-4

Typeset in 11/16 pt Sabon
by Allison & Busby Ltd.

The paper used for this Allison & Busby publication
has been produced from trees that have been legally sourced
from well-managed and credibly certified forests.

Printed and bound by
CPI Group (UK) Ltd, Croydon, CR0 4YY

To Guy Marriott,
President of the Sherlock Holmes Society of London,
with grateful thanks.

And also to 'Suzy',
the laptop expert who saved my sanity
on many occasions.

CONTENTS

FOREWORD

by
Aubrey B. Watson LDS, FDS, D. Orth.

Although some of you may already know how the collections of hitherto unpublished Sherlock Holmes stories came into the possession of myself and my late uncle, for those of you who are unfamiliar with the details, I will recount them as briefly as possible.

My late uncle, Dr John F. Watson, was a Doctor of Philosophy at All Saints' College, Oxford. Because of the similarity of his name to that of Dr John H. Watson, Sherlock Holmes' friend and chronicler, my late uncle made a study of his near-namesake's life and background and consequently became an authority on the subject. It was through this that a certain Miss Adeline McWhirter, an elderly spinster, approached my late uncle with a proposal which she thought might be of interest to him.

It seemed she was related to Mr Holmes' Dr Watson on the maternal side of the family and, on Dr Watson's death, had inherited his tin despatch box containing manuscript accounts of cases that he and Mr Holmes had investigated but which for various reasons had never been published. Because she found herself in straitened circumstances, she offered to sell the box and its contents which had been deposited by Dr John H. Watson at his bank, Cox & Co, at Charing Cross.

Because she seemed honest and respectable, my late uncle agreed and bought the box and its contents for an undisclosed but apparently large sum of money. However, in view of the international situation – it was September 1939 and Britain had not long before declared war on Germany – he decided to place them in his own bank in London. Before doing so, he copied out the papers in case something happened to the originals.

Unfortunately, something did happen.

In 1942, at the height of the Blitz, the bank suffered a direct hit and, although the box was retrieved from the rubble, its contents were reduced to a mass of indecipherable charred paper. Even the original wording painted on the lid – 'John H. Watson, MD Late Indian Army' – was burnt beyond recognition.

Although my late uncle still possessed his own copies of the Watson manuscripts, he had nothing to prove the existence of the originals, nor could he trace Miss Adeline

McWhirter who had moved out of the residential hotel in South Kensington where she had been living, leaving no forwarding address.

Lacking, therefore, any proof of the authenticity of the Watson archives and anxious to protect his own reputation as a scholar, my late uncle decided not to publish his copies of them and, on his death on 2nd June 1982, he left them to me in his will. As there was no mention of the despatch box or its charred contents, I can only assume that the staff at the Eventide Nursing Home in Carshalton where he died threw them away as so much rubbish.

I, too, hesitated over the question of whether or not to publish my late uncle's copies, but as I am an orthodontist and have no scholarly reputation to protect, I have decided to risk rousing the ire of serious Sherlockians and to place them before the public.

However, as I cannot vouch for the authenticity of these manuscripts, I can do nothing more than warn any readers by repeating the old adage: *Caveat emptor.*

THE CASE OF THE
CONK-SINGLETON FORGERY

It was about six years after my old friend Sherlock Holmes returned to London following his apparent death at the hands of Moriarty at the Reichenbach Falls[1] and my own return to our shared lodgings in Baker Street that I became associated with him in a curious case of forgery. It began prosaically enough with the arrival of a visiting card which the boy in

---

[1] The Reichenbach Falls is a series of waterfalls near Meiringen in Switzerland. It was where Sherlock Holmes met his arch-enemy, Professor Moriarty, for a final confrontation in May 1891. In the ensuing struggle, Holmes, who had learned *baritsu*, a Japanese form of self-defence, succeeded in throwing Moriarty off balance and in consequence he plunged to his death in the ravine below. Dr John F. Watson.

buttons[2] brought upstairs to our sitting-room and handed to Holmes who, having studied it with raised eyebrows, passed it to me.

It bore the name of Archibald Cassell followed by the words 'Art Dealer' and an address, the Argosy Gallery, Bond Street, London. Below this was a handwritten message which read: 'I apologise for arriving without an appointment, Mr Holmes, but I have a matter of some urgency about which I wish to consult you.'

'What do you think, Watson?' Holmes inquired. 'Should I agree to see this Archibald Cassell?'

'The decision is entirely yours, Holmes,' I replied, secretly pleased that he should consult me about the matter.

'Very well, then. As we are not overburdened with cases at the moment, I shall say "yes". Show Mr Cassell up, Billy,' Holmes instructed.

Moments later the client in question entered our sitting-room. He was a tall, silver-haired gentleman, distinguished-looking in impeccably cut morning clothes and wearing gold-rimmed eyeglasses. A small leather case under his arm suggested he was a businessman of

---

[2] Billy was the young pageboy who attended Holmes at Baker Street in *The Valley of Fear*. A similarly named pageboy also appeared in several much later accounts, 'The Problem of Thor Bridge' and 'The Adventure of the Mazarin Stone', and it is generally assumed that this is a different pageboy and that 'Billy' was a generic name. Dr John F. Watson.

some sort or another. There was, however, a harassed air about him which I judged to be out of character.

Having shaken hands with both of us and seated himself at Holmes' invitation, he remained silent for a long moment before bursting out, 'In all my years in business, I have never encountered a similar situation, Mr Holmes! I confess I am baffled by it! That is why I have come to seek your advice in the matter.'

'Then pray do so, sir,' Holmes replied coolly. 'I suggest you begin at the beginning.'

'Of course, Mr Holmes,' Mr Cassell replied, making a visible effort to pull himself together. 'As my calling card indicates, I am an art dealer and in my time many hundreds of paintings have passed through my hands, some of enormous value, but until this morning I have never been presented with such a dilemma. It is without precedence and, quite frankly, sir, I am at a loss to know how to deal with it.

'A lady arrived at my gallery yesterday morning who introduced herself as Mrs Elvira Greenstock, the widow of Horatio Greenstock who died two months ago, leaving all his property to her. Among her late husband's effects were a number of oil paintings. It appeared Mr Greenstock was an art dealer in a small way; it must have been a very small way, for I have never heard of him, although I pride myself on knowing most of the dealers and collectors in the world of art. It was one of the paintings from this collection which Mrs Greenstock wished me to evaluate. It is not unusual for members of the public to request such a service, for which, incidentally, I charge a small fee. What they have to show me is generally not of any artistic merit and is worth nothing more than a few shillings. However, I tolerate such clients because there is always the rare possibility that what they have brought may be an unknown or lost work of one of the great masters. It has been known to happen.

'I should perhaps at this point describe Mrs Greenstock to you because her appearance has as much to do with my decision to consult you as the painting she showed me.'

He paused as if gathering together his recollections of his client, a bemused expression on his face as if he were finding it difficult to recall the lady in any detail, a hesitation which was explained by his next remark.

'Forgive me, Mr Holmes, but there is very little I can tell you about her except to say that her appearance was most bizarre. She was tall, with an educated voice, but as she was dressed entirely in widow's weeds, including a long, thick, black veil, I cannot give you any description of her features, not even the colour of her hair or eyes. She was carrying a small leather valise and from it took a painting which she laid before me on my desk and asked me to evaluate.'

As he was speaking, Mr Cassell opened his own portfolio which he had placed at his feet and took from it a canvas which he held up before us so that both of us could see it.

It was an oil painting not much more than eight inches by six depicting a rural scene of trees and hedgerows, richly foliated, as well as meadows and fields of corn stretching back to the horizon, where the spire of a church was just visible. Above was a sky full of sunlit clouds moving towards the right-hand side of the canvas as if propelled by a light breeze.

I confess I am not an art expert and, given the choice, prefer portraits to landscape paintings. Nevertheless, I thought the picture captured most charmingly the beauty of the English countryside as it must have looked at the beginning of the century. I was therefore much taken aback when Mr Cassell remarked in a dismissive tone of voice, 'The lady said it was a Constable[3] but it is, of course, a forgery.'

'Of course,' Holmes murmured in agreement. 'The clouds alone suggest it is not authentic, although the artist is competent.'

'Oh, indeed!' Mr Cassell concurred. 'Whoever painted it is no amateur and might have convinced someone of less experience than myself that it is genuine. It lacks that fluid movement in the clouds that Constable was

---

[3] John Constable (1776–1837). An English landscape painter, some of whose paintings, e.g. *The Haywain*, are world-famous. Born in Suffolk, he is considered, along with Turner, to be one of the greatest painters of the English countryside. Dr John F. Watson.

able to convey by a few brushstrokes, as well as the play of light across the leaves and grass.'

'Given those criticisms,' Holmes remarked, sitting back in his chair and bringing his fingertips together, 'I am at a loss to understand, Mr Cassell, what is the dilemma you referred to. As the painting is a forgery, all you need do is send for the lady and tell her the truth.'

'I agree with you entirely,' his client replied, 'and under normal circumstances I would have acted accordingly. Unfortunately, there are two drawbacks to such a suggestion. In the first place, I cannot send for the lady as I have no address for her. She refused to give me one. She would only arrange to call at my gallery again in a week's time when I shall, of course, act exactly as you suggested.'

As he was speaking, Mr Cassell had laid the little painting face downwards on the table and Holmes glanced across at it as if idly.

I have known Holmes for many years and, although I do not claim to be acquainted with every aspect of his character, I pride myself on being sufficiently familiar with him to recognise signs of excitement on his part, however much he might try to disguise them. They are not glaringly obvious. Indeed, most people would not notice them at all. But on this occasion, a slight lifting of his right eyebrow and a general tightening of the muscles in his shoulders told me that something about the back of the picture had roused his interest.

Aware of this, I looked at it again more closely, trying to gauge what it was that had engaged his attention. But there was nothing that I could see, apart from a piece of quite ordinary brown paper which had been pasted across the edges of the frame, presumably to keep out the dust.

Holmes was saying, 'You spoke of two drawbacks, Mr Cassell. The first was the lack of any address for Mrs Greenstock. That, my dear sir, can be easily rectified, if you will allow me to make some simple inquiries. What was the second drawback?'

Mr Cassell looked a little abashed by the question. Giving a deprecatory wave of his hand, he replied, 'I am almost ashamed to admit it, for it is nothing more than sheer curiosity on my part. Who is this lady who calls herself Mrs Greenstock? As I have already explained to you, she is not to my knowledge the widow of any art collector that I have heard of. And why should she attire herself in a thick black veil, which she never raised once during my interview with her, unless she feared I might recognise her?'

'Excellent, sir!' my old friend exclaimed. 'An admirable piece of deduction on your part!'

His client seemed only partly mollified by this commendation.

'That may be so, Mr Holmes. However, that still fails to answer the question as to her identity. Are you prepared to look into the matter? To be frank, I am uneasy about the whole situation. I shall, of course, not buy the painting from her. But supposing she manages to persuade another dealer or a collector less experienced than myself to do so? I realise the old warning *caveat emptor* should apply to all business transactions, but there is the reputation of the art world to consider. I feel I cannot allow someone whom I know is a forger to pass off her work, or if not hers then someone else's, as a genuine old master. Apart from the aesthetic consideration, it would be condoning a criminal act.'

'I see your point,' Holmes replied suavely. 'To set your mind at rest, I will certainly look into the matter. You said the lady will call again at your gallery in a fortnight's time?'

'That was the arrangement.'

'At what time?'

'At eleven o'clock.'

'Then, with your permission, Dr Watson and I will also present ourselves at your gallery on the same day but a little earlier, at a quarter to the hour. In the meantime, may I keep the painting?'

Mr Cassell seemed a little taken aback by this request but acquiesced with a bow and, having shaken hands with both of us, took his leave.

As soon as he had gone, Holmes gave a delighted chuckle.

'To work, Watson!' he cried.

'On what, Holmes?'

'On the painting, of course! But before I make a start on that, I shall look into the curious matter of the lady's identity. Be a good fellow and run downstairs and ask Billy to bring up a bowl of warm water, a towel, a small sponge and some clean white linen rag while I find the entry I need in my encyclopaedia of reference.'[4]

He was taking the volume in question from his bookshelves in the chimney alcove as I left the room, surprised by his instructions. To what use was he proposing to put the articles he had listed?

I did not find the answer to this question immediately, for when I returned to the room, followed by Billy carrying the requested items, Holmes was standing by the fireplace, his encyclopaedia in his hands, ready to read out the particulars of the entry he had found as soon as the pageboy had left the room.

'Now, Watson,' said he, 'our client suggested the lady in question, Mrs Greenstock, failed to raise her veil in case he should recognise her features. But if, as he himself said, he knew no art collector of that name, it is highly unlikely he has ever met her. It therefore occurred to me that the lady wished to cover up some disfigurement which she preferred not to display in public.

---

[4] Among his library books in the Baker Street lodgings, Sherlock Holmes had an encyclopaedia that he had compiled himself and that contained newspaper cuttings and other sources of material that he considered of particular interest. There are several references to this volume in the canon. Dr John F. Watson.

'The thought recalled to mind a newspaper report of a tragic accident which happened four years ago in which a woman suffered dreadful injuries and which I noted with particular attention because it occurred near Paddington station, where you had your first private practice as a doctor. The name of the lady was also very unusual; in fact, I had never come across it before. I therefore cut out the report from the *Daily News* and pasted it into my encyclopaedia. Here, Watson, you may read it for yourself,' he concluded, handing me the volume of reference open at the relevant page. It was a report under a headline 'TERRIBLE ACCIDENT IN PADDINGTON' and read: 'A lady pedestrian, Mrs Lavinia Conk-Singleton, of Coombe Street, Bayswater, was knocked down and badly injured yesterday afternoon by a runaway hansom cab in Praed Street, Paddington.

'The lady, widow of Mr Horace Conk-Singleton, a retired banker and amateur art collector, suffered severe cuts and bruises to her face. She was taken to the nearby hospital, St Mary's, for treatment. The cab driver, Mr George Packer of Bethnal Green, who was rendered unconscious, was also treated at St Mary's.'

'So her husband *was* an art collector!' I exclaimed.

'Whom our client may have known had she given him her real name. He might even have recognised her, although I doubt that. She wore that thick veil, I believe, to hide her face, which is almost certainly still scarred from her injuries. We might be able to prove

22

that supposition when we meet her in a week's time. Now Watson, we must proceed with the next step in our inquiry. If you would be so kind as to spread the towel over the table, I shall start my investigation of the painting.'

As requested, I spread out the towel and placed the bowl of warm water, the sponge and the clean linen beside it, to which Holmes added a scalpel from his workbench. I assumed his intention was to wipe over the surface of the painting to remove any dirt. To my surprise, however, he laid the picture face down, exposing the back of it and, dipping the sponge into the water, began to dab it along the edges of the brown paper which had been pasted over the frame.

'Holmes!' I expostulated. 'Should you be doing that? I know the picture is a forgery but, even so, it belongs to Mrs Conk-Singleton.'

'Indeed it does,' Holmes replied. 'But I shall not harm the painting itself. I merely want to remove the brown paper which someone, presumably Mrs Conk-Singleton, has recently stuck across the back of it.'

'Recently?'

'In the past few weeks, I believe, judging by its almost pristine condition. But why should she wish to cover up the back of the canvas?'

As he was speaking, he continued to dampen the paper until it was loose enough for him to run the scalpel under the edges and lift the whole sheet away, revealing what lay behind it.

It was another painting, also in oils, but so darkened by dirt and old varnish that it was difficult to make out its subject matter. It seemed to be an interior, for on the left-hand side I could vaguely discern a window through which discoloured sunlight was falling on two figures standing in the middle of the canvas. They were female, for I could just make out their dresses, one a muddy green, the other a dirty blue.

Holmes, who had gone over to his bench, returned with his magnifying glass and, taking the picture over to the window, began examining it more closely under the lens in the full daylight. When he had finished his scrutiny, he handed me the glass so that I could see the effect for myself. It was still difficult to see the painting clearly and, when I remarked on this, Holmes acted in what was to me at first a thoroughly irresponsible, not to say uncouth, manner. Picking up a piece of the white linen rag, he put it to his lips and, having wetted it with his saliva, wiped it across a section of the painting.

'Holmes!' I began, but before I could make any further protest, he had repeated this unseemly action before passing the picture to me.

'Now look, Watson!' he urged.

I looked and was amazed. The portion of the canvas he had treated in this displeasing manner had suddenly and unexpectedly cleared, much as a dirty window will become transparent when it is wiped over with a damp cloth, the discoloration vanishing to be replaced by a clear image of one of the figures which occupied the centre of the painting. It was that of a young woman with a fair complexion, her blonde hair braided on top of her head into an elaborate coronet. For a few seconds she smiled at me and then, as the saliva dried, the image faded and all I could see was a vague oval shape, obscured once again by the brown patina of dirt and old varnish.

Holmes burst out laughing.

'My dear Watson!' cried he. 'If only you could see your face! It is a picture itself of bewilderment and disbelief.'

'It is like a mirage, Holmes!' I replied. 'One second the picture is there; the next it has vanished. What causes it?'

'It is quite simple. When saliva, which is incidentally a mild solvent, is applied to old varnish which has become opaque because of the layers of dirt, it acts as a temporary lens through which one can see the underlying paint.

'However, once it has dried, the effect is lost and all that is left is a blurred smear. It is an old trick used by art dealers when confronted by a dirty canvas. Would you like to try it for yourself, Watson?' he added, handing me the piece of rag. 'The spittle can soon be wiped away with a little clean water.'

Much as I, as a doctor, disapproved of the unhygienic nature of Holmes' method, I was fascinated by its effects and, choosing the face of the second figure which stood slightly to the rear of the first, I applied the cloth to my mouth and, having liberally moistened it, I dabbed it on to that section of the canvas. Once again, the miracle happened. The dirt disappeared and I caught a glimpse of a fresh-faced young woman, rather solemn of expression, wearing a servant's white cap on top of her dark hair.

Such was my excitement that I might have gone on and treated the whole canvas had not Holmes, laughing at my enthusiasm, taken the cloth from my hand and, using the sponge with which he had removed the brown paper backing, wiped over the two areas where we had cleaned the paint.

'Enough is enough, my dear fellow!' he chided humorously. 'We must now finish our examination of the frame itself. I believe it will yield more clues.'

'What clues?' I asked. I could see nothing to suggest it held anything of interest. The frame was made of wood and, unlike the front of it which was gilded and heavily carved, it was undecorated apart from some traces of gold here and there along the edges where the gilding had spread on to the underside.

'Use this,' Holmes suggested, handing me the magnifying glass, but, even with its assistance, I could see nothing which by even the greatest stretch of the imagination could be called a clue, only the rough grain of the wood.

Holmes leaned over my shoulder and, jabbing a long finger, exclaimed impatiently, 'Look here, my dear fellow! And here! And here!'

What he was pointing to were small nails driven into the inner edge of the frame at an angle to hold the canvas in position.

'You mean the nails, Holmes?' I asked.

'Partly, Watson. You are almost there. What else do you see beside them?'

'Ah!' I cried, noticing for the first time that the wood close to some of them was freshly bruised, exposing a cleaner inner surface. 'Someone has damaged the wood, either when the nails were removed or hammered back into place.'

'Suggesting?' he prompted me.

'That whoever forged the Constable first removed the nails and took out the original canvas so that the reverse side was uppermost and then tacked it back into position.'

'And?'

'Well, really, Holmes!' I protested, beginning to find the game a little irksome. 'What more is there to say?'

'Only that whoever replaced the nails was not a skilled picture framer. Mrs Conk-Singleton, for example?'

'Yes, of course,' I agreed, a little disappointed at so simple an explanation. 'Is that all?'

'Not quite,' he said, laughing. 'There is one more clue. If you look at the underside of the upper part of the frame, you will see a small blob of dried glue with a fragment of paper adhering to it.'

And indeed there was. For as soon as I reapplied the lens to the area he suggested, I immediately saw a tiny brown globule, hard and shiny like crystallised syrup, in which an even smaller speck of white material was embedded.

I confess I could not grasp its significance and refrained from asking Holmes, who was bustling into his coat.

'You are going out?' I asked. 'Where to?'

'To Mr Cassell's gallery, of course. Hurry up, Watson, and get ready.'

'Oh, Holmes!' I cried, deeply disappointed. 'I have promised Thurston that I would meet him at the club at noon for luncheon and a game of billiards.[5] It is far too late now to send him a telegram cancelling the arrangements.'

Holmes clapped me on the shoulder.

'Never mind, my dear fellow! The inquiry is by no means finished. You shall join it again, I promise you, at some later stage. And I shall, of course, inform you of any developments which take place this morning.'

Holmes was as good as his word and, when later I returned to our lodgings, I found him already there, his business with Mr Cassell having been concluded.

And what he had to tell me was very interesting. On hearing the name Conk-Singleton, Mr Cassell had become quite excited and had told Holmes all

---

[5] Doctor Watson played billiards with Thurston at their club. Nothing else is known about him, not even his Christian name. *Vide*: 'The Adventure of the Dancing Men'. Dr John F. Watson.

he knew about that gentleman, who had something of a reputation in the art-dealing world. He was a retired banker with private but limited means who, having had an early success in buying a valuable but unrecognised painting for a small sum, had persuaded himself that he was an expert and had haunted the auctions bidding for unlikely paintings in the hope that he could repeat his good fortune and sell them on for a huge profit. Some of the dealers, regarding it as a game, had deliberately bid against him, forcing up the value before withdrawing and leaving him to pay an inflated price for a worthless canvas which he could never hope to profit by. In the end, he died a bankrupt.

As for Mrs Conk-Singleton, Mr Cassell knew a little of her also. Much younger than her husband, she was a talented amateur artist who had had some professional training and, when money became short, had supplemented the family income by selling her work, usually landscapes, for small sums of money. After her accident, which had left her dreadfully disfigured, she had become a recluse, rarely setting foot outside her house in Bayswater.

'And what about the painting?' I asked eagerly.

'Ah, that!' Holmes replied with a twinkle. 'Mr Cassell will have it cleaned by a professional with Mrs Conk-Singleton's permission and will also inquire of her about a possible label which was once stuck on the back of the frame, leaving behind that tiny blob of dried glue. In the meantime, the whole affair is in the lap of the gods.'

'So it could be an old master?' I cried.

'Oh, Watson, Watson! One of your endearing qualities is your habitual optimism, a trait you share with the late Mr Conk-Singleton – and look what happened to him! The painting is probably by an amateur and therefore worth very little. We must wait upon events.'

It was not until a fortnight later that these events reached their climax when Holmes received a telegram from Mr Cassell which read: 'You are both invited to take tea tomorrow afternoon with Mrs Conk-Singleton at four o'clock in my gallery.'

The following day we presented ourselves on the hour and were admitted by Mr Cassell, the premises being closed as it was a Sunday, and were conducted through the gallery itself, hung with paintings, into our host's private office. Holmes was in high spirits and I, too, was full of eager curiosity to meet Mrs Conk-Singleton and to see the painting cleaned and restored.

The office seemed a suitable setting for the dénouement for, like the gallery, its walls were lined with paintings, and furthermore it was furnished with rosewood cabinets on which stood exquisite *objets d'art* in marble and porcelain. It also contained for the occasion a small table laid with a lace cloth and a silver tea service, including a cake stand on which was set out a tempting display of little iced cakes. Four chairs had been drawn up to the table and Mrs Conk-Singleton sat on the one facing the doorway.

She was tall and thin and dressed entirely in black, as Mr Cassell had described her, including the thick black veil which covered her face.

Her sombre attire and her air of sadness cast a melancholy mood over the colour and glitter of the gilt-framed pictures and the beauty of the artefacts which surrounded her, but her voice, when Mr Cassell introduced Holmes and myself, had a gentle sweetness about it which dispelled much of that gloom.

The painting, the reason for our invitation to the gallery that afternoon, was standing to the right of the table, displayed on an easel but covered with a black silk cloth so that, like Mrs Conk-Singleton's features, it was completely hidden from view. I saw Holmes glance towards it from time to time and I myself snatched several sideways glimpses of it, but it was not until tea was finished and Mr Cassell had rearranged the chairs in a semicircle in front of it that he allowed us to see it.

It was clear that our host was hugely enjoying the situation for, when the moment came, he bowed towards us and, showing an unexpected theatrical side to his nature, announced like a magician about to perform his most amazing and difficult trick, 'Madame! Messieurs! The painting!'

And with that, as if to a roll of drums, he whisked away the cloth and the painting was revealed.

What we saw was indeed like a magic transformation, for the picture we found ourselves gazing at was utterly changed from the original dirty brown canvas into an object of such beauty that I felt some sleight of hand must be responsible for it.

It was the interior of a lady's chamber, lit by a brilliant shaft of sunlight which poured in through a window on the left. In its radiance, the indistinct forms of the two women were transfigured, the first into a lady with corn-coloured hair, richly dressed in a gown of pale-green silk, decorated with lace and ruffles. Standing immediately behind her in the act of closing the clasp of a pearl necklace round the lady's throat stood her maid, more modestly attired in a white cap with an apron over a plain blue gown. She was young and pretty, not long up from the country, I imagined, for she wore an anxious, intent expression as she adjusted the clasp as if she were unused to carrying out such a delicate and intimate task.

Against the rear wall stood a table covered with a cloth patterned with blue and green diamonds, a design echoed in the tiled floor, only this time in black and white. A pair of embroidered gloves lay on the table together with a glass vase containing three pink roses. The light and colour were dazzling and so caught up was I in the vivid details of the room and its inhabitants that I heard Mr Cassell's voice as if in a dream.

'A genuine old master!' he was declaring. 'In fact,

a Jan Vermeer, the seventeenth-century Dutch painter who specialised in such interiors.[6] Look at the light falling on the silk of the young lady's skirt! And the roses! They are superb! It is also an unusual subject matter. Vermeer generally included only one lady in his paintings, not two. An expert on his work, a Mr Claude van Heerden at the National Gallery, no less, has examined it and declared it authentic, a claim borne out by its provenance.'

'Provenance?' I inquired.

'Its previous history – in this case the label which Mrs Conk-Singleton found on the back of the frame when she removed the canvas, the presence of which you, Mr Holmes, deduced from the small blob of glue still adhering to the frame. Fortunately, Mrs Conk-Singleton kept the label.'

Mr Cassell bowed to Holmes and the lady, acknowledging the part they had played.

'The label,' he continued, 'was dated 1798 and bore the name Bardwell and the number 275. With a little research, I was able to establish that in 1797 Lord Bardwell died at the great age of ninety-two, leaving a houseful of furniture, paintings and other works of art. His only heir was a great-nephew who, anxious

---

[6] Jan Vermeer (1632–75). A Dutch painter, born in Delft, he was famous for his paintings of household interiors, containing a single female occupant, often occupied with some intimate or domestic task, e.g. *Young Woman Reading a Letter at an Open Window*. Dr John F. Watson.

to benefit by his death as quickly as possible, sold the house and auctioned off its contents. Apparently, nobody recognised the value of the little canvas which, according to the inventories I was also able to consult, had been in the family from at least the end of the seventeenth century. However, by the time Lord Bardwell died, it was probably already discoloured with dirt and therefore when it was catalogued as Lot 275, it was described merely as "An interior; Dutch School". Later it found its way into another auction, still unrecognised for what it was, and was bought by Mr Conk-Singleton.

'It was an extremely fortunate purchase,' Mr Cassell continued, bowing again towards the lady, 'for the painting is now worth a considerable sum of money.'

Mrs Conk-Singleton acknowledged the statement and the bow with an inclination of her veiled head. Speaking in a low, sweet voice, trembling a little with emotion, she replied, 'I do not have the words to express my gratitude to all of you gentlemen for the work you have done in helping to discover the true identity of the painting. I leave the sale of the Vermeer in your hands, Mr Cassell, and offer my heartfelt thanks to all of you.'

She was clearly overcome with emotion and left soon afterwards, Mr Cassell escorting her to the door and summoning a four-wheeler to take her home.

He returned to the office smiling broadly and rubbing his hands together with delight.

'What a truly wonderful outcome!' he declared. 'Mrs Conk-Singleton is indeed a very fortunate lady. She will be financially secure for the rest of her life and there will be no further need for her to paint fake Constables on the back of old masters to save the cost of a new canvas!'

'So it was a happy ending after all, Holmes,' I could not help remarking later as we made our way back to Baker Street in a hansom.

Holmes threw back his head and laughed heartily.

'Your optimism is indeed vindicated, my dear fellow,' he replied, adding with a sly sideways glance at me, 'At least on this occasion.'

THE CASE OF THE
STRAY CHICKEN

It was eight o'clock on a fine June morning and Holmes and I were seated at the breakfast table, he reading some correspondence which the postman had just delivered, I scanning in a desultory manner the pages of the *Daily News* and thinking rather wistfully how pleasant it would be to spend the day somewhere on the coast away from the heat and noise of London, when Holmes suddenly remarked, 'What would you say to a little outing to the seaside, my dear fellow? To Brighton, for example?'

'How extraordinary, Holmes!' I exclaimed. 'The same idea for a day's outing occurred to me only a moment ago. You must have read my mind.'

'Not in this instance, my dear fellow, although I must confess at times your face so clearly expresses what is going on inside your head that it resembles a page in a book. So I might have divined your thoughts from the way you glanced towards the window and gave that pensive little sigh. In this case, however, it was this letter which prompted my remark. It is from a Miss Edith Pilkington, a middle-aged lady to judge from her handwriting, who is staying at the Regal Hotel in Brighton and who writes: "Dear Mr Holmes, I trust you will forgive my addressing you without a formal introduction but I would very much appreciate your advice over a matter which is causing me considerable concern. I am companion to a lady, a Mrs Huxtable, who has recently become acquainted with a certain medical gentleman, Dr Joseph Wilberforce, and his sister Miss Adelaide Wilberforce, who are also guests at the Regal Hotel. Although I have no proof that they are untrustworthy, I have nevertheless become uneasy about their relationship with Mrs Huxtable, who is a widow and has no immediate family to take an interest in her.

'"Because Mrs Huxtable is in poor health and relies on my companionship, it would be very difficult for me to come to London to consult you and, although I am aware I am imposing heavily on your generosity, I wondered if it might be possible to meet you in Brighton one afternoon between two o'clock and three o'clock when Mrs Huxtable has her afternoon rest to discuss the matter with you?

'"I remain, sir, Yours etc. Edith Pilkington."'

'Well, Watson, what do you make of that?' Holmes continued, folding up the letter and returning it to its envelope.

'Make of it, Holmes? I am not sure I make anything of it. It sounds a straightforward enough appeal, although in my opinion she is expecting quite a lot of both your generosity and your time.'

'No, no, my dear fellow. You do not understand,' Holmes broke in impatiently. 'Neither my time nor my beneficence have anything to do with it. It is the situation which is important. Think back a few years. Do you recall a remark I once made regarding foxes and stray chickens?'

'Really, Holmes!' I began to protest but he overrode me.

'Concerning an exceptionally astute and dangerous man?'

As I remained silent, cudgelling my brains to call up any incident from the past which might fit this description, Holmes continued, 'Oh, come, Watson! Your memory deteriorates year by year. You should exercise it as one would exercise any part of one's physical body. Think of your mind as a set of drawers in which you store any information which could be useful to your requirements. Then, when you have need for any of it, you simply open that particular drawer and – hey presto! – the facts are lying there ready to be used.'

He paused for a moment before continuing, 'I see

from your expression that all your drawers are not only closed but securely locked as well. Allow me, then, to provide you with a key to at least one of them. Does the name "Holy Peters" free any recollections for you?'

'Oh, of course, Holmes!' I exclaimed, light suddenly dawning. 'The case of Lady Frances Carfax and that unspeakable clergyman and his wife who attempted to murder her in order to steal her jewels. Now what on earth was his real name?'[1]

Holmes began to chuckle.

'I shall not extend this memory game any further, my dear fellow. It could go on all morning. So let me bring it to a halt by telling you that his name, at least at the time of the Carfax inquiry, was the Rev. Dr Schlessinger and he claimed to be a missionary from South America, whereas he was, in fact, an Australian by birth and one of the most unscrupulous rogues that country has ever produced. His so-called wife, although I doubt if their relationship was ever legally sanctioned, was English and her real name was Annie Fraser. They made their living by preying on lonely spinsters or widows, stripping them of any financial assets they might possess – money, jewels, bonds – anything that could be turned

---

[1] In 'The Disappearance of Lady Frances Carfax', an Australian confidence trickster who works under the alias of Dr Schlessinger, and his so-called wife, rob Lady Frances Carfax of her jewellery and, having rendered her unconscious with chloroform, are about to bury her alive, hidden in a coffin under the body of an elderly woman, when Sherlock Holmes and Dr Watson rescue her at the last moment. Dr John F. Watson.

into ready cash. And once their victim had been bled dry, they had no compunction about dispensing with her as well, either by abandoning her in some out-of-the-way foreign *pension* or disposing of her literally, as they attempted to do in the case of Lady Frances Carfax.

'I believe at the time I described such women as "stray chickens in a world of foxes", an apt simile and one that I am convinced can be applied with equal validity to Dr Wilberforce and his sister, who my intuition tells me are none other than the Rev. Dr Schlessinger and his wife reincarnated in Brighton.'

'Then we must act at once, Holmes!' I declared, remembering with horror the fate that almost befell Lady Frances Carfax[2] who, had not Holmes intervened at the last moment, would have been buried alive.

'My thought exactly,' Holmes agreed, getting up from the table and fetching his coat and stick. 'I propose sending a telegram this very minute.'

'To Inspector Lestrade?'

'Not yet, Watson. First we must begin by making sure of our ground. At the moment, we have nothing

---

[2] Lady Frances Carfax disappeared from her hotel in Lausanne and was reported missing by her former governess, who asked Sherlock Holmes to find her. He traced her to London and saved her life by foiling Holy Peters and his female accomplice who, having robbed her of all her valuables, contrived to have her buried alive. At the end of this case, Sherlock Holmes says to Dr Watson that if they escape justice he 'expects to hear of some brilliant incidents in their future career.' *Vide*: 'The Disappearance of Lady Frances Carfax'. Dr John F. Watson.

but supposition. We need facts first and then a strategy to go with them.'

Before I could offer to accompany him, he strode purposefully from the room. Seconds later, I heard the street door slam shut behind him.

He returned within the hour looking jubilant.

'The first hurdle has been crossed,' he announced. 'As the mountain cannot come to Mahomet, Mahomet shall go to the mountain. I have sent a telegram to Miss Pilkington at the Regal Hotel, arranging to meet her in Brighton this afternoon.'

'At the hotel?'

'No, no, my dear fellow! That would be folly indeed. If you recall, we met Holy Peters face to face at his lodgings in Poultney Square during the Carfax inquiry. He would recognise us at once. I have suggested to Miss Pilkington that she leaves the Regal on the dot of a quarter past two, ostentatiously carrying something in her right hand so that we may identify her, and proceeds to some suitable venue, where we shall meet to discuss the situation. That is the first step. If I am convinced that Dr Wilberforce is indeed Holy Peters, then we can take the second step, which is to book ourselves rooms in the same hotel.'

As I was about to protest at this suggestion, Holmes smiled and held up his hand.

'Rest assured, Watson, that if we do so, Holy Peters will not recognise us for the simple reason that we shall be disguised. Now, be a good fellow and pass me the

Bradshaw[3] and I shall look up the next suitable train to Brighton.'

It was with considerable anticipation that I set off with Holmes later that morning for Victoria station. It was some time since I had accompanied him on a mission and I felt my pulses quicken at the prospect, more especially in this case, for I recalled with a shudder of revulsion that loathsome duo of Holy Peters and his female accomplice. Life with Holmes seldom lacked interest and I realised how much I owed him not only in friendship and companionship but also in that zest for adventure which he always aroused in me.

We arrived in Brighton with a good half an hour to spare before our assignment with Miss Pilkington, and spent the intervening time sauntering up and down the esplanade with the other holidaymakers, enjoying the sun, the sea breeze and the general air of pleasure and relaxation. The prospect was superb. To our left lay the glittering sea and the crowded beach, blossoming like a herbaceous border with gaily coloured parasols; to our right the long splendid vista of hotels and restaurants, their façades painted in pastel shades of vanilla and peach and the pale yellow of rich clotted cream, resembling

[3] *Bradshaw's Railway Guide* was published monthly and contained the times of departure and arrival of the trains of all the railway companies in the British Isles. It also contained information about hotels and places of interest to visit. Dr John F. Watson.

so many delicious pastries temptingly laid out for our delectation.

The Regal was one of the larger hotels, with a glassed-in veranda running the entire length of its ground floor in which we could glimpse some of its guests lounging on steamer chairs amid a miniature grove of potted palms. Waiters moved softly between them bearing trays of tall glasses which appeared at that distance to contain iced sherbet or cordials, or perhaps strawberry ice cream.

At the next corner, directly opposite the newly opened Palace Pier, Holmes consulted his watch and, with a sideways glance at me, remarked, 'It is time we kept our rendezvous with Miss Pilkington, Watson.'

We strolled back towards the Regal Hotel in a leisurely manner and were just drawing level with the steps leading up to its entrance when the doors were thrown open by a flunkey and a small figure dressed in grey emerged from the foyer and, pausing to glance up and down the seafront, set off purposefully along the esplanade in front of us. We were not more than ten yards away and we could see quite clearly the folded newspaper she was carrying in her right hand.

'Our correspondent, I think,' Holmes remarked as we fell in behind her, keeping our distance but making sure we did not lose sight of her among the crowds.

We continued in this manner for several minutes until, with a backward glance at us, she turned down a side street and entered a modest little tea shop with lace curtains at the window and a sign, 'The Copper Kettle', hanging above the door. Holmes and I followed her inside and joined her at a small round table tucked away in a discreet corner.

'Miss Pilkington, I assume?' Holmes remarked pleasantly. 'I am Sherlock Holmes. May I introduce my colleague, Dr Watson?'

We shook hands in turn with a short, plain, little woman in her fifties, I estimated, with grey hair drawn back into a neat, no-nonsense bun and whose crisp, forthright manner suggested an experienced governess or schoolmistress.

'Now,' Holmes continued as all three of us were seated and he had ordered tea and cakes from the elderly waitress, 'as I stated in my telegram to you, Miss Pilkington, I am most interested in the account you put before me in your letter, but before I take the matter any further, there are certain facts which I must first establish. You will, I trust, have no objection to that?'

'No, of course not,' Miss Pilkington replied. 'I am only too happy to assist you as it is the facts of the situation regarding my employer, Mrs Huxtable, that are causing me so much disquiet. I wish to know if these new acquaintances of hers, Dr Wilberforce and his sister, are to be trusted.'

'Ah, Dr Wilberforce!' Holmes murmured. 'Could you please give me a few details about him? His age, for example, and his appearance?'

'Well,' Miss Pilkington drew a deep breath before

beginning an account of such fluency that I suspected she had rehearsed it in her mind several times already, 'Dr Wilberforce is a well-built, middle-aged man, bald-headed and clean-shaven, with a rather florid complexion.'

'An excellent description!' Holmes remarked and I was amused to notice that she blushed a becoming pink at the compliment. When he wished to, my old friend had an enviable talent for setting his clients, especially women, at their ease.[4] 'Now were there any distinguishing features about him that you also noticed, such as a scar or a birthmark?'

As he spoke, he cast a quick sideways glance in my direction as if to draw my attention to a certain significance in his remark, but it meant nothing to me at the time and neither, apparently, to Miss Pilkington, who shook her head.

'Not that I noticed,' she replied.

Holmes seemed disappointed but continued smoothly as if her answer had had no effect on him at all, 'Very well, then. Let us move to another aspect of the matter, that of the doctor's personality. What was it about him that roused your suspicions?'

This time Miss Pilkington hesitated before speaking, which made me conclude that she had not given this side of the matter the same attention she had applied to his

---

[4] In 'The Adventure of the Dying Detective', Dr Watson remarks that Sherlock Holmes had 'a remarkable gentleness and courtesy in his dealings with women', even though 'he disliked and distrusted the sex'. Dr John F. Watson.

physical appearance and that probably she was relying on her intuition rather than any rational consideration. However, after a long moment she said in a rapid little burst of words, 'It sounds ridiculous, Mr Holmes, but he smiles too much.'

'Ah!' Holmes said softly as if he perfectly understood. '"A man may smile and smile and be a villain."'

Miss Pilkington's face lit up.

'Shakespeare, is it not, Mr Holmes?'

'Indeed it is; from *Hamlet*, to be precise, and refers to Claudius, one of the Bard's most cunning villains.'

'Together with Iago,' she riposted, before adding with greater certainty, 'I feel most strongly that he and his sister have wheedled their way into Mrs Huxtable's good books with dubious intentions.'

'Is that your belief? Then tell me about your employer, Mrs Huxtable,' Holmes continued, leaning back in his chair in a comfortable manner, inviting her confidence. 'How old is she, for instance? I deduce from your letter that she is in her late sixties. Am I correct?'

'Yes, you are.'

'And she is also a widow in poor health?'

'Her late husband was George W. Huxtable, a manufacturer of Sheffield tableware.[5] They had no

---

[5] Sheffield tableware. A method of coating a layer of sterling silver which was fused on to both sides of a copper base was developed *circa* 1770, having been accidentally discovered by Thomas Boulsover of the Sheffield Cutlers' Company in 1743. Dr John F. Watson

children and as far as I can ascertain there are no close relatives. He died about four years ago, leaving the house and a considerable fortune to his widow. After his death, she advertised for a companion to accompany her on foreign travel. As I have lived abroad for several years – tutoring the children at various embassies and overseas delegations – and wanted a change of occupation, I applied for the post and Mrs Huxtable engaged me. Since then we have been travelling on the Continent together, largely in the Mediterranean, staying at spas and seaside resorts. She suffers from a bronchial complaint, you see, and her doctor has advised a dry, warm climate. We returned to England this summer so that Mrs Huxtable could settle one or two financial arrangements with her bank and oversee the sale of the house in Sheffield, which she had been leasing to tenants. The transaction took longer than expected and, rather than remain in London during the height of summer, she decided to move to Brighton so that her agent and solicitor could visit her fairly easily by train.'

'Tell me about Dr Wilberforce and his sister. How did they become acquainted with Mrs Huxtable?'

'That is another aspect of the situation which causes me anxiety,' Miss Pilkington continued. 'They were already staying at the Regal when we arrived, and as soon as they met that first morning at breakfast, they seemed – now, how can I describe it? – drawn to her like bees to a honeypot. She is a lonely lady and was greatly flattered by their attentions, particularly those of Dr Wilberforce.'

'And the sister? What can you tell me about her?'

'Judging by her accent, she seems to be of English origin. His accent is difficult to define but is definitely not English.'

'South American?' Holmes suggested.

'Possibly.' Miss Pilkington sounded dubious.

'Or Australian?'

'That is more likely,' she agreed. 'But I would not wish to swear to it. I am not well acquainted with Australian speech. She is a tall lady with a strong personality, I would have said, although she is much overshadowed by her brother, if that is indeed the relationship between them.'

'You doubt it?' Holmes inquired sharply.

'I can see very little physical resemblance between the two of them but that is no real proof, is it? They could be half-brother and -sister or step-relations. But whatever the connection, Miss Wilberforce is closely involved with the doctor.' Reaching into her reticule, she produced a small oblong of white cardboard which she passed to Holmes. 'I found this in Mrs Huxtable's pocket yesterday evening when I hung up her clothes. She herself has not yet noticed it is missing but, knowing you were coming today, I thought it might be of interest to you.'

After looking at it carefully, Holmes passed it to me so that I, too, could read the words printed on it, which were: 'The Hollies, Randolph Road, Harrogate, Yorkshire. Private Spa Treatments for Rheumatism and other Related Illnesses, including Circulatory Complaints, Chest and Lung Ailments, Blood and Heart Disorders and General Infirmities. Remedies include Hydrotherapy, Mesmerism, Galvanism, Magnetism and Herbal Physic under the Strict Supervision of a Fully Qualified Physician and Matron.'

'A very comprehensive list indeed. It seems to cater for all the ailments that flesh is heir to,' Holmes commented wryly, passing the card back to Miss Pilkington, who replaced it in her reticule. 'I assume the matron is none other than Miss Wilberforce?'

'That was my assumption,' Miss Pilkington agreed, adding with an anxious air, 'Will you take the case, Mr Holmes? I am becoming more and more concerned about Mrs Huxtable's well-being. She spoke this morning about seeking treatment for her breathing difficulties and I fear she may turn to the Wilberforces for help. I should very much like to know more about them before she places herself in their care.'

'I understand your concern and shall indeed make inquiries on your behalf. By the way, is there any chance of our covertly observing Dr Wilberforce, and also his sister if that is possible? I should prefer a more public setting than the foyer or the dining room of the Regal Hotel, say, where they are more likely to be aware of the scrutiny of other people.'

'I believe I know the very place, Mr Holmes!' Miss Pilkington declared. 'Dr Wilberforce is in the habit of taking a stroll along the Palace Pier at about eleven o'clock each morning before returning to the hotel for luncheon. His sister sometimes accompanies him.'

'Excellent!' Holmes declared. 'Then that is one aspect of the case which is already settled. Are there any questions you would like to ask me before we take our leave?'

Miss Pilkington looked embarrassed.

'About your fees, Mr Holmes . . .' she began.

Holmes waved an airy hand.

'Do not concern yourself with those, Miss Pilkington. I am sure we can come to some amicable arrangement. Now, Dr Watson and I will return to London, where I shall immediately telegraph the manager of the Regal Hotel requesting a booking for two rooms for tomorrow evening. And I should warn you not to be surprised if we have changed our appearances as well as our names when you next see us. You see, we have met Dr Wilberforce and his sister before under other circumstances and it would ruin our plans if either of them should recognise us on this occasion. You must behave as if you have never seen us before.'

'What plans?' I inquired when, having paid the bill and taken leave of Miss Pilkington, we emerged from the Copper Kettle into the dazzling sunshine.

'To lay the Wilberforces by the heels, of course,' he replied crisply. 'There should be no difficulty in identifying Dr Wilberforce as Holy Peters. Judging by your lack of response, Watson, when I asked Miss Pilkington if Dr Wilberforce had any distinguishing marks or scars, you have clearly forgotten that Holy Peters was bitten on the ear in a bar-room brawl in Adelaide in '89, which has literally left a mark.[6] However, he may have tried to alter his appearance in certain ways, grown a beard or dyed his hair, for instance. He has evidently changed his lure . . .'

'Lure?' I asked, puzzled by his use of the word.

'My dear Watson, do try not to be obtuse. I am referring to his speciality in using religion to tempt his victims into his net. It was for this reason he earned the soubriquet of Holy Peters. Apparently he has abandoned this ploy for another equally attractive to lonely ladies of a certain age who like to talk about themselves, in particular their health. So we may assume his title of "Doctor" refers in this particular instance not to any assumed religious qualification but rather to a medical degree. However, no matter what changes he makes to his name or professional title,

---

[6] In 'The Disappearance of Lady Frances Carfax', Sherlock Holmes, who wishes to identify Dr Schlessinger as Holy Peters, the confidence trickster, asks the Englischer Hof hotel (where Schlessinger had stayed) for confirmation that the man he suspects has a 'physical peculiarity' of the left ear, caused when he was badly bitten in the bar-room brawl. His suspicion is confirmed by a telegram sent by the hotel. Dr John F. Watson.

he cannot change that one detail of his appearance, his damaged ear, which will identify him beyond any doubt. And as soon as this can be established, then he and his sister can pay the price they owe to justice, for it is time those unspeakable villains were behind bars for the attempted murder of Lady Frances Carfax.' He broke off to hail a passing cab. Having hustled me inside and given the driver the instruction to take us to the railway station, he added, 'I am sorry to cut short our little excursion to the seaside, my dear fellow, but, God willing, we shall return tomorrow to make free of the delights of sea, sun and sand which this charming town has to offer.'

We had hardly set foot in our Baker Street lodgings than Holmes dashed out again to send a telegram to the Regal Hotel requesting two rooms for the following night. Within the hour, having received confirmation of the booking, he set off once more, this time to call on Inspector Lestrade at Scotland Yard, and after that to buy any extra necessities we would need for our disguises when we returned to Brighton.

'Nothing too elaborate,' he decided. 'We do not want to draw unnecessary attention to ourselves. Something in the holiday mood, I think, but not excessively ebullient. Modesty shall be our maxim.'

It was hardly a suitable precept for Holmes, I thought with some amusement as I followed him up the attic stairs to the lumber rooms where he stored the appurtenances of his many disguises,[7] although I had to admit that it was because of his tendency towards the theatrical that he was able to assume the appearance and identity of another person with astonishing ease.

In this case, it was that of a City gentleman with a weakness for fashionable attire setting out for a few days' relaxation away from the tedium of a London office. He wore flannels and a blazer, a little too extravagantly striped for my taste, and a boater which, tipped at a jaunty angle, gave him a festive, holidaymaking air. A silver-topped cane, a brown wig *en brosse*, a small clipped moustache and a pair of gold-rimmed eyeglasses completed his transformation.

As I lack Holmes' skill at carrying off a disguise with confidence, mine was similar to his but far less conspicuous, consisting of a light-brown moustache with a matching wig, worn with a plain navy blazer and a pair of grey flannels. Thus disguised I felt, as we sauntered along the esplanade towards the hotel, that we blended in perfectly with the other visitors enjoying the sea air.

On Holmes' advice, I had packed my army service revolver into my portmanteau, for, as he reminded me,

---

[7] During his long career, Sherlock Holmes used many disguises, including that of an elderly lady, a young plumber, an Italian priest and a sailor. His longest-maintained disguise was as Altamont, an American/Irish spy in 'His Last Bow: The War Service of Sherlock Holmes'. He had at least 'five small refuges' in different parts of London where he kept his disguises. *Vide:* 'The Adventure of Black Peter'. Dr John F. Watson.

Holy Peters was a dangerous villain who would stop at nothing to avoid arrest. His own preferred weapon was a weighted riding crop.[8]

We saw nothing of Miss Pilkington or her employer Mrs Huxtable until we strolled down to the dining-room for dinner later that evening and saw them sitting at a table overlooking the sun veranda and the more distant view of the passing crowds against the glittering backdrop of the sea. Seated with them were the unforgettable figures of Holy Peters and his loathsome companion, now masquerading under the false identities of Dr and Miss Wilberforce.

They had changed very little since the last time we had confronted them in their shabby lodgings in Poultney Square. They were older, of course, but still easily recognisable despite the fact that Holy Peters had put on weight over the intervening years so that his jowls were now quite pendulous, while in contrast his so-called sister was thinner than I remembered, her cheekbones more protuberant and her lips more tightly compressed. They were both well dressed and gave the impression of a successful, professional couple, at ease in the marble and plush surroundings of the Regal Hotel.

Unfortunately, we were seated too far away from

---

[8] In 'The Adventure of the Six Napoleons', Dr Watson remarks that this was Sherlock Holmes' favourite weapon. He used it on several occasions: for example, to smash the last of the plaster busts of Napoleon and to strike the gun from the hand. Dr John F. Watson.

their table to see details of any individual feature, such as signs of damage to Dr Wilberforce's ear.

Miss Pilkington was aware of our arrival but, intelligent woman that she was, showed no sign of having recognised us, her glance merely passing casually over us as we took our places at a vacant table while she continued listening to the lady seated at her left, whom I took to be her employer, Mrs Huxtable.

She was a plump lady in her late sixties, fashionably attired and with an air of self-satisfaction about her which only wealth and the certainty of always getting her own way could have given her. There was a stubborn set to her lips and an imperious tilt to her head. Here was a woman, I thought, who demanded attention and was easily persuaded by flattery. The raised colour in her cheeks suggested high blood pressure, exacerbated, I suspected, by an overindulgent lifestyle. Her weight may also have contributed to breathing difficulties. Had I been her physician, I would have put her on a strict diet which excluded all cakes, cream and sugar as well as any form of alcohol. I noticed that she frequently sipped from a glass of Madeira wine which stood by her plate and which an obsequious wine waiter kept replenishing.

'A perfect example of a stray chicken ready for plucking, wouldn't you say, Watson?' Holmes murmured, not raising his eyes from studying the menu. I had no opportunity to agree to this remark, for a waiter arrived to take our order and the subject was dropped until later that evening when, dinner over, we set off at Holmes' suggestion for a brief walk along the Palace Pier where, according to Miss Pilkington, Dr Wilberforce, or Holy Peters as I preferred to think of him, was accustomed to take a pre-luncheon stroll.

Now that the sun had set, the air was cooler and the crowds of holidaymakers had dispersed a little, although a festival atmosphere still lingered in the flags and bunting which decorated the stalls and kiosks lining the pier. Here and there were gaps in the railings opening on to steps leading down to landing stages where passengers from the pleasure steamers could disembark and from which swimmers and fishermen could have easy access to the sea at different levels. As we passed them, some of the anglers were already putting away their rods and keepnets in readiness for going home and Holmes and I decided to follow their example and return to the hotel.

There was no sign of Holy Peters, his sister nor Miss Pilkington, although, when Holmes invited me to join him upstairs after dinner to confirm the plans for the following day, he discovered, on letting himself into his bedroom, a folded slip of paper lying on the carpet just inside the room which someone had evidently slid underneath the door – Miss Pilkington, as he ascertained, when he had unfolded it and scanned its contents before passing it on to me.

There was no superscription to the message which was short and to the point.

'I believe Dr Wilberforce intends to act soon over the matter of my employer. This evening after dinner she announced that she had arranged to move to his clinic as a patient in two days' time, that is on Friday.

'She has agreed to pay me a month's salary in lieu of notice. I thought I should notify you of this fact as soon as possible as I have very serious concerns over her future welfare. Edith D. Pilkington.'

'Concerns which I myself share,' Holmes said gravely as he refolded the note and placed it in his pocket book. 'Well, Watson, the stakes have been raised and we must accordingly elevate our own game. Early tomorrow morning I shall telegraph Lestrade, explaining the situation to him and requesting his presence here in Brighton with arrest warrants for both the Wilberforces. There is a fast train from Victoria at 8.07 which arrives at 9.49. I shall arrange to meet him at the entrance to the Palace Pier at a quarter past the hour. All we can do in the meantime is trust that we have chosen the right villains.'

Lestrade was only a few minutes late for our rendezvous the following morning, and as Holmes and I lingered outside the ticket office wearing the disguises we had worn the day before, we surveyed the crowds of people who were already making their way on to the pier, including a number of anglers equipped with rods and some with folding stools who were taking up vantage points along the railings and the steps of the landing stages.

Holmes and I were also suitably equipped, although in our case for a quite different catch, he with his loaded riding crop, I with my Webley No. 2 revolver which fitted snugly into the pocket of my blazer.

Within ten minutes we were joined by Lestrade, dressed like us in flannels, blazer and boater and looking so unfamiliar in this holiday attire that I failed to recognise him. It was only when he approached Holmes and shook his hand that I realised with a start who he was.

'Everything is arranged as you suggested, Mr Holmes,' he remarked *sotto voce* as we bought our tickets and strolled on to the pier. 'The local constabulary have agreed to put a dozen men on duty, some mingling with the crowds, some stationed as anglers along the length of the pier.' He nodded towards the fishermen gathered by the railings. 'If needed, I can summon them with a double blast on my whistle.'

'Excellent, Lestrade!' Holmes replied. 'And what of Holy Peters' sister?'

'She, too, is taken care of,' Lestrade assured him. 'Two matrons from the Brighton police force will be despatched to the hotel and will arrest her on the stroke of eleven o'clock.'

'So all we have to do is to await the arrival of our own big fish,' said Holmes, with a satisfied air. 'No doubt he will come in with the tide.'

The tide was indeed rising and, despite the potential danger of an imminent confrontation with Holy Peters, Holmes seemed to be enjoying himself immensely, walking briskly with his head flung back as he breathed in the crisp, salt-laden air, his eyes darting eagerly this way and that as he absorbed every detail of the scene, from the colourful dresses of the ladies as they promenaded up and down the pier to the more distant view of the beach, with its canvas changing tents and bathing machines for the convenience of the swimmers, the goat carts and donkeys for the children, the horse-drawn wagonettes along the seafront ready to convey the holidaymakers to such places of interest as the Devil's Dyke.[9] Although it was by then essentially a pleasure centre, Brighton's origins as a fishing port were still evident in the nets spread out to dry on the shingle and the stalls set out along the beach selling the proceeds of the latest trawl.

Further off still, and almost lost in the dazzle of the sun on the waves, were boats of all shapes and sizes – rowing boats and skiffs, yachts and dinghies – and beyond these the looming shape of the paddle steamer, the *Brighton Queen*, nosing up to the pier to unload its passengers at one of the landing stages.

I was so absorbed myself with all this colour and activity that I almost missed the sudden appearance of Holy Peters from among the crowds, and it was only when Holmes tugged at my sleeve that I noticed him.

---

[9] The Devil's Dyke was a beauty spot, not far from Brighton, that was popular with tourists for its splendid views, and still draws visitors. A deep V-shaped valley, said to have been excavated by the Devil, led from the Downs to the sea. In Sherlock Holmes' and Dr Watson's time there was a small fairground there to entertain the tourists. Dr John F. Watson.

Holmes set off after him, Lestrade and I following suit, falling in behind our quarry who, unaware of our presence, was striding out purposefully on this morning stroll of his, ignoring everyone about him until a few minutes later when his real motive for being there became apparent. Suddenly the crowds parted to allow an invalid chair free passage. It was coming towards us as if making for the exit and we therefore had a clear view of its occupant, an elderly lady who, despite the sun, was well wrapped up in shawls, a plaid blanket spread over her knees. A middle-aged woman was in charge of the chair, a qualified nurse-companion, I assumed, judging by her dark-blue cloak and bonnet which gave her a professional air.

Holmes, Lestrade and I lingered at the railings among the anglers, watching with fascinated interest as Holy Peters set about his work.

To give the man his due, he was very good at it. The surprised delight with which he greeted the old lady as if the meeting was entirely fortuitous, the solicitous manner in which he bowed his head over her hand as he raised it to his lips, could not have been bettered.

'Another stray chicken almost ready for the pot,' Holmes murmured in my ear as Holy Peters, having concluded conversation with the old lady, which involved more sycophantic attention, took his leave with apparent reluctance, once more kissing her hand and standing almost to attention as she was wheeled away and her chair disappeared among the crowds, her daily intake of ozone evidently over for the day. It was only then that he turned away and set off briskly for the far end of the pier.

'Well, gentlemen, shall we strike now?' Holmes inquired.

Lestrade and I nodded our agreement and the three of us fell in behind Holy Peters, gradually converging in on him until we were so close on his heels that he could not fail to be aware not only of our presence but also that of several of the anglers, who, realising that events were beginning to reach a climax, had abandoned their rods and keepnets and had joined our posse.

Whether Lestrade had tutored his men in the more subtle arts of arrest or whether, like hunting dogs, they knew by instinct the skills of the chase, I do not know. I was only aware that, little by little, Holy Peters was being edged towards the railings at the point where a set of wooden steps led down to a small landing stage.

It was only then that he realised he was being forced into a trap. The expression on his face as he glanced back over his shoulder made this obvious. The remnants of the unctuous smile which still lingered on his lips from his parting with the elderly lady, no doubt already chosen as his next victim, had vanished completely to be replaced by a look of fearful apprehension. In that moment, the very flesh of his face seemed to shrink and his full, well-fed jowls shrivelled to loose bags of trembling skin.

He could have jumped or attempted to escape down the steps but the tide was now lapping over them and inching its way up to the top.

Perhaps it was this insidious creeping of the water, silent and inexorable, that made Holy Peters hesitate.

It was at that moment that Lestrade, with impeccable timing for a man of whom Holmes had once remarked dismissively that he lacked imagination, acted.[10] A double blast on his whistle, shrill and urgent, brought the scene to even more vivid life. Several of the erstwhile anglers moved forward as if galvanised by the sound and one of their number, a tall young man with the build of an athlete, threw himself at Holy Peters and brought him to the ground with a flying tackle, the skill of which I had not seen so superbly executed since my old student days at Blackheath Rugby Club.[11] The next instant the young plain-clothes policeman had, with the help of two of his colleagues, turned Holy Peters briskly over on to his face, his arms doubled up behind his back, and a pair of handcuffs was snapped into place. To the spontaneous applause of a small crowd of spectators, who were uncertain as to who were the heroes and who the villains in this unexpected drama until this final moment, Holy Peters was hoisted to his feet and hustled away to the exit.

---

[10] In 'The Adventure of the Norwood Builder', Sherlock Holmes says of Inspector Lestrade that 'he did not add imagination' to his 'other great qualities'. Dr F. Watson.

[11] When Dr Watson was a medical student at St Bartholomew's Hospital, he joined the Blackheath Rugby Club, said to be the oldest in the world. Games took place on the heath itself. It is not known in which position Dr Watson played. Dr John F. Watson.

Head high and chest out, Lestrade strode proudly at the front of this procession and even Holmes was impressed enough to declare, 'Well done, Inspector!' – a rare accolade on his part.

We fell in behind them, Holmes pausing for a moment to gather up some small object from the decking of the pier which he slipped into his pocket and which he only revealed when we had arrived at the police station, where we learned that not only had Holy Peters been charged, but his erstwhile sister had also been arrested at the Regal Hotel and that the pair of them were in custody in the cells downstairs, accused of the abduction and attempted murder of Lady Frances Carfax.

Once these formalities were over, Lestrade drew us to one side to thank us, Holmes in particular for the part he had played in bringing these two criminals to justice.

'The most infernal pair of villains I've ever clapped eyes on, Mr 'Olmes,' the inspector declared. 'It's a pity in a way that we can't 'ang the two of them and be done with them for good. But at least we can be sure they'll serve long sentences in gaol, thanks to the efforts of both you gentlemen. You'll be returning to London, I assume?'

'I have one more small task to perform,' Holmes replied, 'and one small gift to give to you, Inspector.'

'A gift?' Lestrade's sallow features lit up with pleasurable anticipation.

'Only a trifle, my dear Inspector, but I thought it might amuse you,' Holmes replied with a smile, plunging his hand in his pocket and displaying on his open palm the object which he had picked up from the decking of the pier.

Lestrade bent to examine it and then drew sharply back, his expression turning to one of mixed bewilderment and distaste.

'What on earth is it, Mr Holmes? It looks like an ear!'

'That is exactly what it is. An ear,' Holmes assured him. 'To be more precise, the ear which Holy Peters wore over his own to hide the injuries his real ear suffered when it was bitten in that bar-room brawl in Australia in '89. The damage to it was too conspicuous a means of identification, so Holy Peters contrived to conceal it by attaching this wax ear over it.'

Lestrade gave a little nervous laugh as if still not entirely comfortable with the sight of the object lying in Holmes' palm.

'It's a very good likeness,' he ventured at last, clearly at a loss as to what to say.

'Made by an expert, I should imagine,' Holmes replied. 'Possibly by Monsieur Oscar Meunier of Grenoble who, if you recall, made a wax bust of myself to display in the window of our sitting-room in Baker Street to fool Colonel Moran into thinking I was at home and to draw his fire.[12] Now if you will excuse me, Inspector. As I

---

[12] Sherlock Holmes had a bust of himself specially made by a French sculptor which he set up in his sitting-room window to convince any of Moriarty's colleagues who might be keeping watch on the house that he was at home. Mrs Hudson was given the task of periodically turning the bust to make it appear that he was alive. Dr John F. Watson.

said, I have a small task to perform before Dr Watson and I return to London.'

'What task, Holmes?' I asked as we emerged from the police station.

'To inquire after Miss Pilkington and Mrs Huxtable,' Holmes replied, breaking off briefly to hail a cab. 'I should like them to know what has happened and to reassure myself that both the ladies are well.'

I know that on occasions in the past I have criticised Holmes for his lack of warmth and sympathy for others but at times like these, when he reveals the more caring side to his nature, there cannot be a more considerate person in the whole world.

As soon as we had returned to the hotel and collected our luggage, we went in search of Miss Pilkington, whom we found seated alone in the ladies' drawing-room, Mrs Huxtable, it seemed, on Holmes' inquiry, having retired to her bedroom to recover from the shock of witnessing the arrest of Miss Wilberforce and of learning the truth about the criminal career of the lady and her so-called brother.

'Thank goodness I wrote to you, Mr Holmes,' Miss Pilkington declared. 'I dread to think what would have happened to Mrs Huxtable had she gone to that clinic in Harrogate.'

'Indeed,' Holmes replied gravely. 'But it is your future which concerns me at the moment, Miss Pilkington. Will you remain in Mrs Huxtable's employ?'

'I think not, Mr Holmes. I have come to the conclusion that children and elderly widows do not make the most agreeable of companions. I have a friend in Paris whom I met when I was working there as a governess. She owns a private school where she teaches English to French businessmen. She offered me a position there but unfortunately I had already accepted the post with Mrs Huxtable so I had to refuse. However, her offer is still open and I have decided to accept it. In fact, I have written a letter to her this morning. As soon as I receive her reply, I shall give my notice to Mrs Huxtable.'

'A very wise decision,' Holmes replied, rising to his feet and holding out his hand. 'I wish you well.'

It was sincerely meant and so, too, was her gratitude for the part Holmes had played in averting what could so easily have been a tragedy.

There was one loose thread, however, which still remained.

'What of Mrs Huxtable, Holmes?' I asked, anxious that the lady should not be disregarded.

'Ah, our stray chicken!' Holmes replied with a smile. 'In her case, I think there is nothing we can do but hope that she has learned her lesson and does not allow any more foxes into her henhouse but keeps the door securely locked and bolted.'

THE CASE OF THE
ONE-EYED COLONEL

In 1880, after my return from Afghanistan, I was invalided out of the army where I had been serving as a medical officer and was granted a pension, awarded because of the wound I had received at the Battle of Maiwand.[1] Uncertain what to do or where to go, I decided to settle in London, which at least was familiar to me from my old days at Bart's,[2] and a year or

---

[1] After Dr Watson was wounded at the Battle of Maiwand in July 1880, he was repatriated to the Royal Victoria Hospital in England and was later invalided out of the army with a pension of 11s 6d a day, equivalent to 57 pence. Dr John F. Watson.

[2] Before joining the army and being sent to India, Dr Watson had studied medicine at St Bartholomew's Hospital in London. Dr John F. Watson.

so later I found lodgings at 221B Baker Street which I shared with Sherlock Holmes. However, until my relationship with him had developed into a real friendship, rather than a mere acquaintanceship between fellow lodgers, I felt rather at a loose end and, as Holmes was frequently absent, occupied with various activities about which I knew nothing at the time, I drifted about looking for diversions and trying to decide what I should do with the rest of my life.

It was during these inconsequential rambles that I came across the Kandahar Club in Sutton Row, a turning to the north off Oxford Street. It was a modest, rather shabby establishment, founded specifically for junior officers in the Indian army, like myself,[3] for minor officials in the Civil Service, and for a handful of undistinguished explorers, mostly bachelors, who liked to spend their leisure time travelling through the more far-flung and exotic regions of the British Empire.

Unlike the grander clubs in Pall Mall such as the Army & Navy, and The Travellers, which cater for the upper echelons of these disparate groups, the fees at the Kandahar are more moderate and the food plain and unpretentious, the kind of English fare that you might be served at home or at school, such as beef steak casserole and rice pudding; the type of food, in fact, that Mrs Hudson, our landlady at Baker Street provided, although for those members who had a taste for a genuine curry,

---

[3] Dr Watson was never a member of the Indian army but was an officer in the English regiment, the Royal Berkshire, which served in India. Dr John F. Watson.

the Kandahar could also serve up a very good vindaloo, hot enough to take the skin off the roof of one's mouth.

It was here that I met Thurston,[4] with whom I soon struck up a friendship. Like me, he was retired, in his case from his post of deputy chief accountant in the Public Works Department, and his connections with Afghanistan were civil rather than military. Apart from occasional tours of inspection, he was based at the department's main offices in Calcutta and was what we army men used to refer to rather disparagingly as a 'desk-wallah',[5] although, unlike many of us, he had learned Hindi, a necessary requirement demanded by the Civil and Military Examination Board. He had also come to love the country and took an active interest in its history and culture. A bachelor of forty-one with few close friends, he had a pleasant, easy-going nature and, like myself, was rather lonely at times, I suspected. We soon found we had several interests in common, in particular billiards, a game which I had taken up as a student at Bart's. Although billiards is not my first choice of sports, rugby being my preference,[6] the

---

[4] Dr Watson played billiards with Thurston at their club. Nothing else is known about Thurston, not even his Christian name. *Vide*: 'The Adventure of the Dancing Men'. Dr John F. Watson.

[5] '*Wallah*' is a Hindi word for 'servant'. A *desk-wallah* would have been a clerk or an office worker. Dr John F. Watson.

[6] While a medical student at St Bartholomew's Hospital, Dr Watson had played rugby for the Blackheath Rugby Club. Dr John F. Watson.

injury to my leg had made it impossible for me to take part in any vigorous games and, as billiards requires only a minimum of physical exertion in the way of running about and tackling one's opponent, I accepted Thurston's invitation to play. I was, by the way, a fairly competent player, having had plenty of practice while I was in the army and while recovering from my wound, both at the hospital at Peshawar and later at Netley.[7] From that time on, we used to meet once a fortnight at the Kandahar for lunch, followed by a game of billiards.

It was during one of these fortnightly meetings that Thurston introduced me to Colonel Godfrey Carruthers, a new member of the club.

Having arrived a little early, I was waiting in the bar when Thurston arrived accompanied by a tall, upright, handsome man in his fifties with sandy hair and a small, neatly clipped moustache who was wearing a patch over his right eye. Judging by his bearing and the eyepatch, I assumed he was a former army man who had been wounded on active service.

As Thurston introduced us, Carruthers shook my hand with a firm, manly grip. At the same time, I was aware that he was scrutinising me with a keen, blue gaze.

---

[7] There is some confusion as to where Dr Watson was wounded. In *A Study in Scarlet*, he states that he was wounded in the left shoulder by a bullet from a jezail rifle which shattered the bone and grazed the subclavian artery. He was also injured in the leg, a wound that had longer-lasting effects. Dr John F. Watson.

'Thurston tells me you served in Afghanistan,' he remarked. 'I was there myself; at least my regiment was part of the army under Major General "Bobs" Roberts which relieved the siege at Kandahar.'

'Were you indeed!' I exclaimed enthusiastically. 'Then I and all my army colleagues owe you a great debt of gratitude. Without your troops, we might have been defeated and suffered the same fate as our comrades at Maiwand.'

'You are referring, of course, to the *ghazis*[8] and their rather unpleasant habit of dismembering anyone left on the battlefield, whether alive or dead?'

'Indeed, I am. And it was not just the men; their womenfolk joined in with just as much gusto.'

'A bad business,' Carruthers commented, pulling a wry face.

Something about his voice and demeanour warned me that he preferred not to discuss the subject any further and I respected his reticence. I myself still find it difficult to put into words some of the horrors I had witnessed during that particular battle. He, too, must have suffered much the same experiences in that forced march of three hundred and twenty miles across the mountains from Kabul to attack Ayub Khan's camp where, by putting the rebels to flight, Carruthers and his comrades had lifted the siege of Kandahar.

---

[8] A *ghazi* was a particularly fierce Islamic soldier who had a reputation for courage in battle. Dr John F. Watson.

However, I was left with a number of questions I would have loved to hear the answers to, such as: When was he wounded? Was it during that lifting of the siege? I knew over one hundred and ninety of our men were among the casualties. Perhaps, like me, he had been transferred to the base hospital at Peshawar. If so, I wondered if he had come across Lieutenant Wilkes or Captain Goodfellow, both fellow patients. And what about that formidable ward sister with the totally unsuitable name of Dear, who was almost as terrifying as a sergeant major and about whom Wilkes had made up a rather saucy ditty to the tune of 'Do ye ken John Peel'?

But I dismissed such questions from my mind and instead remarked, 'Let me buy you and Thurston a drink. What would you like?'

Waiting at the bar to be served, I glanced back over my shoulder and, seeing Thurston and Carruthers chatting together like old friends who had known each other for years, I experienced a strange and unexpected sensation.

Even now I find it difficult to describe it exactly. It was not quite jealousy, although I confess to feeling a little piqued that Carruthers, a total stranger, should seem so much at ease with Thurston who was my friend. There was also a touch of professional animosity that Carruthers had taken part in that heroic forced march to relieve our beleaguered forces while I had been struck by a bullet when carrying out the much less dramatic role of tending the wounded.[9] The fact that he was a colonel while I was a mere lieutenant also rankled, much to my shame. Mixed up with this general feeling of animosity was a more vague disquiet which I could not rationalise and which I dismissed from my mind as just another symptom of my resentment.

Trying not to let these unworthy thoughts show in my face, I made an effort to smile and to assume a friendly expression as I walked back across the bar towards them.

Thank goodness, he did not join us for lunch, as evidently Thurston had expected he would, but instead he made some hurried excuse that he had suddenly remembered a prior appointment with an old army friend and, shaking hands with us both, he left, much to Thurston's disappointment, as I could see from the look on his face. As for myself, I was extremely relieved not to have to share a table with him and to join in reminiscing with him about our mutual experiences in Afghanistan.

However, there was no respite from Colonel Carruthers, even in his absence, for hardly had we sat down to luncheon in the dining-room than, like

---

[9] Dr John Watson was present at the Battle of Maiwand (1880) during the Second Afghan War in which he served as an army surgeon. After the defeat by the Afghans of the British army, he witnessed the dismemberment of those left behind on the battlefield, both the living and the dead. Dr John F. Watson.

Banquo's ghost at the feast,[10] his name came up. It was Thurston who introduced it.

'Interesting man, don't you think?' he remarked.

I knew whom he was referring to but, in a futile attempt to kick the subject into the long grass, so to speak, I replied with feigned ignorance, 'Who do you mean?'

'Why Carruthers, of course!' Before I had time to say anything more, Thurston continued enthusiastically, 'I thought you would take to him. As soon as I was introduced to him, I said to myself, "That's someone who my old friend Watson would like to meet." You have so much in common: the Indian army; Afghanistan; both wounded . . .'

'Yes, it is quite a coincidence,' I agreed. 'Does he play billiards?'

'Probably not. After all, he only has one eye,' Thurston pointed out with a touch of sharpness in his voice that drew attention to my foolishness in asking such an obviously ridiculous question, and, at the sound of it, my antipathy for the wretched man grew even stronger.

It took all the pleasure out of our game of billiards after luncheon. I could not concentrate and, in consequence, Thurston won hands down, another

---

[10] In Act 3 of *Macbeth*, Macbeth murders Banquo (whose children, it has been prophesised, will succeed to the Scottish throne) in order to seize the throne himself. Banquo's ghost appears at the banquet to celebrate Macbeth's succession. Dr John F Watson.

blow to my self-esteem and another reason to dislike Carruthers even more, a quite unfair reaction on my part, as I shamefacedly admitted to myself at the time.

I was therefore not in a good mood when I returned to Baker Street, a state of mind that Holmes, with his usual acuity, was aware of from the moment I entered the room.

'So what happened this afternoon to put you in such low spirits?' he inquired.

'Nothing,' I replied.

'Oh, come, my dear fellow! I have shared these lodgings with you for long enough to know your moods almost as well as my own. Despite women claiming that they alone possess the powers of intuition, we mere men can be just as sensitive – more so in some cases. Was it Thurston who has put you in this frame of mind?'

Without intending to say anything specific, I heard myself replying, 'No; it was a new member of the club, a man called Carruthers – Colonel Godfrey Carruthers.'

'And?' Holmes persisted, raising an inquiring eyebrow.

'That is the trouble, Holmes!' I burst out. 'I just do not know why I have taken such a dislike to the man.'

'Is it because he is a colonel?' he suggested gently.

'And I am just a lieutenant? I do not think so, Holmes; at least, I hope it is not so. All I can say in the way of explanation is that there is something not quite pukkah about him.'

I used the word involuntarily, dredging it up from my

memory of Anglo-Indian words and phrases which had been familiar during my army days, and I was surprised by this and also by Holmes' apparent knowledge of the meaning of the word.

'And how is he not quite genuine?'

'That is the trouble. I do not know. I just felt . . .'

And here I broke off, unable to offer a coherent explanation.

'Ah, your intuition again!' Holmes exclaimed. 'But behind all these intuitive reactions, there must be some rational explanation. At least, that is my belief. So let us examine your feelings as one would dissect a body, looking for the causes of a medical condition. Was it his demeanour which was not genuine?'

'No, not really. He looked and behaved much as any former army officer.'

'His manner of speech, then?'

'That, too, seemed quite normal.'

'Did you take into consideration his reason for joining the club?'

It was a new and unexpected aspect of Carruthers' disposition to which I had not given any thought and I hesitated before replying.

'Well, I suppose he wanted to meet up with former army men like myself . . .'

'But is not he a colonel? Is it usual for officers of such a high rank to become members of the Kandahar?'

'Not really, I suppose, now I come to think of it. They are usually captains or majors at the most . . .'

'Then does not his decision to join your club strike you as a little strange? Not that I am casting any aspersions on the Kandahar, Watson. I am sure it is an excellent establishment. But even so . . .'

'I just assumed that, as a pensioned officer, which he must be, he could not afford the fees anywhere else. It is a perfectly respectable place, Holmes.'

'Of course it is, my dear fellow. I do not doubt that in the least. It just occurred to me that the reason you find him not quite pukkah is because . . .' He broke off here to exclaim with a smile and a shrug, 'Oh, this is ridiculous, Watson! Here we are, going round and round in circles discussing an individual whom you have met only once and I have not met at all. The answer to the dilemma is more information. Therefore I suggest that the next time you meet the colonel at the Kandahar you find out as much as you can about his background, in particular about his military career.' Seeing my doubtful expression, he added, 'It is one of the basic tenets of investigation when your suspicions are aroused. You must quietly and discreetly search out the trail he leaves behind him and follow it to its logical conclusion. You know my methods. Are you prepared to put them into practice on your own behalf? I shall be at hand, of course, to advise you on any aspect of the situation you find disturbing.'

Knowing that Holmes was at the time involved in several important cases including the Barnaby-Ross case and the mystery of the disappearance of Lord

Penrose's private secretary, I agreed immediately, feeling somewhat ashamed that I should burden him with my trivial concerns and very grateful for his offer of help. So it was agreed that on Wednesday week, the date of my fortnightly appointment with Thurston at the Kandahar, I would confer with Carruthers along the lines that my old friend had suggested and then report back to him on the outcome of the interview.

In the event, however, I did not see the colonel on that particular date. Thurston was there at the club but Carruthers was absent. On my inquiring into his whereabouts, Thurston replied that he did not know.

'I have not seen him since the last time we met here.'

'Oh, what a pity!' I remarked with more honesty than Thurston could possibly have realised. 'I was looking forward very much to seeing him again.'

'Were you really? I had the impression you did not much care for the fellow.'

I hurried to cover up the faux pas I had made, at the same time warning myself that Thurston was much more perceptive than I had given him credit for and that I would have to tread a great deal more carefully in the future. The tactics that Holmes had referred to were more complex than I had imagined and I found myself admiring my old friend's techniques more than ever.

However, my self-confidence was restored a little by Thurston's next remark, which helped to convince me that I had handled the situation a lot better than I had imagined.

'I am not sure when he will call in again at the club but perhaps this fellow will know,' Thurston continued, raising a hand to summon a passing waiter, who came over to our table. After listening to Thurston's request for information regarding Carruthers' plans about future visits to the Kandahar, the man replied without any hesitation.

'Indeed, sir. I understand from the manager that the colonel has changed his regular luncheon booking from Wednesdays to Fridays at eleven o'clock. Is that all, sir?'

Thurston cocked an interrogative eyebrow in my direction and, when I shook my head, he thanked the man before dismissing him.

'It is such a pity he has changed his arrangements,' Thurston remarked when the waiter had left.

'Indeed it is,' I agreed with genuine disappointment. I had hoped to quiz Carruthers the next time we met over luncheon and, by so doing, to learn more not only about the man himself but also about my own confused feelings about him. I also felt that I would be letting Holmes down if I failed to carry through my inquiries.

Unaware of these private feelings of mine, Thurston picked up the thread of our earlier conversation.

'Yes, a very interesting man. Before you arrived on that Wednesday, he talked at some length about his army experiences,' he remarked and, as he did so, it suddenly occurred to me that Thurston could serve as a secret conduit to Carruthers and that all was not yet lost.

'What did he have to say?' I asked, trying hard

not to sound too keenly interested. 'Did he mention Afghanistan?'

'Oh, at some length. He was clearly much taken with the country and its culture, in particular its fighting men for whom he had a great deal of admiration, despite its tendency to unseemly behaviour at times.'

I nodded solemnly, trying not to look too aghast at Thurston's inappropriate use of language. The gruesome habit of dismembering any enemy soldiers left lying on the battlefield, whether alive or dead, with the aid of their womenfolk, struck me not so much as 'unseemly' as downright barbaric. It was only through the swift action of my orderly, Murray, who threw me over the back of a packhorse when I was wounded at Maiwand and led me to safety at Kandahar,[11] that my life was saved. As a desk-wallah in Calcutta at the time of the battle, Thurston had a reason for not being fully aware of the facts, but I could think of no excuse for Carruthers' ignorance.

'Indeed they are brave to the point of fanaticism,' I replied. 'Did he mention the siege of Kandahar?'

'Several times. It must have been an appalling experience that you, too, of course, had to endure. Thirty days with no food and very little water! The suffering you had to go through! You must have been so thankful when Carruthers arrived with the relieving army.'

---

[11] Kandahar, or Candahar, is a garrison town in Afghanistan which was occupied by the British army. Dr John F. Watson

'Indeed we were! Very relieved in both senses of the word, although for my part I was still recovering from my wound and at times was not really aware of what was going on. Did Carruthers by any chance mention when he was wounded?'

'No, I don't think he did. Is it important?'

'Not at all, Thurston, not at all,' I said dismissively, at the same time inwardly rejoicing that Thurston had unwittingly placed in my hands the information I needed to prove I was right. As I had suspected, Carruthers was certainly not pukkah! Indeed, so great was my jubilation that afterwards I beat Thurston at billiards by two frames to one.

Something of my delight must have shown in my expression, for when I returned to Baker Street later that afternoon, the first remark Holmes made when I entered our sitting-room was, 'I see from your face that you have won a victory. I assume you beat Thurston today at billiards.'

'Not only that, Holmes, but I now know without a shadow of a doubt that Carruthers is a wrong 'un!'

'Really? That is good news! Draw a chair up to the fire, my dear fellow, and tell me how you came to this conclusion. Was it something he said at the Kandahar this afternoon?'

'No; he was not there and I have the feeling that he absented himself on purpose to avoid meeting me again. On the contrary, it was something Thurston said. A fortnight ago before I arrived at the club, he was having a conversation with Carruthers. Apparently, Carruthers spoke in some detail about his experiences in Afghanistan, in particular about the siege of Kandahar.'

'Do go on,' Holmes urged as I paused for a moment to draw breath and put my thoughts into a more coherent order.

'Well, Holmes, in this conversation, Carruthers evidently referred to the fact that, during the siege, I and my fellow soldiers had to suffer thirty days at Kandahar with no fresh water.'

'So?' Holmes inquired, raising his eyebrows. 'What is the point, Watson? I assume there is one.'

Chastened by this remark, I hurried to make good my mistake.

'The point is, the siege lasted twenty-four days, not thirty, and there was no shortage of water. There were enough wells in the garrison to keep all the troops supplied. Had he been there, he would have known this. If you want my opinion, I think he was using information he had picked up from soldiers who had been at the siege but who had exaggerated the facts in order to make the situation more dramatic.'

'Could he not have exaggerated the facts himself?'

'That is a possibility,' I conceded, 'but I think not. Any officer worth his rank would have kept to the truth. It is generally the other rankers who add colour and excitement to their accounts. This could explain Carruthers' change of arrangements at the Kandahar. I think he wanted to avoid another meeting with me in case I became suspicious about him for, to be perfectly frank, Holmes, I do not believe for a moment that he was in Kandahar or even in Afghanistan.'

Rising to his feet, Holmes took two or three turns up the room, chin in hand, and, knowing him in this reflective mood, I said nothing to interrupt his thoughts. After a few minutes of silent contemplation, he seemed to come to a decision, for he strode back to his chair by the fire where he sat down bolt upright, his eyes bright.

'You say Carruthers now comes to the club on a Friday?'

'Yes; according to the waiter who spoke to Thurston. He apparently arrives at eleven o'clock.'

'Then I shall make sure to be in the vicinity of the Kandahar at the same hour.'

'Shall I come with you?' I asked eagerly, keen to witness Carruthers' downfall.

'No; not yet. It is too early in the case. Besides, if he saw you, he might leave at once and ruin the whole plan. Let me reconnoitre on my own to begin with. I may need your assistance later in the investigation.'

'Then would you like a more detailed description of him?' I asked, keen to contribute something, however small, to the inquiry.

Holmes laughed out loud.

'That is hardly necessary! The eyepatch alone should mark him out!' he replied, much to my discomfiture.

* * *

85

The following Friday, Holmes set off in good time to arrive at the Kandahar a little before eleven o'clock. Knowing he would not be back until after lunchtime, possibly later if he followed Carruthers after he had left the club, I tried to settle down to the exasperating business of waiting on events, an exercise in patience in which I confess I am not very accomplished.

I tried reading the *Daily Gazette* in an effort to while away the time, but after an hour I gave up and, laying aside the newspaper, I decided to walk to the Metropolitan Railway station[12] in Baker Street before returning home, but a thin cold drizzle drove me back to the fireside in our Baker Street lodgings with no sign yet of Holmes.

It was nearly four o'clock and getting dark before he finally arrived back from what had evidently been a successful foray, for I heard the street door slam shut behind him before he came bounding jubilantly up the stairs.

'You were right, Watson!' he announced, bursting into the room. 'Carruthers is definitely a wrong 'un, as you so pertinently observed. So congratulations, my dear fellow! I do not think I could have done better myself!'

It was praise indeed, for Holmes rarely paid compliments unless they were fully deserved, and I felt the warm blood course up into my face with pleasure.

---

[12] The Metropolitan Railway was an underground railway system, the first of this type to be introduced in London. Baker Street was a station on this line. Dr John F. Watson.

'What did you find out?' I asked eagerly.

'Oh, really, Watson! Let me tell my account from the beginning. You of all people should know the importance of not giving away the ending before first building the story up to its climax. Well, then, to begin. I strolled up and down Orchard Street for a good ten minutes before Carruthers emerged from the Kandahar. From there, he walked into Oxford Street, where he caught a Bayswater omnibus,[13] alighting from it in Holborn. Having arrived there, he set out on foot down the Gray's Inn Road before he turned into that maze of little streets in the Clerkenwell area, finishing up eventually in Pickard's Close, at number 14, to be precise, where he let himself in at the front door.'

'What sort of place is it?' I asked, thinking that from what Holmes had said about it, the district hardly sounded a suitable address for an army colonel – an unspoken criticism which my old friend expressed more succinctly out loud.

'It is a terrace of shabby, run-down little houses,' he said. 'I am sure you know the type: no front gardens, grubby lace curtains at the windows . . . I leave the rest to your imagination, Watson. Anyway, Carruthers'

---

[13] London was well served by various omnibus companies, the vehicles of which were distinguished by their colour. The Bayswater omnibus was light green and served the area from Notting Hill to Whitechapel via Oxford Street and Holborn. Although it was a cheap and convenient means of travel, Sherlock Holmes and Dr Watson rarely used it, preferring to take cabs. Dr John F. Watson.

disappearance inside number 14 placed me in something of a dilemma. I had no idea how long he would remain within the house and I could hardly knock on the front door and ask to speak to him. That would have given the game away immediately.'

'What did you do, Holmes?' I asked, as tense with anxiety over the situation as if I had experienced it myself.

'Thank goodness we English are a nation not so much of shopkeepers, as Napoleon would have had us believe, but of topers. There was a convenient little tavern on the corner named, most inappropriately, I thought, in view of the sooty bricks and the muddy doorsteps, "The Farmer's Boy", complete with a hanging sign depicting a cherry-cheeked, curly-haired youngster dressed in a spotlessly white smock and carrying an equally freshly laundered lamb on his shoulder.

'I retired there and ordered half a pint of ale – a suitable beverage, I thought, given the circumstances – and carried it over to a table by the window, from which I had a clear view of Pickard's Close and the front door of number 14. I should add that I had dressed down for the occasion in a short jacket, pepper-and-salt trousers and a bowler hat.

'Even so, I attracted some attention from the other customers. Thinking it over later, I came to the conclusion that my shoes were too clean. One has to be so careful in some districts of London such as Clerkenwell, which are almost tribal in their exclusiveness and regard any stranger as a potential enemy. So after looking me over suspiciously, they turned their backs on me as a man to show their disapproval. They may have concluded from my bowler hat that I was a debt collector or perhaps a nark: a police informer to you, Watson.

'I waited for at least half an hour before Carruthers emerged, wearing a shabby overcoat and carrying several letters in his hand. There was also one other significant change in his appearance. He was no longer wearing the eyepatch, which was obviously a prop, such as an actor would wear, in his case to win public sympathy. There is nothing like a crutch or wooden leg to increase one's earnings as a beggar or a confidence trickster. Remind me, by the way, to give you an account of the three-handed widow one of these days.'

'The three-handed widow . . . !' I began but Holmes, ignoring my interruption, pressed on with his own account.

'Anyway, to return to Carruthers. His was a remarkable transformation. In that short time, he had changed from an officer and a gentleman who had lost an eye, presumably in battle, to a down-at-heel individual, although he still walked with the brisk, upright gait of a soldier, which led me to believe that he had been in the army at some point in his life.'

'How extraordinary, Holmes!' I declared. 'Why do you suppose Carruthers went to such lengths to falsify his appearance?'

'The answer, I believe, lies in the letters he was

carrying, which he posted in the nearest pillar box.' Seeing my puzzled expression, he continued with the kindly air of a schoolmaster explaining some abstruse mathematical equation to a not-overly-bright pupil. 'He is a screever, Watson, a writer of begging letters to you and me, or, if you prefer a more succinct description, a professional cadger. He probably has other methods of persuading innocent citizens to part with their money. Gagging, for example.'

'Gagging?'

'Convincing a complete stranger that they are old acquaintances and, on the strength of that supposed friendship, borrowing money from him. Here is a possible scenario. The gagger pretends to recognise the victim, perhaps just a passer-by in the street, as an old acquaintance and, to celebrate their reunion, invites him to join him in a tavern or a hotel bar for a celebratory drink. However, when he is presented with the bill, he discovers, on searching through his coat, that he must have lost his wallet. The victim, of course, offers to pay not only for the drinks but to supply a little extra cash so that his "friend" has the fare for a cab home. They exchange addresses so that the cadger can reimburse his victim. Of course, he never does but the cadger makes a pound, say, from the "lay".'

Seeing my puzzled expression, Holmes hastened to explain.

'A "lay", my dear fellow, refers to the particular method used to deceive or defraud. In this case, it would be a "gagging lay", which could bring in an extra bounty on top of the original "gag" because the cadger now knows the address of the victim, which he can then sell on to a "screever", who in turn makes money from the innocent citizen.'

'Oh, Holmes! How despicable! Is there nothing we can do? I hate the thought of a bounder like that preying on the members of the Kandahar.'

'Well, I suppose I could speak to Lestrade about him. He may already be known to the police. But better still, I could approach Sammy Knox, an old acquaintance of mine, who used to be a "shofulman", and before you ask, Watson, that is someone who passes on counterfeit money; banknotes, in Knox's case. He used to buy them from a pair of brothers, the Jacksons, who were experts in producing false banknotes, or "gammy soft", as they are known in the trade. They owned a small but apparently respectable printing firm in New Cross producing visiting cards, invitations, that sort of thing. Sammy, who was a keen gambler on the horses, used to pass on the "soft" at the various race meetings, not just on the course itself, but at various public houses which flourished in the neighbourhood. If anyone knew about any unlawful business involving money it would be Sammy.'

'Is he still a – what was the word? – a "shofulman"?' I asked, fascinated by my old friend's knowledge of the sporting underworld.

'Officially, no,' he replied. 'He was arrested a couple

of times and had spent time in "stir", but when I last met him he was adamant he had given up his old, bad ways, although I rather doubt it. Leopards and spots, Watson, if you take my meaning.'

'Should I warn Thurston and the other members of the Kandahar about Carruthers? He seems a thoroughly bad lot.'

'Heavens, no! That would send him running for cover. Give me time to find out where Sammy Knox is living these days and to ask for his help in the matter before we speak to Thurston and the club members, even Lestrade. Now we have the man in our sights, it would be a pity to lose him through hasty action. As the old saying goes: "Softly, softly catchee monkee".'

I do not know how Holmes set about finding out Knox's whereabouts but within four days he had evidently been successful, for on the Tuesday afternoon I was invited by Holmes to a rendezvous at the Crooked Billet in Castle Street, off Holborn, to meet Sammy Knox.

It was a discreet public house partitioned off by wooden panels into separate cubicles like loose boxes or narrow railway compartments. The one Holmes had chosen faced the door and I felt, as we took our seats on one of the settles, that my old friend was familiar with the place and had used it before for similar meetings. We had not long to wait, for, soon after our own arrival, the door opened and a man entered: Knox, I assumed, from the way Holmes immediately sat up in readiness to greet him.

He was not at all what I had been expecting from Holmes' account of him. He was a small, slightly built man and, seen from a distance, looked very boyish, with a youthful flush to his cheeks, his billycock[14] hat tilted at a jaunty angle and his checked suit a little too loud to be considered in good taste. A flower in his buttonhole and a yellow waistcoat marked him out to be a 'sporting' gentleman, typical of the sort you can see at any racecourse during the season.[15] It was only when he drew closer that I realised that he was, in fact, quite elderly, for his face was a network of tiny wrinkles, like the craquelure one sees in the varnished surface of an old master, while the boyish flush to his cheeks was caused by the dozens of broken veins under the skin.

He seemed pleased to see Holmes, for he shook his hand warmly, and greeted me with a gentlemanly courtesy which I found quite disarming.

''Ow are things with you, Mr 'Aitch?' he inquired of my old friend. 'And you, too, sir?' he added with a little bow in my direction.

But Holmes clearly wanted these preliminaries over and done with so that he and Sammy Knox could get down to business as soon as possible and he plunged straight in.

'Now, Sammy, the reason I wanted to meet you

_____

[14] A billycock was a type of bowler hat. Dr John F. Watson.

[15] As Dr Watson was in the habit of betting on horses, he was presumably familiar with the 'sporting' gentlemen who met at the various racecourses. Dr John F. Watson.

here is very important. You know a great deal about the underworld. Have you ever met a certain gentleman who calls himself Carruthers and claims to be an army officer – a colonel, no less?'

'I might,' Sammy conceded cautiously. 'What does 'e look like?'

Holmes glanced across at me, clearly expecting I would supply the answer and I strained my memory to recall as vivid an image of Carruthers as I could, as well as the words to describe it.

'Tall; very upright, military bearing; well spoken; sandy-haired; claims to have served in Afghanistan.'

I kept my eyes on Sammy Knox's face, looking for the slightest sign that he had recognised my description, but his features remained impassive until I finished my account when he said in a voice of quiet authority, 'Barty Cheeseman,' and then fell silent.

What happened next occurred so quickly that I was unaware of it until it was all over. Holmes held out his right hand, the fingers tightly closed, and at the same time extended his index finger and drummed it gently on the table.

'Tell me,' he said softly, 'and tell it straight, if you please, Sammy. My friend is not very familiar with "cant".'[16]

Sammy glanced across at me with an amused

---

[16] 'Cant' was a special form of language used by certain classes, in this case by the criminal underworld. Dr John F. Watson.

expression and then decided to accept whatever terms Holmes was offering.

'Right!' he said. 'Straight it shall be, Mr 'Aitch. First of all, about Barty Cheeseman. 'E used to be in the army – batman to a major, by all accounts, which is 'ow he learned 'is manners and 'ow to speak proper. 'Is favourite "lay" is smashing – passing false money, to you and me. 'E prefers to work alone and in the best cribs;[17] no backstreet publics for 'im. It's the fancy 'otels and clubs and he offers, say, a finny – sorry, Mr 'Aitch – a five-pound note to pay for drinks and a meal; so 'e gets them free and the change into the bargain. Or 'e'll go into a baccy shop and buy the best cigars. Or if it's bigger swag 'e's got 'is eyes on, like a gold watch or a swanky ring for 'is dolly bird, then 'e'll pay by cheque, 'aving discovered 'e 'asn't got 'is wallet on 'im – left it at the 'otel, is 'is usual blab. Rather than lose the sale, the shopkeeper will accept the fakement. S'matter of fact, that's one of Cheesey's specialities, passing a stiff – a cheque or bill of exchange, either a dud or a stolen one.'

'Is it indeed?' Holmes asked and I could tell by the way his shoulders stiffened that the information had caught his attention. He gave a quick sideways glance in my direction, the significance of which I failed to grasp at the time, although I was a little puzzled at first by my old friend's apparent carelessness as he posed the

---

[17] A crib could be a house or a room or lodgings. It could also refer to a place which was to be robbed or burgled. Dr John F. Watson.

following questions. His manner was a little too offhand to be entirely genuine. However, I had known him long enough to realise that he was at his most engaged when he seemed the most indifferent. Unaware of this quality in Holmes, Sammy Knox replied to his queries with the pleased self-satisfaction of a man who thinks he knows all the answers.

'How would Cheeseman have set about acquiring someone's cheque book?' Holmes inquired. 'I assume he would simply pick the man's pocket?'

Sammy grinned broadly at Holmes' innocence.

'Nah, guv'nor! Cheesey's not a dip. He ain't got the skill. 'E might pick a pocket if a coat was 'anging up somewhere 'andy or lying across the back of a chair. That's more 'is line of business.'

'Oh, I see!' Holmes declared, as if light had suddenly burst upon him. 'So then he would fill in the cheque and present it at the man's bank?'

Again that knowing smile spread over Sammy's face.

''E might do, but 'e wouldn't last very long as a knapper[18] if 'e did.'

'So what would he do?'

''E'd take a few of the stiffs from the back of the book so the man 'oo owned it wouldn't fink anyfin' was wrong until later, and then pass 'em on at some other bank, not the one named on the cheques. Or 'e might sell 'em on. There's plenty of coves 'oo deal in stolen

---

[18] A 'knapper' was the cant word for a thief. Dr John F. Watson.

stiffs. Is that the lot, Mr 'Aitch, or is there somefin' else you'd like to know?' Sammy concluded. 'Only I've got a pretty little dolly waitin' for me at my crib. Lovely, she is!'

On Holmes replying that there was nothing more, Sammy Knox rose to his feet, shook hands all round and, with a sleight of hand that would not have shamed a professional magician, he scooped up the piece of crumpled paper lying on the table and transferred it to his pocket. Then, raising his billycock hat not without a certain grace, he left the bar.

'What was in the paper?' I asked as the door closed behind him.

Holmes laughed.

'A couple of what Sammy would call "thickers",' he replied. 'Pound notes to you and me, Watson. But worth every penny. Thanks to Sammy, I now know how we can "nab" Colonel Carruthers, alias Cheeseman, and see him safely in "stir". And that is the last time today I shall make use of "cant", fascinating though it is as an alternative language.'

'How will you set about arresting him?' I asked, agog with curiosity.

'Guests are allowed at the Kandahar, are they not?' he asked with an offhand air.

'Yes, they are,' I replied.

'And there is a back door to the club?'

'I have no idea,' I said, quite bewildered by this time.

'Then that must be ascertained before we proceed

any further. I must also speak to the manager and alert Lestrade, for I shall need their assistance, along with a couple of constables. I shall call on Lestrade this morning and make a start on my little strategy.'

Holmes and I parted company on the return journey, I to make my way back to Baker Street, Holmes presumably to Scotland Yard to call on Lestrade and to lay before him whatever plan he had in mind for the arrest of Carruthers, alias Cheeseman, an event I was looking forward to with eager anticipation, for I felt the man had not only taken advantage of Thurston and the Kandahar Club but had also, in some manner which I could not quite rationalise, besmirched the reputation of the British army in India and the gallant colleagues in my regiment who, from the most senior officers down to the humblest private, had fought, and in many cases had died, for the reputation of our country and the Berkshires in particular.

The interview with Lestrade must have gone well, for not long before luncheon Holmes returned, looking pleased.

'Lestrade is very keen to lay Carruthers by the heels,' he announced, settling himself in his armchair and lighting his pipe. 'The colonel has been a thorn in his flesh ever since the Fitzgibbon case last summer.'

'The Fitzgibbon scandal!' I exclaimed. 'Was Carruthers involved in that?'

'Apparently so; or so Lestrade believes, although there was not enough evidence to take the case to court.'

'Good heavens!' I murmured, too shocked to make any further comment.

'Indeed!' Holmes agreed wryly.

At the time, it had been the main topic in the more sensational newspapers. Although he was not mentioned by name, to avoid the risk of the editor being sued for libel, it was clear to anyone who had even the most rudimentary knowledge of the comings and goings of the aristocracy that the 'beautiful daughter of a distinguished member of the House of Lords' was none other than Lady Vanessa Fitzgibbon, daughter of Lord Wellesley Fitzgibbon, whose secret engagement to a dashing Guards officer, Montagu Orme-Wiston, hinted at in the society pages of the *Daily Echo* and the *Morning Star* for the past three months, had been broken off and that Lady Vanessa and her mother had departed for a prolonged visit to the Seychelles.

'So,' Holmes continued, 'Lestrade believes that the arrest of the colonel would be a considerable feather in his inspector's hat.' In an apparent non sequitur he added, 'You have a cheque book, Watson?'

'Not at the moment. If you remember, Holmes, you confiscated it three days ago and locked it up in your desk.'

'Of course! I had completely forgotten about that little incident. But if you agree to my plan, I shall release it back into your possession immediately.'

'What is your plan?' I asked, wondering what part my cheque book would play in it.

'We shall present ourselves at the Kandahar . . .'

'*We?*' I interposed. 'You mean I shall be there as well?'

'Lestrade and I will be your guests for lunch followed by a game of billiards.'

'When exactly?'

'On Friday.'

'But Carruthers will be there! If you remember, he changed his day for lunching at the club from Wednesday to Friday – on purpose, I believe, to avoid having to meet me.'

'Then it will be a happy reunion for both of you,' Holmes remarked with a chuckle of amusement which I did not share.

'I do not think—' I began in protest.

'Just as well, my dear fellow. Better to leave any mental effort to me. I am more practised in that field than you are. And now,' he continued, striding to the door, 'I must call briefly on Lestrade again to put the finishing touches to my plan. If I were a cricketing man, which I am not, I would enlarge on the metaphor by saying that in the game I am proposing, Lestrade shall act as longstop, you shall be the wicketkeeper and I shall be the bowler who delivers what I believe is known as a "googly".'

'And Carruthers?' I asked.

'Oh, he will be the batsman who is bowled out for a duck!' Holmes declared and, laughing loudly, he went running down the stairs.

* * *

Holmes and I started off together for the Kandahar on the following Friday to set in motion Holmes' 'little game of cricket', as he insisted on calling it. He was in one of his excitable moods and was clearly relishing the thought of the coming adventure and its consequences which, if all went well, would result in the downfall of Colonel Carruthers.

Before we went inside the club, he insisted that we made a quick reconnoitre of the back of the building to check that Lestrade had made sure the rear exit was covered; not that he thought the inspector was unreliable but, like a general before a battle, he needed to confirm for himself that everything was arranged according to plan, a meticulous attention to detail which extended to his own appearance, for he insisted on wearing a small black moustache in case Carruthers might have seen likenesses of him in the illustrated papers and would recognise him.

We discovered that Lestrade who, though lacking imagination, according to Holmes, is nevertheless an efficient officer in other matters, had indeed secured the rear exit by positioning a costermonger selling apples from a barrow by the back door while two other policemen in plain clothes were strolling up and down the street, chatting to one another and trying to look inconspicuous.

At the sight of them, Holmes nodded approvingly and we set off round the corner to the front of the building where Lestrade, also in civilian clothes, was waiting for us on the doorstep of the Kandahar.

After I had signed in my two 'guests', we moved into the dining-room where we were shown to a table facing the door on the far side of the room which, on Holmes' instructions, the manager had reserved for us and, having been served, we began our meal. As arranged, I was sitting with my back to the door so that Carruthers would not see me when he entered and be frightened off. He came when we were finishing the first course and were about to order the pudding. As a signal of his arrival, Holmes gently nudged my foot with his under the table.

I must admit I was tempted to turn my head to look at him, not out of curiosity so much as to satisfy myself that the description of him I had given to Holmes was correct. But I resisted and concentrated instead on the food that was in front of me and on the conversation that was struck up among the three of us, trying as hard as I could to behave naturally, a difficult task when I was tingling with anticipation and desire to see the infamous fraudster arrested and marched out of the club in handcuffs.

I did, however, allow my feelings to overcome my prudence and, on the way out of the dining-room, I risked a quick sideways glance in his direction. I need not have felt so anxious. Carruthers was tucking into a portion of steak and kidney pie and, between mouthfuls, was absorbed in reading a copy of the *Morning Herald* which was propped up in front of him against the salt and pepper pots.

There he was, as handsome as ever, his hair and moustache carefully brushed, and his black eyepatch neatly in place.

He appeared not to have seen us and continued eating and reading as we made our way through the door and across the lobby to the billiard-room.

Holmes had instructed us meticulously as to how we were to play out the last part of our little drama. So, following his directions, I took off my jacket and hung it over the back of a chair that was within reach of the door and that itself had been deliberately left half open. Lestrade placed himself near the billiard table, as if he intended watching the game. Meanwhile, Holmes and I chose our cues and went through the pretence of setting out the balls and tossing a coin to decide who should go first. Holmes won the toss. After that, all we had to do was to push the balls about, Holmes taking the initiative, while I was careful to stand with my back to the door so that Carruthers, when he came, would not see my face.

The trap was set. From then on, it was simply a matter of waiting for Carruthers to arrive.

He came.

With my face averted, I did not actually witness his arrival. All I heard was Lestrade's voice calling out, 'Hey, you! Wait a moment!', followed by the clatter as Holmes' cue fell to the floor and then the sound of footsteps running across the parquet floor.

I whirled round and was just in time to see Holmes

and Lestrade struggling in the doorway with Carruthers, who was fighting in a most ungentlemanly manner that obeyed no rules that I was aware of, certainly not Queensberry's.[19]

It was Holmes who brought him down with a rapid uppercut to the jaw[20] and he fell as if he had been poleaxed, the skill and swiftness of the blow giving rise to an outburst of spontaneous applause from the small group of bystanders comprising waiters and club members who had been attracted to the scene by the noise.

Lestrade immediately despatched one of the waiters to collect the plain-clothes men who had been guarding the back door before sending another to call up a four-wheeler. While waiting for its arrival, he snapped a pair of handcuffs on Carruthers' wrists and began swiftly searching his pockets.

As he had suspected, several cheques, torn from my cheque book, were found on him and these Lestrade promptly confiscated along with the book itself, as evidence of the man's larceny. So for the second time in as many months, I was deprived of my cheque book.

But it was a small price to pay for having the

---

[19] The 8th Marquess of Queensberry, a keen patron of boxing, supervised the formation of a new set of rules to govern the sport in 1867. Dr John F. Watson.

[20] Sherlock Holmes was a skilled amateur boxer who, according to the professional prizefighter McMurdo, could have turned professional himself. Dr John F. Watson.

satisfaction of Cheeseman alias Carruthers alias half a dozen other assumed names sent for trial and sentenced to several years' hard labour by the judge who, in his summing up, referred to his long career of theft, fraud and forgery, not to mention his general moral turpitude.

'I have not felt so much pleasure over the outcome of an inquiry since the arrest of the three-handed widow,' Holmes remarked, laying down the *Morning Chronicle,* which contained a detailed report of the trial.

'The three-handed widow?' I exclaimed in surprise, for it was the second time my old friend had referred to this particular individual.

'Indeed, Watson. And a more demure and prim little woman you could not wish to meet in a month of Sundays. Remind me to tell you about the case one of these days. You can add it to your collection of highly coloured narratives concerning my career. In the meantime, I would appreciate a little silence while I finish reading this account of Lady Petersham and the gypsy fortune-teller.'

And with that, he shook out the pages of the newspaper and disappeared behind them.

THE CASE OF THE
THREE-HANDED WIDOW

In the event, it was nearly January before Holmes found the time to recount the case of the three-handed widow. Several other investigations came up which demanded his immediate attention, among which was an urgent request on behalf of the Bishop of Sunderland to inquire into the identity of the person who was ordering quite unsuitable merchandise to be delivered to the palace, cash on delivery. It was only after that embarrassing business had been successfully cleared up that he found the leisure to turn to that other case, the details of which, I must confess, I was impatient to hear.

A three-handed widow! Could Holmes be joking?

As I remember, it was a bitterly cold day and strangely

silent, for an overnight snowfall had deadened all sound from the street outside our windows, where there was no movement of either people or traffic. The whole world, it seemed, had turned white, against which the branches of the leafless trees and the lamp posts stood out stark and black under the pewter-coloured sky.

Inside our sitting-room, however, all was warmth and light. The gas lamps were lit and a cheerful fire burned in the hearth, its bright glow reflected in the bowl of oranges on the table.

Holmes and I sat close to the fire, both of us silent, as if the snow had cast its stillness over us as well, until suddenly my old friend roused himself and, taking his pipe out of his mouth, remarked, 'Tell me, Watson, did I ever give that account I promised you?'

'Which one?' I asked.

'The three-handed one.'

'No, you have not told me about that yet.'

'Ah! I thought not. I had forgotten about it myself until this recent inquiry regarding the bishop and the chaplain, which reminded me of that other investigation which also concerned members of the church, a vicar and a curate in that particular case. Would you like to hear it, my dear fellow?'

'Indeed I would,' I replied warmly.

'Then,' said Holmes with a smile, 'I shall begin.

'It happened while I was still living in Montague Street and had not long begun to earn my living as a consulting detective, although my reputation was starting to grow and I was developing quite a satisfactory circle of clients. Among the most interesting to come my way in those early days were a pair of clergymen, the Rev. Samuel Whittlemore, the vicar of St Matthias the Less of Fountain Square, Chelsea, and his curate, James Thorogood.

'I had received by post a request from the Rev. Whittlemore for an appointment at half past three on a Wednesday afternoon in October but the letter gave no clue for the reason behind this request, nor the fact that he would be accompanied by his curate, and it was much to my surprise that *two* clerical gentlemen were shown into my sitting-room in Montague Street.

'The senior of the two, the Rev. Whittlemore, was a tall, elderly, stoop-shouldered man with a beaky profile and thin white hair through which patches of shiny scalp were visible. He had about him an air of disapproval, some of which was directed at me but some, I felt, was also turned on his companion, James Thorogood, perhaps simply for being young and good-looking and of a normally cheerful disposition, although at the time of our meeting he seemed uncharacteristically cast down.

'I was soon to discover the cause of his low spirits.

'As I might have guessed, the Rev. Whittlemore took charge of the interview from the beginning. Eyeing me with considerable suspicion, he remarked, "I assume you *are* Mr Sherlock Holmes? Only you look far too young and inexperienced to be an expert on any subject, let alone crime."

'After I had assured him of my competence by pointing out that, on occasion, Scotland Yard officers had consulted me[1] about certain investigations, he climbed down as far as to remark, "Well, young man, we shall see how successfully you handle my particular case," in a tone of voice which suggested he had no great trust in my competence.

'As you may imagine, this little exchange had left me rather annoyed with my reverend client and I was about to suggest that he looked elsewhere for another older and wiser consultant to take my place when his animosity shifted from me to his curate, on whom he cast a condemnatory glance before announcing in a high-pitched, nasal voice, "The matter I wish to lay before you, Mr Holmes, is quite outrageous. It concerns a member of my congregation, an elderly lady of high reputation and social standing, who shall be nameless. Last Sunday morning, she was robbed of her reticule containing a considerable sum of money after attending matins in *my* church."

'The tone of his voice suggested that some outraged comment was expected on my part, but I could raise nothing more than a low murmur of disapproval, not even a "tut-tut" .

'There is nothing I dislike more than having my

---

[1] Sherlock Holmes assisted the official police in several investigations, for example in the adventure of 'The Man with the Twisted Lip', in which he uncovers the true identity of the beggar for the benefit of Inspector Bradstreet. Dr John F. Watson.

emotions orchestrated for me, particularly when the person doing the orchestration is a cold, humourless individual such as Whittlemore. I also suspected that the lady in question was almost certainly wealthy and contributed generously to the upkeep of St Matthias the Less, and probably also to Whittlemore's stipend, hence his grievance.

'So I replied in a non-committal voice, "I see. When exactly did this robbery take place? Was it during the service?"

'"No, after the service," he corrected me sharply, as if I ought to have known this simple fact. "When matins was finished, I went, as usual, to stand in the porch to shake hands with the members of the congregation as they left and to thank them for coming. It is, I feel, a courtesy on my part which is much appreciated. Mr Thorogood stands on the other side of the porch to carry out a similar duty."

'This last sentence was spoken dismissively as if the curate's presence was of little consequence.

'"I should explain," the Rev. Whittlemore continued, "that my services are very popular and always draw a large congregation so that the porch can become quite crowded on occasions. In fact, it was only after the last person had left that I was aware that anything untoward had happened. The lady in question returned to the porch in some distress. It seemed that a purse containing three guineas," and here he paused to give me time to register the exact value of the sum of money which had been stolen, before repeating it with greater emphasis, "*three guineas* had been taken from her reticule!"

'I felt I ought to make some response this time, so I remarked, "Quite a large sum."

'"Indeed it is!" he concurred. "The point is it must have been stolen when the lady was leaving the church. There was quite a crowd of people in the porch waiting to shake hands and, in the crush, someone must have taken a knife or a pair of scissors and slit open the lady's reticule, which she was carrying on her wrist, before slipping a hand inside the receptacle and removing the purse. Besides the money it contained, the purse itself was quite a valuable object. It was of embroidered satin that must have cost at least a guinea in a West End emporium."

'Again, this emphasis on money, I noticed.

'"Did anyone witness the theft?" I asked.

'The Rev. Whittlemore turned deliberately towards his curate who was perched in silence by his side, looking uncomfortable, his pleasant features contracted into an expression of acute anxiety.

'"Well?" he demanded.

'"I am afraid I was nearest to Lady . . ." he began, and then fell guiltily silent when the Rev. Whittlemore cleared his throat as a warning not to mention any names.

'"I am so very sorry," the curate stammered. "I meant to say the lady concerned . . ."

'I decided it was time I intervened, partly to put the

poor young man out of his misery but largely, I must admit, to bring the interview forward and to prevent Whittlemore from holding up the proceedings any further.

'"As you are clearly anxious to protect the lady's anonymity, may I suggest we refer to her as 'Lady Dee?' I announced and was pleased to see the young curate looked grateful for the suggestion. Even the Rev. Whittlemore bowed his head in agreement, a minor victory, I felt.

'"So please continue," said I, addressing the curate. "You said you were standing near Lady Dee when the theft must have taken place. Did you notice anyone in particular close by; almost certainly another woman?"

'"You seem very sure it was a woman, young man," Whittlemore interjected in a condescending tone of voice.

'"Indeed I am!" I retorted sharply, for by this time I was becoming exasperated by his superior attitude. "I have some experience of pickpockets, both male and female. It would be most unusual for a male thief to approach close enough to a female victim under those circumstances to pick her pocket, or in this case her reticule. Had a man done so, the lady would have instinctively drawn away and by doing so would have attracted attention to him. The art of picking pockets is to be inconspicuous. That is why I suggested a female thief."

'I was pleased to see that Whittlemore himself

withdrew to the extent of leaning back in his chair and thereby signalling that I had won that particular round in the battle of wits, which gave me a little triumphant thrill. I was then still young and brash enough to delight in getting the better of an opponent, especially of a clergyman who had too high an opinion of himself.

'"Well, there was one lady," the curate began hesitantly. "But I cannot believe she could be responsible . . ."

'"Why?" Whittlemore demanded. But I was determined not to let him take charge again, so I overrode him, despite his years and his clerical standing.

'"Please describe her in as much detail as you can recall," I said, pointedly addressing my remarks to the young curate, who seemed relieved by my assumption of authority.

'"She was in her twenties, I should think," Thorogood replied. "About five feet six inches in height; recently widowed, for she was dressed completely in black which looked new, including her bonnet and her reticule that she was carrying in one hand. With the other she was holding a little girl about three years old, also dressed in black. The child had fair hair and was very pretty, like her mother."

'The last detail seemed to slip involuntarily from the curate's lips, for no sooner had he spoken the words than he looked flustered and the blood ran up into his cheeks. It was quite obvious that the young man had been attracted to the widow and was embarrassed that he had made this apparent to a stranger and, more pertinently, to his vicar, who cleared his throat in a most disapproving manner.

'Witnessing this little scene, I was convinced that for all his mature years and priestly training, Whittlemore was still human enough to experience the more corporeal emotions such as envy, one of the deadly sins, perhaps even physical desire, although he would never admit that in a thousand years. These feelings were, I thought, probably the root cause of his dislike of his young curate. My own reaction was unexpected and I was considerably taken aback for, in that moment, I felt I had learned more about human nature than I had ever acquired before in all my years of book learning.

'It was therefore with this newly won enlightenment that I turned back to the Rev. Whittlemore and asked in as pleasant a manner as I could muster, "I understand your dilemma, sir, and I shall do my very best to resolve it. Your curate has given me an excellent description of the person who almost certainly carried out the theft and I shall do all I can to trace her."

'It was evident that Whittlemore had not himself experienced an equivalent moment of personal enlightenment for he snapped back at me with his old animosity, "With discretion, I trust."

'I dared not reply in case I made my exasperation too obvious, so I merely bowed my head in agreement before escorting the two of them to the door.

'It was only after I had returned to my chair that

the full consequences of what I had done dawned on me. Foolishly, I had allowed myself to be forced into a commitment which I had no idea how to carry out. That was another lesson I learned that morning, Watson. Never raise the hopes of a client about the outcome of a case unless you know you can fulfil them. Self-confidence is one thing; complacency is quite another.

'As I sat there that morning, the reality of the situation became painfully apparent. I had assumed from the beginning that the young woman whom Thorogood had described so vividly was indeed the thief. But what if I were wrong and someone else in the crowded porch had stolen the old lady's purse? Or the theft had occurred inside the church?

'I realised I had been arrogant in acting so dismissively towards the Rev. Whittlemore, who might himself have valuable evidence regarding the young woman and the child. Perhaps she was a regular member of his congregation whose name and address were known to him.

'I saw there was no other recourse but to seek out the Rev. Whittlemore and eat humble pie. So I learned another painful lesson that morning, Watson. Never antagonise your potential witnesses if you can possibly avoid it.

'Thank goodness, I had at least kept Whittlemore's visiting card which gave me his address, and consequently the following morning I set off by cab for St Matthias the Less in Fountain Square, trusting that the vicar would be at home and willing to receive me.

'The church was an elegant eighteenth-century edifice set in a quiet part of Chelsea. The vicarage was not so charming. Built of white stucco, it faced a burial ground crowded with gravestones and enclosed by high black railings which put me in mind of the Rev. Whittlemore. It had the same severe, forbidding look about it and it was with considerable misgivings that I mounted the steps to the front door and rang the bell.

'An elderly black-clad woman answered the door, Whittlemore's housekeeper, I assumed, and I half-expected the kind of grudging welcome that he would have given me and was therefore surprised and relieved when she took my proffered card with a smile and invited me into the hall, where I waited for a few moments before she ushered me into the rector's study.

'It could have been a handsome room, for it had the proportions of the Georgian period, with an elegant plaster cornice and a single long sash window. Unfortunately, it was full of large, ugly, dark oak furniture and the view through the window was of the churchyard, with its gravestones crammed shoulder to shoulder and only an occasional angel of discoloured marble to relieve the severity of the melancholy rows.

'The Rev. Whittlemore had already taken up his position on the hearth rug where he stood waiting to receive me, hands clasped behind his back and an expression of considerable disfavour on his face.

'"Yes?" he inquired, not giving me the courtesy of addressing me by name.

'I felt like a pupil summoned by the headmaster to his office for transgressing some sacred school rule such as whistling in the corridor or walking into chapel with my hands in my pockets.

'I said, trying to keep my voice and face as pleasant as I could, "I have been reconsidering that most interesting case which you spoke of yesterday and, after careful thought, I have come to certain conclusions."

'"Indeed?" he replied, raising his eyebrows. It was not a very encouraging response but I thought I perceived a softening of his granite features and a brightening of that hard, disapproving stare.

'I continued, "I cannot, of course, be positive at this early stage of the inquiry but it is my belief that the lady in black, who almost certainly stole the purse, is an accomplished pickpocket who chose your church quite deliberately. However, there are two or three factors concerning this theory which need clarifying. So, if you would be so good as to answer a few additional queries, I should be much obliged."

'"What are these factors you refer to?" he asked, regarding me with an expression which, while it could not be exactly described as approving, was considerably more tolerant than before.

'I pressed on.

'"Is it possible that this woman could have attended your church before last Sunday?"

118

'He considered this question with grave attention and seemed about to deny it when I, fearful of losing the initiative, continued, "Perhaps wearing different clothing or sitting behind a pillar where she might not have easily been seen?"

'"Yes, that is possible, I suppose," he grudgingly agreed, "But the child . . ."

'"She may not have had the child with her on these other occasions."

'"Oh!" He seemed put out by the idea. "Well, I suppose that is possible but I did not particularly notice anybody, although, now you have mentioned it, there was a woman who seemed young and who was wearing a veil, but not widow's weeds. She sat at the back of the church and slipped out before the rest of the congregation left. I certainly did not shake hands with her and neither did my curate. He was detained at the door."

'"Was he indeed? By whom?" I asked, aware suddenly of a more complex plot than I had at first imagined.

'"By a man; not one of my regular congregation, for I had never seen him before. He was middle-aged, stockily built, wearing spectacles, with grey hair and a moustache. I noticed him particularly because he kept Mr Thorogood talking in the porch for several moments, about what, I have no idea, but I remember being annoyed at the time. It meant the people behind him were delayed in leaving. I said to Thorogood afterwards, 'Never let them chat. Just shake hands and wish them good morning or evening, whichever applies. We are not a Friendly Society.' In fact, I thought I saw him again last Sunday. Seen from the back, he resembled the man who kept Thorogood talking, but as soon as I saw his face, I realised I had been mistaken."

'"Really? May I ask what was the difference?"

'"The second man was much younger. He had dark hair and was clean-shaven. There was also a most distinctive mole on his face which I am sure I would have noticed before. I am rather proud of my ability to remember faces. One has to learn the skill when one has large congregations."

'There was an exasperated note in his voice when he made the last remark as if he suspected me of doubting his word and, aware that I was treading on dangerous ground, I changed the subject.

'"Tell me," I said, "was last Sunday a special occasion?"

'"Special? Of course it was! It was our saint's feast day. That was why there were so many people in church."

'"And this special feast day was known about in the parish?"

'"Certainly! There were announcements posted on the churchyard gates and in the porch itself." He spoke sharply as if I had accused him of neglecting his parochial duties.

'I decided to leave it there, Watson, at least for the time being.'

'You did not interview the curate again?'

'No. I thought I had enough information to be going on with for the time being. If more were needed, I could always call back at the rectory when I was more sure of my ground.'

'What ground?' I asked, a little puzzled by his reply.

'The whole of it, of course! Remember, I was then a young man and, to be frank, a little overconfident of my detective skills whereas, in fact, I was very much a greenhorn when it came to certain aspects of crime, especially those connected with the professional criminal and the underworld he, or she, inhabits. Take fraud as an example. I had very little idea of its complexity, the training of its perpetrators, the myriad subterfuges, the countless tricks of the trade. It even had its own language, "magsman", for example, or "neddy", or "shofulman". These are just a few instances of the variety of its vocabulary.[2]

'The same applies to pickpockets, or "dippers" as they are known in the trade. In my ignorance, I had assumed they were all young street urchins, like the Artful Dodger,[3] and, although I realised there was more

---

[2] These words are examples of 'cant', a language used by the criminal underworld. A 'magsman' is a cheat, a 'neddy' is a cosh and a 'shofulman' is a person who passes on fake or forged money. Dr John F. Watson.

[3] The Artful Dodger is a character from Charles Dickens' novel *Oliver Twist,* who is a member of the gang of young boys trained by Fagin to be pickpockets. Dr John F. Watson.

to it than that, at the time I was quite unaware of how much more I had to learn, and quickly, too, if I were to solve the case of the stolen purse to the satisfaction of the Rev. Samuel Whittlemore. And I had to succeed. It would have hurt my *amour propre* exceedingly if I had been forced to admit defeat.

'So I went back to my lodgings in Montague Street, shut the door firmly and sat down to think over what action I could take to bring the inquiry to a successful conclusion.

'The facts of the case were easily established. "Lady Dee", or whatever her real identity might be, had been robbed of a purse containing three guineas in the porch of St Matthias' Church virtually under the noses of two clergymen and members of the congregation. The "dipper" was apparently a young and attractive widow with a three-year-old child, who had cleverly slit open "Lady Dee's" reticule and removed the purse.

'But how had she contrived to carry out this theft? She was holding the child by one hand and carrying her own reticule on the wrist of the other. It seemed impossible.

'As for apprehending the thief, it seemed quite out of the question. I had no idea who she was or where she came from, although some aspects of the crime seemed significant and might lead eventually to an arrest. For example, the theft had been carried out in a public place – a church – and among a crowd of people. Was it possible that the thief had deliberately chosen that place and that time? I then remembered that the Rev. Whittlemore had pointed out that the service was a special occasion and had been advertised in the neighbourhood.

'In addition, there was the stockily built man who was seen among the congregation on both occasions. The changes in his appearance – the moustache, the spectacles, the large mole on his face – suggested theatrical disguises and these alone intrigued me. As a young consulting detective, I was becoming increasingly aware of the usefulness of wigs and greasepaint and all the other paraphernalia that actors use to change their appearance.[4] Although I was at the time ignorant of all the tricks "dippers" used, I was aware they frequently acted in pairs, one to carry out the actual theft, the other to take the stolen item when it was passed to him, or her, by the "dipper" and then to disappear from the scene as quickly as possible.

'I must admit, Watson, that by the time I had thoroughly thought the matter over, I was extremely pleased with the results. I now knew the method that was used by the thief, or rather, thieves, and this knowledge in turn gave me a brilliantly inspired notion of how I might bring about their arrest.

'I therefore went to Scotland Yard and put my plan before Inspector Lestrade who, I felt, was in my debt as I had assisted him in solving several inquiries while I

---

[4] Sherlock Holmes was himself an adept in the use of disguise. Dr John F. Watson.

was living in Montague Street, the first being a case of forgery.[5] We came to an arrangement on a quid pro quo basis, that I would help him over a recent investigation into a burglary while he, in turn, would provide me with the services of a constable, a certain Herbert Pound, a young, intelligent officer who later moved quickly up the ranks and became an inspector. Incidentally, to jump forward in time, it was Pound who arrested Dawkins, the notorious blackmailer who murdered Jenny McBride and threw her body into the Thames. You may recall the case, Watson. The papers were full of it at the time.

'However, to *revenir à nos moutons*, as the French say, my plan was this. I had no doubt my suspects would strike again using the same method. Criminals on the whole are the most conservative of creatures. They live and operate in the same districts, pursue the same illegal activities, use the same modus operandi to commit the same types of crime. Once you have identified these similarities, you can follow the criminal's spoor like that of a wild beast in the jungle, visit his watering holes, identify his lairs and the places where he lies in wait for his prey.

'The same precept applied to my pickpockets who,

---

[5] In *A Study in Scarlet*, Dr John H. Watson lists 'the many acquaintances' who called on Sherlock Holmes soon after they had moved into their new lodgings at 221B Baker Street. Among them was a 'little sallow, rat-faced, dark-eyed fellow' who Sherlock Holmes later explains was a 'well-known detective' whom he had helped over a forgery case. The reference is to Inspector Lestrade. Dr John F. Watson.

for convenience's sake, I christened the Widow and her Beau, for I was convinced the relationship between the two of them was more than a mere professional fraternity. They would hunt out their prey, not in the streets but in crowded public places, and their preferred choice of victim would be found among the middle classes, who were more likely to be wearing or carrying on their persons objects worth stealing such as gold watches and well-stocked purses and notecases.

'So, following this theory, I searched the newspapers looking for advertisements for special events that would interest a well-heeled clientele, such as bazaars, charity fairs and fund-raising concerts. You would be amazed, Watson, at how often these events were held, many of them for charitable causes, and how the better class of citizens flocked to them to spend their money on home-made cakes or hand-painted bookmarkers for the sake of benighted natives in Borneo, shipwrecked mariners or destitute seamstresses in Shadwell.

'Knowing that the Widow and her Beau would find such events a valuable source of well-to-do victims, I also surmised that they would almost certainly follow the same procedure as they had at St Matthias the Less. In other words, they would make a preliminary visit to these places to size up the situation; for example, to discover where the exits were placed and how tight was the general security. They would then return later to carry out the actual robbery. As Pound had other duties beside assisting me, I usually carried out these preliminary forays on my own.

'Oh, it was such a lonely and dispiriting business, my dear fellow! I cannot tell you the number of times I called in at the various venues where these bazaars were held, usually church halls or similar premises, and how I would wander about for hours at a time, trying to look interested in the goods for sale and occasionally buying something in order not to make myself conspicuous by my miserliness. At the end of five days, I had nothing to show for my trouble except half a dozen handkerchiefs embroidered with the letters S.H. in one corner and a shelf full of hand-painted pots for holding collar studs and small change.

'I was on the point of abandoning the whole project when, on the last Wednesday of the month, I ran them to earth in an assembly room in Kensington. I was so jubilant that I almost danced a hornpipe on the spot but managed to restrain myself. For there they were! The Beau was grey-haired on this occasion, wearing spectacles and a trim, little moustache. He had the respectable air of a senior bank clerk or the manager of a superior gentlemen's outfitters. No one in their right mind would have picked him out as anyone of disrepute, let alone a professional thief.

'Having discovered the Beau, I now set about finding the Widow among the crowds of eager customers and I soon ran her to earth quietly examining a display of bunches of lavender sold for the benefit of the widows of impecunious missionaries.

'She was a young woman, petite of figure and modest of bearing, although I could understand why Thorogood was attracted to her. There was something very appealing about her – a shy vulnerability that the black widow's weeds she was wearing emphasised in a most charming manner, as no doubt they were intended to do. She was accompanied by a little girl of three years, I estimated, who was also dressed completely in black from the top of her dear little bonnet down to the toes of her dainty boots.

'I stood back and studied them from a distance, trying to solve the riddle of how she had managed to slit open Lady Dee's reticule and steal the purse it contained when both her black-mittened hands were fully occupied, the left with a reticule of her own, the right with one of the little girl's hands, which she was holding tightly as if to make sure they were not separated in the crowds that jostled between the stalls.

'Together they formed a charming pair: a mother and daughter, recently bereaved by the death, no doubt, of a husband and father, standing there, hand in hand, examining the bunches of lavender with such captivating innocence.

'For a moment, I too was seduced by the sight of them. How could they possibly be guilty of any misdemeanour? They were the personification of virtue and honesty. And then common sense prevailed. I believe I have mentioned to you before, Watson, that the most winning woman I ever knew was hanged for poisoning three little children for their insurance money.[6]

'So I hardened my heart and left in search of a cab to take me to Herbert Pound at Scotland Yard, with whom I made arrangements there and then to meet him at the Kensington Assembly Rooms the following afternoon, trusting to luck that the Widow and her Beau would keep to their usual schedule.

'In the event, it was three days later before they reappeared and, having given up hope of seeing them again that day, I was in the middle of apologising profusely to Pound for the waste of his and police time, when we saw them; or rather, Pound saw them first, having recognised them from my description of them. Giving me a nudge with his elbow, he indicated them with a nod of his head. And there they were, the Widow and the child, hand in hand as before, but not examining the goods for sale on this occasion. Instead, they were following purposefully a few paces behind an elderly lady and her younger companion who were walking slowly between the rows of stalls, the old lady leaning on a stick, an old-fashioned reticule in her other hand, her companion carrying several small parcels, no doubt purchases they had already made.

'Several seconds later, I caught sight of the Beau as

---

[6] In *The Sign of Four*, Sherlock Holmes remarks that 'the most winning woman' he had ever known was hanged for poisoning three little children for their insurance money. Dr John F. Watson.

well, keeping a discreet distance from the two ladies, his appearance slightly altered from the last time I saw him, the moustache replaced by a neatly clipped goatee beard.

'There was an air of purpose about the two of them which convinced me that they had chosen their victim and would carry out the theft within a very short space of time.

'When, a few seconds later, they actually performed the crime, I had to admire their skill. Their timing and coordination were impeccable. They hung back until they were within yards of the exit doors and only then made their move when other people were either entering or leaving the building so that the area round the doors was crowded. The only warning Pound and I had was the Beau's sudden change of pace. Instead of tagging along behind the Widow and her chosen victim, he stepped smartly forward so that he was ahead of them.

'The next second, the Widow had also moved forward so that she was alongside the elderly lady and her companion. It was then that she pounced. Brushing past her victim, she seemed to lose her balance momentarily, as if someone had pushed against her. In that moment, something was passed to the Beau who, picking up speed, hurried towards the exit doors, thrusting whatever he had been given into the pocket of his ulster.

'The theft was carried out with such audacity and

professionalism that the old lady seemed unaware that her reticule was no longer hanging on her arm. Then the truth dawned on her and she gave a little cry of alarm, but rather too ladylike to arouse much response in the people milling about in the aisles. By the time her lady-companion was aware of the incident, the Beau had left the building and the Widow and the little girl were also about to disappear through the swing doors.

'I had already arranged with Constable Pound that we would split forces when it came to making an arrest: he would tackle the Beau while I would take on the Widow. Therefore the two of us sprinted off on our separate missions, he in close chase of the man, I following hard on the heels of the woman who, aware by now that they had been "rumbled", to use the slang term they themselves would have employed, was struggling to rid herself of the little girl who was still clinging to her hand and was impeding her progress, as the child was having difficulty in keeping up with her.

'It was only later that I realised what the Widow was doing as she plunged about under her cloak. All I saw was the child's sudden release and the Widow who, lifting up her skirts, was running ahead of me like a black hare into the crowds, leaving the little girl standing alone on the pavement and, to my utter bewilderment, still holding the woman's hand.

'That, of course, was impossible!

'If I was confused, so, too, was the child. For a moment or two she remained standing hand in hand with what I now realised as I drew nearer was an artificial arm and hand, the latter wearing a black mitten, the whole contraption attached to a sort of shoulder harness. As soon as I saw it, light dawned.

'So that was how the theft was carried out! What a fool I had been not to realise it before!

'Before setting out to commit the crime, the Widow had strapped on a shoulder harness to which a false arm and hand were attached. These were then passed down through her mantle, the child taking hold of the fake hand when it emerged from the sleeve. The Widow's real hand and arm were then allowed to hang loose inside this outer garment which had an opening at the side through which the Widow could either snatch at the victim's reticule or cut it loose with a knife or a pair of scissors.

'When the theft had been accomplished, the Beau would then move forward and the Widow would pass the stolen reticule to him, which he would swiftly conceal in his own pocket. In the meantime, the Widow and the child, still apparently hand in hand, would walk away from the scene of the crime, looking the very picture of innocence.

'It was unlikely she would be arrested, for there would be few, if any, witnesses to the theft. It was over in a matter of seconds and who would be callous enough to accuse a young, widowed mother of such a felony, let alone lay hands on her and proceed to stop and search her?

'The whole affair was devilishly cunning, Watson, and, in a perverse way, I had to admire the sheer ingenuity of the crime. A false arm! A widowed mother! A pretty, young child! And the choice of venue and victim were also inspired. The crime took place in a middle-class setting and the victim herself looked respectable. People from that social category do not expect to be robbed by three-handed widows and, should they suspect that such a crime had taken place, they are unlikely to make a scene in public.'

'So the Widow and her Beau were not arrested?' I said, assuming that was the end of the story. Holmes quickly corrected me.

'Certainly not, Watson! The law had to be allowed to run its course and I had to follow it to the very end. Pray allow me to finish.

'Once the theft had taken place and the reticule had been handed over to the Beau, it was Constable Pound's turn to bring the curtain down on part of this little drama. As I have already explained, Pound and I had come to an agreement. He was to arrest the Beau, I the Widow. So, as soon as the Beau made off for the exit doors with the stolen reticule concealed in his ulster, Pound acted. Shouting "Stop thief!", he bounded forward. I, too, made ready to seize the Widow. But she was an extremely slippery fish. Dropping the false hand and arm, she, too, made a run for the doors.'

'Abandoning the child?' I asked in horrified disbelief. 'Oh, Holmes, what a dreadful thing to do!'

'That is exactly what I thought at the time. How utterly disgraceful! But I need not have wasted my sentiment. As soon as the Widow disappeared, the child also vanished, wriggling her way through the crowds and out of the door. By the time I reached the exit, the Widow had disappeared but the child, whose legs were much shorter, was still visible, running for dear life, her charming little black bonnet bobbing up and down as she went.'

'So what did you do?' I asked, aghast at the situation.

'Followed her, of course,' Holmes said crisply. 'There was no other choice. Over the years, I have in my professional career trailed various criminals and, on occasions, dogs as well.[7] But never have I acted like a bloodhound in pursuit of a child. Oh, she was very nimble, Watson! A veritable little terrier! In and out of the crowds she went, down alleyways and through passages with me hot on her heels. She was unaware I was following her, for she did not once glance over her shoulder. But one thing was clear to me: young though she was, she was

---

[7] In 'The Adventure of the Creeping Man', Sherlock Holmes states that he had 'serious thoughts' of writing a small monologue upon the use of dogs in the work of a detective. Dogs feature in several inquiries including 'The Adventure of the Missing Three-Quarter' in which he uses a dog called Pompey to trace the whereabouts of Godfrey Staunton, a missing rugby player. The dog follows the tracks to a cottage where the missing man is found at the bedside of his dead wife. Dr John F. Watson.

fully familiar with the backstreets of that area of London, which convinced me that she had been taken there on other thieving excursions in the past.

'Down Oxford Street we went before turning left in the direction of Warren Street, where we entered one of those indeterminate areas of London composed of shabby little side streets that are neither disreputable enough to be called a slum, nor respectable enough to be considered genteel. Here our journey ended in front of a small terraced house, in design not unlike the type where Colonel Carruthers lived, only much neater and better kept. In the complex strata of the English class system, I would have placed it three rungs up from the bottom of the social ladder. It had clean lace curtains at the windows and a brightly polished door-knocker in the shape of a mermaid. There were even pots of geraniums standing on the sill.

'I paused outside for a moment or two, earnestly studying my notebook that I had taken from my pocket as if verifying the address, before lifting the mermaid by the tail and rapping smartly on the door.

'It was opened by a plump, motherly-looking woman in a clean pinafore carrying a baby on one arm, wrapped in a shawl. Just beyond her, I caught a glimpse of a door partly set open, which afforded me a view of the room beyond: a parlour, by the look of it, with a cheerful fire burning on the hearth, the shelves of the overmantel crowded with little ornaments in glass and china and fretted wood.

'And there, before the fire, sitting on a velvet-covered pouffe, her bonnet off and her plump little legs extended comfortably towards the flames, was the pretty child who had clung so loyally to the Widow's third hand.

'There was no sign of the Widow nor, come to that, of the Beau but there were three or four other children of various ages seated about the room, playing quietly together; nicely dressed children with neatly combed hair, their little faces shining with health and cleanliness.

'It took a moment or two for the significance of the scene to dawn on me and, when it did, I was deeply shocked. The little girl and the other children, including the baby, were the means whereby the woman made her living. She rented them out by the day to people like the Widow and the Beau who, in turn, made their own livings by begging or stealing or any other fraudulent activities in which the presence of a child would help to enhance their professional takings.

'My train of thought was interrupted by the woman who had answered the door, the owner of those children.

'"Yes, sir; can I 'elp you?" she inquired in that soft, wheedling tone of voice that door-to-door sellers of trinkets or lucky white heather tend to use and that I always find particularly nauseating for its obvious insincerity. But, not wishing to rouse her suspicions, I asked in as normal and pleasant manner I could muster if I could speak to Mrs Harrison.

'"I think you've come to the wrong address, sir," she replied. "There's no Mrs 'Arrison livin' 'ere."

'So I thanked her and moved on.

'I was also anxious to find out from Constable Pound, whom I had already arranged to meet once the arrests had been carried out, if the Beau had been taken into custody and to pass on to him the information regarding the Widow and, in particular, the child.

'We met in a discreet little coffee shop not far from Scotland Yard, a rendezvous which he had apparently used before, because the waitress, a middle-aged lady, greeted him as an old friend, addressing him as "Bert" and showing us into a small back room, empty apart from the two of us.

'Yes, the Beau, alias Johnny Wilkins, had been arrested, Pound informed me, and, as the old lady's reticule had been found in his pocket, he was charged with theft for which, considering his criminal record, he would probably serve two or three years in Pentonville.

'As for the Widow, Wilkins had given him an address in the Clerkenwell area, but when he called there, she had either flown the roost or Wilkins had deliberately misinformed him.

'"But there's no need to fret," Pound assured me cheerfully. "They'll pick her up some other time for sure."

'When I mentioned the false arm, Pound burst out laughing.

'"Oh, that old trick!" he declared. "Sometimes they don't even bother with the extra arm. They'll use a sling or keep their arm inside their coat and pin up the empty sleeve to look as if the arm's been amputated. It works wonders, that one does, 'specially if the 'dipper' plays the 'old soldier's lay' and wears a row of medals across his chest!"

'When I came to the subject of the child, his smile disappeared.

'"Yes, you're right," he replied. "They hire the little kiddies out at so much a day."

'"And later, when the children are older?" I asked.

'"Well, not to put too fine a point on it, they're rented out for other purposes, 'specially the girls."'

'Oh, Holmes!' I interjected, horrified by the information. 'What can we do about it?'

'For that particular child, nothing at all. You have forgotten the case took place years ago. But, in fact, something was done at the time and by a most unlikely person. Can you guess who?'

'Someone who took part in the inquiry?' I asked, intrigued by the riddle.

'Yes, indeed.'

'And someone unlikely?'

'Extremely unlikely.'

I was silent for a few moments while I tried to guess to whom he was referring. And then the answer came to me in a flash.

'Obviously not the young curate, Thorogood. He is

137

too likely a candidate. Now, if I were a betting man—'[8] I continued, breaking off as Holmes burst out laughing.

Seeing my expression, he straightened his face before adding, 'You are getting warmer, my dear fellow!'

'Then,' I continued, 'my money would be on a rank outsider, the Rev. Samuel Whittlemore.'

'Oh, well done, Watson!' Holmes exclaimed, clapping me on the shoulder. 'To change to another sporting metaphor, you have hit the bullseye! It was indeed Whittlemore, and to extend the image even further, he came up trumps! When I returned to the rectory to inform him about the arrest of Wilkins, who was involved in the theft of his parishioner's reticule – "Lady Dee" as I named her – I happened to mention the little girl and the circumstances in which I found her and the other children. Whittlemore in turn must have passed on the information to Lady Dee who, being an extremely wealthy lady, founded the charity called "The Little Flowers of St Matthias the Less", not a name I would have chosen myself but, as she was paying the piper, so to speak, she called the tune.

'And her goodwill did not end there. Knowing your predilection for happy endings, Watson, it gives

---

[8] Sherlock Holmes is amused because Dr Watson *was* a betting man and spent almost half his army pension on betting on horses. At one point, Holmes locked his cheque book in his desk to prevent him spending any more money at the races. Dr John F. Watson.

me great pleasure to announce that the child, who is now rechristened Ruth, alias Pity, was adopted by Lady Dee, who still must remain anonymous, and is now a charming heiress, happily married to a member of the House of Lords, and is the patroness of her late adoptive mother's charity. So, you see, my dear fellow, to use another well-thumbed metaphor, or in this case, an aphorism, "every cloud has a silver lining".'

THE CASE OF THE
PENTRE MAWR MURDER

'What do you know about Wales?' Holmes inquired one morning, looking up from the letter he had been reading.

'Whales?' I inquired, misunderstanding his question. 'Not a great deal, Holmes, except they are large sea mammals which are hunted for their blubber and are—'

I broke off as he burst out laughing.

'No, not whales, my dear fellow! I am referring to the principality to the west of England. W-A-L-E-S.'

I joined in the laughter for, although I was a little piqued at his amusement at my quite understandable mistake, I was also secretly relieved that Holmes had shown so positive a reaction. For the past few days, he had been in a very low state of mind brought on by the lack of any interesting investigations to stimulate his intellectual powers. I knew from experience that this could be a dangerous situation. Despite my best efforts to wean him off the habit, I was aware that he still occasionally indulged in the use of cocaine when, as he himself expressed it, he was feeling the 'insufferable fatigues of idleness'.[1] The only antidote to this state of affairs, apart from an injection of the drug, was some new and challenging inquiry on which he could hone his unique skills.

'I am afraid I know very little either about Wales,' I replied, 'except it is well known for coal mining and male voice choirs. But what on earth prompted the question?'

'This letter,' he replied, flapping a sheet of paper in my direction. 'Rather than read it to you, I will summarise its contents as it is rather garrulous in places. It is from a certain Dr Gwyn Parry, the general practitioner in a village called Pentre Mawr – at least, I assume that is how it is pronounced – who requests my assistance in what he refers to as "a deeply tragic situation". It appears a patient of his, a local farmer called . . .' and here Holmes glanced briefly at the missive, 'Dai Morgan was stabbed to death two days ago at his farm. His

---

[1] In *The Sign of Four*, Sherlock Holmes states that 'idleness exhausts me completely', a reaction he reiterates in the same account with the remark, 'My mind rebels at stagnation.' Dr John F. Watson.

son, Hywel, has been arrested for his murder and is at present languishing in Abergavenny gaol awaiting trial.

'Dr Parry was evidently called to the scene of the crime by Hywel Morgan, who found the body of his father and it was Parry who made an initial examination of the victim. According to him, and here I quote his very words, "Hywel is a hard-working, God-fearing young man, who is incapable of such a dreadful act of patricide." Dr Parry, it seems, delivered Hywel as a baby, and therefore claims he knows him very well, although I am not sure that the logic of such an assertion would stand up to close cross-questioning in a murder trial. So what do you think, Watson? Shall I accept the good doctor's invitation and investigate the case?'

I was considerably flattered by Holmes' request for my advice; it was not often he asked for help over any matter that touched on his professional life, although I knew in this particular instance that he had no cases on hand and was consequently at a loose end, a state of affairs which left him bored and restless. A trip to Wales might well alleviate that tedium and raise his spirits.

I was therefore quick to agree. Apart from the matter of Holmes' needs, the idea also appealed to me from an entirely selfish point of view, for the prospect of sharing lodgings with a morose and unsociable companion for an uncertain period of time was far from alluring.

'Why not, Holmes?' I replied. 'I have never been to Wales. It would make a change from London, would it not?'

'I suppose so,' Holmes replied, but only half-heartedly. 'Oh, very well, then, Wales it shall be, although I have serious doubts about the location of the inquiry. A farm in the Welsh countryside hardly seems to hold out much promise of excitement. One can only hope there are not too many cows. They are the most boring of animals in my opinion – worse even than sheep. And I should warn you, Watson, the journey is going to be tedious in the extreme. According to the itinerary Dr Parry has given us, there are two changes of train, one at Hereford of all places.'

Nevertheless, he sent the telegram to Dr Parry confirming our arrival and the following day we set off from Paddington for Abergavenny, a journey that was indeed long but not as tedious as Holmes had predicted. He was, however, still in a dispirited frame of mind and refused to be diverted by the passing scenery, sinking instead into a heavy silence, the flaps of his deerstalker cap pulled down about his ears. I greatly missed his sprightly conversation on a variety of topics that had entertained me on similar train journeys in the past.

It was only after we had changed at Hereford, a charming town as far as I could judge from the carriage window and not in the least deserving of Holmes' rather dismissive comment on it, that he began to sit up and take notice of the names of the stations we were passing through.

'An interesting language, Welsh,' he commented. 'It is, of course, Celtic in origin and is said by some scholars to have its roots in the ancient British tongue spoken by the inhabitants of this island before it was overrun by the Anglo-Saxons.'

And with that, to my infinite relief, he plunged into a fascinating discourse on the influence of Indo-European, the protolanguage from which, it seemed, a great number of other languages, including Celtic, had sprung. This explanation continued until our arrival at Abergavenny where we were met by Dr Gwyn Parry, an eager-looking little man, short of stature but brimming over with energy that seemed to set the air about him crackling with an electric charge. Even the weather seemed affected by him, for the low clouds which had persisted for most of the day began to scatter, torn to tatters by a sharp little breeze. By the time we had left the outskirts of Abergavenny and were proceeding at a brisk trot in the doctor's smart little pony and trap into the countryside beyond, the landscape itself began to lift, much like Holmes' spirits, into a series of mountain slopes, rising one behind the other, across which the sun chased the cloud shadows in a game of hide-and-seek.

At first, all three of us were silent, Holmes and I in contemplation of the view, while Dr Parry, I surmised, was turning over in his mind the circumstances that had brought the two of us to this location and how he was to broach so tragic and personal a subject to a pair of strangers.

It was Holmes who broke the silence.

'Tell me, Dr Parry, about the murder of Dai

Morgan,' he said in a down-to-earth but kindly tone of voice. 'I gather from your letter that he was a local farmer, well respected in the community, and that his son—'

The remark seemed to act as a stimulus to the little doctor. The words gushed out of him in a torrent made more excitable by the rise and fall of his Welsh accent.

'Hywel had nothing to do with his death, Mr Holmes! He's a good lad who wouldn't harm a fly, let alone his own dada. Inspector Rees has got it all wrong! He's a townee, see, from Abergavenny. He doesn't understand us hill people. We're like foreigners to him!'

'So Inspector Rees is in charge of the investigation,' Holmes remarked evenly. 'What is his opinion? Does he think it is a case of murder rather than suicide or a terrible accident?'

My old friend's down-to-earth attitude had its desired effect on Dr Parry for, with an apologetic sideways glance at Holmes, he replied in a more temperate manner.

'Oh no, Mr Holmes, it was murder without a doubt. No man can stab himself twice in the heart either on purpose or by accident. And you must forgive me for taking on so. I've known Dai and Hywel Morgan for most of my adult life. They are like family to me. I'm certain Hywel is not guilty.'

'You examined the body?'

'I did indeed.'

'How soon after the incident?'

'Within the hour. Hywel came down to the village

146

from the farm as soon as he found Dai's body in the barn. It was still warm when I examined it.'

'When was this?'

'The day before yesterday, at about half past nine.'

'And the body was where?'

'In the barn, lying on its back on the floor.'

'You said he had been stabbed twice in the heart?'

Dr Parry looked a little abashed.

'To be honest, it was only once directly in the heart. The other wound was in the chest a little to the left of the heart.'

'I see. Any sign of a weapon nearby?'

'No, and nowhere else in the barn either. I had a good look round myself, as did Inspector Rees and a constable who came with him. There was nothing that any of us could see that could have caused those injuries. They were very strange, those wounds, unlike anything I have ever seen before.'

'Strange? In what way?'

'Whatever caused them was a narrow blade, more like a rapier than a knife, and they were about six inches apart. The entry was downward and curving—'

'Curving?' Holmes broke in sharply. 'Are you sure, Dr Parry?'

'I would stake my life on it. I used a probe to follow the thrust of the injuries. Whoever killed him must have stood in front of him and plunged the weapon twice into his chest with sufficient force to knock Dai backwards off his feet on to the floor of the barn, so it was someone of more-than-usual strength. Dai wasn't a big man but he was strong. He was used to lugging sheep about, see, or holding them down when he was shearing them. So the muscles in his arms and chest were well developed.'

'Very interesting!' Holmes remarked musingly. 'Would it be possible for Dr Watson and myself to inspect the scene of the crime?'

Dr Parry gave us a conspiratorial sideways glance.

'It could be arranged. The barn's all locked up but I know where to find the spare key to the padlock on the door. The police have gone, so you would have the place to yourselves. But you'll have to keep mum about it. If Inspector Rees found out I had let you in, he'd make a proper fuss. Officious he is, see – likes to be in charge.'

'When could we see it?' Holmes asked eagerly.

'Now, if you wish. I've arranged for you and Dr Watson to stay in the village inn, Y Delyn Aur, "The Golden Harp" in English. I would offer to put you up at my house but my wife's an invalid and I think you'd be better off at the inn; as my guests, of course. It's a comfortable little place and Emrys Jenkins, the landlord, speaks English. You could come and go as you wish and you might pick up some of the local gossip from Emrys. We could drop off your luggage there and then go on to Plas Y Coed.'

'Plas Y Coed?' Holmes inquired. It was obvious from the tone of his voice that he was fascinated by the Welsh names and, aware of this, Dr Parry was delighted to translate them.

'The House of Trees,' he explained. 'Dai Morgan's farm. It's about a mile outside the village.'

'Which I gather from your letter is Pentre Mawr, is it not?'

'Indeed it is, Mr Holmes. It means "The Big Village" and the name of the hill near to the farm is Bryn Mawr, Bryn meaning "hill" . . .'

'And Mawr therefore meaning "big",' Holmes said, completing the sentence for him.

The little doctor laughed out loud, clearly enjoying this linguistic game as much as Holmes himself, and I, too, was delighted at Holmes' change of mood from his earlier low spirits to this more cheerful frame of mind.

Despite its name, Pentre Mawr seemed a small enough place to me, a collection of stone and brick cottages and houses clustered along a pair of interconnecting country roads barely wide enough to allow two vehicles to pass side by side. Its central crossroads were dominated by its most impressive features: a chapel of dark-red brick with a steep gable end and pointed, Gothic-style windows, and the village inn of whitewashed stone, sporting a hanging sign of a golden harp against a bright-red background.

Here the pony and trap was drawn to a halt and Dr Parry, having secured the reins to a convenient post, carried our bags into the inn, emerging shortly afterwards to resume his seat in the trap. We then set off once more in the direction of the mountains that loomed over the village like the curtain wall of some ancient fortress.

Below it were fields dotted with the pale shapes of grazing sheep moving slowly across the pasture, with here and there an isolated farmhouse of stone and slate crouching low to the ground as if cowering from the scrutiny of unseen enemies lying in wait up there among the crags.

After about a mile, we came to one of these farmhouses set back a little way from the road and surrounded by trees. As we turned in at the gateway, I heard Holmes murmur beneath his breath, 'Ah, Plas Y Coed!', a remark which Dr Parry immediately translated into English.

'The House of Trees. Indeed, Mr Holmes, you are an excellent scholar. We'll make a Welshman of you yet!'

The pony, which had slowed to a walk, proceeded down a short drive to the house itself. It was a plain building of stone with a low, slated roof that gave it a top-heavy appearance, and it faced a cobbled farmyard that was surrounded on two sides by outbuildings, the largest of which appeared to be a barn.

As soon as the pony halted, Dr Parry jumped down and, having secured the reins, produced a large door key from his pocket, explaining over his shoulder, 'Hywel has given me this in case of need. I shan't be more than a few moments, gentlemen, fetching the key to the barn, and then you can examine the place were Dai Morgan was murdered at your leisure.'

He was as good as his word and a few moments later was unlocking the double doors to the large stone building which faced the house and which put me in mind of drawings I had seen of Saxon churches. It had the same simple architecture, the interior open and uncluttered, the floor paved with large, uneven stone slabs and the roof supported on a structure of ancient beams, held together by larger cross braces. Old cobwebs hung down from these beams like the tattered banners of some long-ago battle. At the far end was an open-fronted loft, the ladder that would have given access to it lying on the floor amongst a scattering of hay. The sweet scent of the hay pervaded the whole interior and the air was filled with a cloud of glittering dust mites caught like fireflies in the shafts of sunlight from the arched window set in the rear wall.

Dr Parry was pointing to an area of the floor a little distance from the hayloft.

'That's where Dai's body was lying,' he said in a low voice, as if he were indeed not only in church but also in the presence of death. He added in the same hushed tone, 'There was a muddy footprint in the centre of Dai's chest as if someone had stamped on him.'

'Was there indeed?' Holmes commented but he said no more, merely walking over to the spot that the little doctor had indicated, where he stood without speaking for a moment looking down at the strewn hay before, shifting his attention, he glanced up at the hayloft and then looked across at the barn walls. I had seen him before at other scenes where a crime had been committed looking about him with the same rapid, keen-eyed scrutiny.

Dr Parry and I waited for him to make some remark that might indicate that he had noticed something of significance but he said nothing apart from asking me to help him to set up the ladder against the edge of the loft, which he then briskly mounted. To my surprise, however, he made no attempt to clamber into the loft itself but remained on the ladder, his head level with the loft floor, before climbing down again. It was only then that he spoke.

'Did Inspector Rees go up into the loft?' he asked.

'No, he did not,' Dr Parry replied. 'In fact, he said something about the dust up there and not wanting to get it on his clothes.'

'And what about the other policeman who came with him?'

'He didn't either.'

Holmes made no rejoinder but wandered off towards the right-hand side of the barn, which seemed to serve as a storage area for various farm implements. Several were leaning against the wall, among them a large wooden rake and a scythe, while suspended from pegs on the wall itself were several smaller pieces of equipment including billhooks, knives of various sizes, sieves and large woven baskets which I took to be used for winnowing grain.

'Interesting!' Holmes murmured, tilting his head to one side and lapsing once more into silence.

Dr Parry, who was watching Holmes with the rapt attention of a cat at a mouse hole, was perceptive enough to realise that some significance should be attached to Holmes' movements and occasional remarks but was frustrated by his silences.

As if aware of this, Holmes turned to him with a smile.

'You must not mind me, Dr Parry,' he said. 'I have my own methods. And this case reminds me of the curious incident of the dog in the night.'

Dr Parry looked merely bewildered by this remark which must have meant nothing to him. Even I, who had accompanied Holmes on this particular investigation, was taken aback. What possible connection could there be between that case, involving a missing racehorse and a dog which failed to bark, and this present inquiry which, as far as I could ascertain, concerned neither a dog nor a horse, but a Welsh farmer and a barn containing a hayloft and a collection of farm implements?

Holmes was aware of my perplexity and, catching my eye, gave a small smile accompanied by an almost imperceptible shake of his head. I knew my old friend well enough to understand the signals. I was to regard the subject as closed, at least for the time being, although he might, if so inclined, explain the enigma at some future stage in the inquiry. In the meantime, he strode forward to address the doctor, who was making his way to the barn door, key in hand, as if to indicate that the examination of the barn was finished.

'A few more questions before we go, Doctor Parry. Inspector Rees must have thought Hywel Morgan had some strong motive for murdering his father, otherwise he would not have arrested him. What was that motive?'

There was a long moment of silence before the doctor replied, and when he did speak, it was with obvious reluctance.

'It was just gossip, Mr Holmes.'

'Never mind that!' my old friend retorted sharply. 'I need to know everything about the case, including the gossip. Unless you are prepared to be completely frank with me, Dr Parry, I shall be forced to abandon the inquiry and Dr Watson and I will return immediately to London. The choice is entirely yours.'

I saw Dr Parry was trying to avoid Holmes' gaze and I thought he was about to brush aside this ultimatum with some vague reply but, where his professional standing is concerned, Holmes is adamant. There is no compromise and Parry must have recognised this in my old friend's stern, inflexible expression. I felt quite sorry for the little doctor as he hurried to make good his error, stumbling over his words as he did so.

'Well, you see, Mr Holmes, there was talk in the village about Dai marrying again. He's a widower, see; has been for the past seven years. And there's this widow, Carys Williams, a pleasant enough woman, owns a farm out at Bryn Teg on the other side of the village. People had noticed them chatting together after chapel and they added two and two together and made, well, more than five, if you ask my opinion. Before you could say "knife", they had the two of them married off and Carys moving into Plas Y Coed with her younger son helping Dai to run the place while her eldest son took charge of the farm at Bryn Teg.

'The talk apparently caused ill feeling between Dai and Hywel. Had Dai remarried, Hywel could have felt his claim to Plas Y Coed was threatened.'

'Is there any evidence that this was indeed his reaction, or was that also simply gossip?'

Dr Parry shuffled his feet uncomfortably.

'Well, the postman evidently heard Dai and Hywel arguing one morning when he delivered some letters. Hywel was saying, "If that woman and her son come here, I'll pack up and leave." Then he went slamming out of the house.'

'Is that all?' Holmes demanded.

'They stopped drinking together at Y Delyn Aur. Dai would sit on one side of the bar, Hywel on the other . . .'

His voice trailed away miserably.

But Holmes had not finished with him yet.

'In your opinion, was the situation bad enough to give Hywel a motive for murder?' he demanded.

Dr Parry looked down at the ground and then, drawing himself upright, he looked Holmes full in the face.

'It could have been, Mr Holmes. Hywel has a quick temper. But I'll still lay any wager you care to name on his innocence. And that is all I'm prepared to say on the matter.'

'I see,' Holmes replied, obviously impressed by the little doctor's conviction. 'Then on your recommendation, I shall continue with the case, but I warn you, Dr Parry, should any evidence arise that proves Hywel's guilt, I shall hand it over to the police without a moment's hesitation. Do you agree with those terms?'

'I do indeed, Mr Holmes,' Dr Parry replied, looking crestfallen.

'Very well, then,' Holmes said briskly. 'Let the inquiry continue. Now, Dr Parry, a few more answers, if you please. Who else beside Hywel Morgan was at the farm at the time the murder was committed?'

'Owen Madoc and his daughter Rhian,' Dr Parry replied promptly, as if to confirm there would be no holding back from now on.

'And who are they?'

'Owen works on the farm and Rhian is a sort of housekeeper, I suppose.'

'Where were they when Dai was killed?'

'Owen was out feeding the pigs, I believe, and Rhian was somewhere in the house. Inspector Rees would know. He took statements from them both.'

'Can I speak to them myself?'

'I don't see why not but they're not at the farm today, apart from Owen who had permission to call in briefly to feed the animals. Otherwise Rees told them to stay at home until the police had finished searching the place.

But you should find them at Plas Y Coed later this morning.'

'So they are not live-in staff?'

'Oh, no. Owen has a bit of a farm – well more like a smallholding, I suppose – about half a mile up the road; keeps chickens and a pig or two, that sort of thing.'

'I would very much like to speak to them both. Would tomorrow morning suit you? Say, at ten o'clock? The journey here has been quite tiring and I would like the opportunity for a rest before we continue with our inquiries. I am sure Dr Watson will agree.'

He turned to me and I nodded in agreement.

'But I should not wish to inconvenience you in any way,' Holmes added, addressing the little doctor who waved away such a suggestion.

'No trouble at all, I assure you, Mr Holmes. I have a locum who will see any patients on my list. I suggest we drive back to the village, where I will drop you off at the inn and where you will find excellent lodgings for the night.'

He was right about the inn. The rooms were small but comfortable, the linen clean and smelling of lavender and the evening meal plain but delicious; far better, in fact, than some I have eaten in London restaurants. I went to bed tired but content, drifting easily into a deep sleep in which the puzzle of the link between this case and the one about the dog that had not barked occupied my mind for no more than a few minutes.

* * *

Dr Parry was as good as his word and promptly at ten o'clock the following morning called at the inn, ready to take us on the next stage of the investigation. I, too, was eager after a good night's sleep and an excellent breakfast to discover what was the connection between the Silver Blaze inquiry and this present murder case. But Holmes, who, much to my relief, was back on form, fended off any questions I tried to put to him.

There was no opportunity to quiz him anyway, for no sooner had I opened my mouth than Dr Parry arrived and Holmes began to make his own inquiries of him concerning the people we were about to meet.

In the conversational stakes, Dr Parry was almost as fluent as Holmes. Obviously delighted that Holmes was once more committed to the investigation, he began with great enthusiasm.

'Now then, gentlemen, let me give you the full story. Owen Madoc is a widower with just the one daughter, Rhian. There is a son as well but he left home years ago for Cardiff, looking for adventure, see, though I doubt if he found it there. Owen must be in his late fifties, the daughter is . . . well, thirty-five at a rough reckoning; unmarried; speaks only Welsh, as does her father; not much spark to her, if you know what I mean. They live about half a mile up the lane from Dai Morgan's farm in a small house called Cartref – "Home" to you, Mr Holmes, knowing your interest in the language. If you like, I could take you for a little drive tomorrow into the mountains to look at the view. The road passes their place. It would be a shame to come all this way and not see the countryside.'

On receiving Holmes' assent to this plan, Dr Parry continued with his account of the Madocs. 'They both help out at Plas Y Coed, Owen with the sheep and the pigs. Rhian works in the house: does the çooking and cleaning; sees to the hens as well as the butter and cheese-making.

'I feel sorry for the pair of them. Cartref is isolated, as you'll see for yourselves when we drive past it, although they should be back at Plas Y Coed by then. Rees gave them permission to return later this morning. So if you'd like to meet them, I could make some excuse for stopping by there.

'As I was saying, it's not much of a life for Rhian. As for Owen, he's a very bitter man in my opinion. He would like to have had his own place but he was the younger son and the family farm went to his older brother. It's left him hard; ill-natured. His wife died, too. Oh, a terrible death! He thinks life has been unfair to him and, to give him his due, I can sympathise. He's concerned, too, about what will happen to Rhian when he dies. She'll lose the cottage – it's tied; goes with the job. She'll be without a home. It's all such a great worry!'

While he had been speaking, he had turned the pony into the gateway of Plas Y Coed and had drawn up at the farmhouse door, which on this occasion was standing open. Even before Dr Parry had time to climb down from the trap, a woman, Rhian Madoc, I assumed, appeared on the threshold where she stood regarding us with a suspicious air.

She was in her thirties, as Dr Parry had described her, but looked older, her black hair, which was speckled with grey, drawn back tightly from her forehead, giving her features a gaunt, hungry look. The shabby brown dress she was wearing, together with the coarse apron that looked suspiciously like a piece of sacking, did nothing to enhance her appearance, although she might once have looked handsome in a dark, Romany fashion.

Although she and Dr Parry spoke to one another in Welsh – she in short, reluctant sentences, he more volubly – it was possible from their gestures and expressions to follow a little of their conversation. He was evidently explaining who we were and asking where her father was, for she pointed across the farmyard to one of the outbuildings before setting off herself in that direction, presumably to fetch him, as Dr Parry's subsequent remarks verified.

'She said we are to wait in the house while she calls her father,' he explained, leading the way into a stone-paved passageway and opening a door on the right that led into a parlour overlooking the yard, that was furnished with a horsehair sofa and matching armchairs. A huge dresser of dark oak together with a white-faced clock framed in the same sombre wood and wallpaper patterned with sepia leaves gave the room a cheerless, funereal air. A more sinister note was struck by the presence of a double-barrelled shotgun propped up by the fireplace.

'By the way,' Dr Parry continued, 'I've told her you are friends of mine from London and I'm taking you on a little tour of the area so I thought I'd call in as I was passing and see how her father is. He's had a bad chest for the past three weeks.' Seeing Holmes' attention had been drawn to two large photographs in oval frames which were hanging side by side over the fireplace, he added, 'Those are of Dai and Hywel.'

The family likeness was immediately apparent. Apart from similar self-conscious expressions at having to face a camera, both had the same firm chin and frank, open features, although the older man had a stubborn set to his mouth and, noticing this, the thought occurred to me that I would not care to cross him in any way. I was reminded of the account Dr Parry had given us the previous day on the drive back to Pentre Mawr concerning the quarrel between the two men about Dai Morgan's relationship with the widow Carys Williams and I could understand how it might have arisen.

I was about to ask Dr Parry about this aspect of the case when I heard footsteps approaching the house and, glancing through the window, I saw Rhian Madoc crossing the yard in the company of a man in his fifties who had grizzled hair and beard and was wearing a collarless flannel shirt and a pair of old corduroy trousers well worn about the knees.

Like the Morgans, father and son, there was a strong

family likeness between the Madocs. Both were tall and dark and gave the impression of physical strength about the arms and upper body. Like Rhian, her father was also taciturn to an embarrassing degree. When Dr Parry introduced Holmes and myself, our presence was acknowledged with nothing more than a curt nod of the head, while Parry's explanation in Welsh of the reason for our visit there was heard in complete silence, although at the end of this soliloquy Owen Madoc made some dismissive remark which I took to be the equivalent of 'Is that all?', before he turned as if to leave the room.

I could tell Holmes was exasperated by the difficulty of communicating with the man, not simply because of the language barrier but by Madoc's reticence. Just before he reached the door, Holmes said unexpectedly, addressing Dr Parry, 'Would you convey to Mr Madoc and his daughter our condolences on the death of Mr Morgan? It must have come as a great shock to both of them.'

The comment was obviously made with the intention of rousing a response and it succeeded, although perhaps not as dramatically as Holmes might have wished. Owen Madoc stood for a long moment in silence, his face as hard and as expressionless as a rock, before, muttering something in reply, he turned rapidly on his heel and left the room. His daughter's reaction was more positive. One hand flew up to her mouth and a little cry escaped her lips. The next moment, she had run out of the room after her father and, catching up with him on the far side of the yard, they stood facing each other, Rhian talking animatedly, her father listening in silence. The next moment they had disappeared from view into the outbuilding from which they had first emerged.

'She has taken Dai's death badly,' Dr Parry remarked, looking embarrassed at the little drama which had just taken place. 'I think she looked on him as a father figure. And then Hywel's arrest . . .'

He broke off, as if he could say no more.

'Yes, of course; I understand,' Holmes replied. 'Well, Dr Parry, shall we go on that little excursion you promised?'

'Indeed we shall,' Dr Parry said heartily, clearly relieved at the change of subject and the prospect of a jaunt into the countryside. Leading the way, he started off across the yard towards the barn where the pony and trap were standing, Holmes and I at his heels.

We set off towards the mountains this time, away from the village, along an increasingly steep, stony lane which grew narrower the further we went until it dwindled to a mere track, passing on the way a small cottage which crouched low in a hollow between sloping pastures. Dr Parry flourished his whip at this nondescript building.

'Cartref,' he announced. 'Where the Madocs live.'

It was indeed isolated as he had described it earlier and, apart from the sheep grazing on the coarse grass and a few black-winged birds – ravens, perhaps – wheeling overhead, the place seemed empty of all life and I wondered, as we clattered past it, how Owen Madoc, and Rhian in particular, could survive the bleak loneliness, especially in winter.

Even so, there was a beauty about the scene which grew more majestic as we progressed up the hill and the mountains began to dominate over the lower pastures. Rock outcrops thrust themselves upwards, like the bones of some huge prehistoric monster, stripped bare of the soft, grassy flesh of the meadows below and, as the crags grew higher, the landscape dropped away, revealing a magnificent view of distant fields and farms, the houses as tiny as children's toys, the roads mere brown ribbons curling their way round the patches of green pasture scattered with the pale forms of sheep, reduced by the distance to nothing more than moving dots.

The layout of Plas Y Coed was also revealed, not as we had seen it before at ground level as a huddle of outhouses gathered indiscriminately, it seemed, round the yard and the great barn, but as a series of separate buildings fanning out from this central point and each one distinct from its neighbour. Even at that distance, it was possible to differentiate their separate uses, from a row of pig sties, each with its own little yard, to a much larger construction, evidently the cowshed, with a separate lane leading to the adjoining field where some black and white cows were grazing. I could even distinguish a tiny brown heap like a miniature pyramid in one corner which I took to be the dungheap and from the top of which the handle of some farm implement was protruding. Amazed at seeing so much detail at such a distance, I drew Holmes' attention to it but he merely shrugged his shoulders indifferently.

As we progressed, the hill grew steeper until, at Dr Parry's suggestion, we dismounted from the trap to ease the pony and proceeded on foot to a large, flat rock at the side of the track, clearly a favourite lookout post for the little doctor, for he sat himself down with a sigh of satisfaction.

'There now, gentlemen!' he declared proudly, extending an arm towards the distant view. 'Have you ever seen anything as beautiful as that!'

Indeed, I had not, and I suspected Holmes had not either, for he perched himself on the edge of the rock, arms crooked about his knees, where he remained in silence contemplating the view, his keen profile looking even more like an eagle's surveying its kingdom from its lofty eyrie.

We stayed there entranced for at least half an hour, held by the magic of the place, Holmes silent and so totally absorbed that I dared not interrupt whatever train of thought he was following with such close attention.

He did not even rouse himself on the return journey except, when we passed Plas Y Coed, the Place of Trees, and the site of Dai Morgan's murder, he twisted his head round to catch a last glimpse of it before the trap moved on and the house and outbuildings disappeared from view round a bend in the road.

In fact, he said nothing until we reached the village

of Pentre Mawr, when he turned to Dr Parry and said abruptly, 'May I speak to you in private about the case?'

'Of course!' Dr Parry replied, looking a little puzzled at this sudden request.

'Not at your house,' Holmes continued. 'I should not wish to inconvenience your wife. The inn has a private room in which we have taken our meals. Could it be made available for our use if the landlord agrees?'

'I'm sure Emrys won't object. I shall ask him straight away.'

The little doctor wasted no time on arranging the matter. Two minutes later, the three of us were ushered into the small room opening off the main bar that in an English public house would be referred to as 'the snug'.

Here we seated ourselves at the table and Holmes, after a moment's hesitation, opened the discourse with a declaration that astonished me and, judging by his expression, astonished Dr Parry as well.

For without any preamble, Holmes announced, 'Gentlemen, I know who murdered Dai Morgan and the method used to kill him. But I shall need your cooperation to bring the murderer to justice.'

As no doubt he had intended, his words provoked gasps of amazement from Dr Parry and myself, although, knowing Holmes' love of the dramatic[2] as well as I did

---

[2] In 'The Adventure of the Naval Treaty', in which Sherlock Holmes astounds Dr Watson and Percy Phelps by serving up the missing document at breakfast under a dish-cover, he admits that 'I never can resist a touch of the dramatic.' Dr John F. Watson.

after all the years of close acquaintanceship with him, I suspected he found a great deal of satisfaction in the situation and so I sat back, letting Dr Parry ask the inevitable questions.

'How on earth did you come to that conclusion, Mr Holmes?'

'From the evidence, of course,' Holmes replied coolly.

'But where was this evidence?'

'In the barn and its vicinity.'

I took 'vicinity' to mean the yard and its surrounding buildings, but quite where the evidence had been found, I had no idea. As for Dr Parry, he merely shook his head in bewilderment. It was Holmes who broke the silence.

'Well, gentlemen,' said he, 'as the case has been satisfactorily solved, I suggest we turn our attention to the final stage of the investigation – that of bringing the guilty person to justice – and for that I have devised a plan for which I shall need your assistance. This is what I propose.'

Leaning forward across the table, he explained his plan, or 'little drama', as he described it, in detail.

That following afternoon, we returned to Plas Y Coed, leaving the pony and trap in the yard as we had on the two previous occasions we had called at the farm. Once more, Dr Parry entered the house to collect the key to the barn, only this time, when he emerged, he was accompanied by Rhian who, instead of joining us, set off up the yard to the gate that led into the fields to fetch her father who was attending to a sheep that had injured its foot, as Dr Parry explained in English for our benefit. Holmes also set off on his own mission, an action which he had warned us he would make but the purpose of which he had so far refused to explain. Meanwhile, Dr Parry had unfastened the padlock on the barn doors and had swung them open.

The interior of the barn was just as we had left it on the first day we had examined it. The ladder to the loft was still lying on the floor among the scattered hay, the farm implements arranged against the left-hand wall.

Following Holmes' instructions, I set the ladder up against the edge of the loft. No sooner had I done so than we were joined by the other participants in what Holmes had referred to as the 'little drama' he had devised and for which he had carefully instructed the players.

First to arrive was Inspector Rees, a tall, lugubrious man who had been summoned by telegram from Abergavenny the previous day and who had arrived that very morning in a wagon, hired for the occasion from the station, accompanied by a sergeant and a constable. The three of them had then followed us to Plas Y Coed at a discreet distance. Now obeying, albeit reluctantly, Holmes' orders, they took up their allotted positions at the rear of the barn where their presence would not be obvious to anyone entering through the double doors.

Holmes entered next, returning from his mysterious errand carrying something that surprised me greatly, although I hardly had time to consider its relevance before, having nimbly climbed the ladder, he was standing on the edge of the loft as if on the stage of a theatre. And the scene was indeed theatrical, with the figure of Holmes towering over us like a celebrated actor while Dr Parry and myself, together with the policemen, stood below forming the audience, much like the groundlings in Shakespeare's Globe gathered to watch a performance of one of the great tragedies. Long shafts of dusty sunlight slanted down from the window on to the scene with a strange, shifting luminosity.

By some unspoken agreement we waited in silence for the two missing participants in the play and their arrival, heralded by the heavy creaking of the barn doors as they were swung open, had all the dramatic impact of the knocking on the gate in *Macbeth*.

They came in hesitantly, Owen Madoc first, followed by his daughter Rhian, and for a moment they stood without moving just inside the barn, their faces lifted up towards the figure of Holmes posed there above them on the edge of the hayloft, as motionless as they were.

And then slowly and deliberately, like a warrior lifting his javelin, Holmes seized the pitchfork he was carrying that he had retrieved on our arrival from some unknown location, and, raising it to shoulder height, held it there, quivering in his clenched fist and aimed at the two of them standing there below him.

Rhian broke first. With an inhuman scream, like an animal in pain, she covered her face with her hands. Madoc remained silent but on his face was stamped the same agonised horror.

We remained motionless, holding our positions as if in a tableau at the end of a melodrama, waiting for the curtain to descend.

And then suddenly the scene disintegrated, its participants scattering in every direction, Madoc leading the way towards the barn door, which he tore open like a madman before setting off at a run across the yard to the house. By the time the rest of us had reached it, the door to the hall was shut and bolted. Rhian threw herself against it, banging on it with her fists and shouting, 'Dada! Dada!'

While Dr Parry and I stood dumb and motionless, Holmes had darted forward. Tearing off his ulster, he wrapped it about his arm before punching out the glass in the parlour window beside the door. Reaching in, he unfastened the latch and a moment later was scrambling through the open casement. The next thing we heard was the sound of his feet on the stone floor of the hallway and the muffled and discordant noise of a struggle accompanied by raised voices.

I could distinguish Holmes' voice, very loud and clear and carrying with it a note of masterful command that, like the accompaniment of a bass to a tenor in an operatic duo, served to heighten the emotional content of the exchange.

He was shouting, 'Don't be a fool, Madoc! Put the gun down!' and then Madoc's voice, high-pitched and hysterical, screamed out a reply in Welsh that I could not understand.

The next moment, his voice was cut short and there followed the thunderous explosion of a gun being discharged.

By this time Inspector Rees and I, closely followed by the two policemen, had crossed the yard and reached the door. In the turmoil that followed, none of us thought to make entrance, like Holmes, through the parlour window that was standing open. Instead, we threw ourselves futilely against the solid oak of the front door, on which not even the sturdy bulk of the two policemen had the slightest effect, and we might have gone on with our pointless efforts had not the door suddenly opened, nearly precipitating the four of us headlong into the hall. Much to my fervent relief, Holmes appeared on the threshold, looking calm and uninjured, and with a little ironic bow, he stood aside to let us in.

It was the sprawled figure of Owen Madoc that first met our gaze. He was lying on his back on the flagstones, a double-barrelled shotgun at his side, blood running from one corner of his mouth and a quantity of broken plaster lying scattered about him.

As I ran forward to feel for the carotid artery in his neck, Holmes remarked in a dismissive manner, 'Oh, do not distress yourself, my dear Watson. He is not dead.

He is merely knocked out by an uppercut to the jaw.[3] If anyone needs medical attention, it is myself. The blow has split the skin on my knuckles, but no doubt I shall survive.'

'But I heard the gun go off!' I protested.

'It did indeed. In fact, it nearly deafened me. But by that time, I had managed to wrench the weapon sideways in Madoc's grasp so that when he pulled the trigger, the barrel was pointing upwards, hence the hole in the ceiling and the broken plaster.' Turning to Rees, he continued, 'I suggest you handcuff him now, Inspector, in case he decides to continue the struggle after he comes round. He is a very powerful, and more to the point, desperate man.'

But Holmes had misjudged him for, when Madoc regained consciousness, he was subdued and contrite rather than aggressive and he put up no further resistance when he was led out of the house to the station wagon that was waiting in the yard. Accompanied by Inspector Rees and the two policemen, he was driven away to Abergavenny gaol, there to await trial for the murder of Dai Morgan.

As for the rest of us, we too dispersed, Holmes and I to walk to the Golden Harp to await for the arrival of

---

[3] Sherlock Holmes was an expert boxer, having practised the sport when he was at college. He was so good that when he fought three rounds with McMurdo, a professional prizefighter, on his benefit night, McMurdo claimed he could have turned professional himself. *Vide*: *The Sign of Four*. Dr John F. Watson.

Dr Parry who, in the meantime, drove Rhian Madoc to a neighbour's house to be cared for there.

By a common unspoken agreement, neither Holmes nor I discussed the morning's events until Dr Parry returned and the three of us retired to the snug, where I was able at last to ask my old friend the questions that had been foremost in my mind since the previous day.

'How on earth did you know that it was Owen Madoc who had killed Dai Morgan and not Hywel Morgan? And what was the relevance of your remark about the dog in the night?'

Holmes, who was lighting his pipe, took a moment or two to reply before, leaning back in his chair, he blew a long stream of smoke up to the low ceiling of the little room, its once whitewashed surface tanned brown like a kipper by layers of nicotine.

'If you remember, my dear fellow, the dog failed to bark. That was its significance.[4] It was the *absence* of something that should have happened. In this inquiry, it was also the absence of something, not of a sound but of an object. If you recall, various farm implements were hanging on the wall of the barn or propped up against it, but one implement was missing that, considering the

---

[4] Sherlock Holmes is referring to a remark he made during the Silver Blaze inquiry, in which he investigates the death of John Straker, the trainer at Colonel Ross's stable, and the disappearance of the racehorse Silver Blaze. 'The curious incident of the dog in the night-time' refers to the fact that the dog left on guard in the stable yard failed to bark when the horse was stolen, thereby proving that the thief was known to the dog. Dr John F. Watson.

other features of the place – the hayloft and the hay lying scattered on the floor – should have been present. It was, of course, a pitchfork.

'I asked myself: Why was it missing? I then recalled Dr Parry's description of the two wounds in Dai Morgan's chest, which we all assumed were the result of a double stabbing with a single-bladed weapon. According to you, Dr Parry, there was also something unusual about the wounds themselves. They suggested a blade that was narrow and tapering but also *curved*, a description which matched no knife or sword I had ever encountered. But the very word "knife" brought to my mind another implement, common enough but often associated with a knife that one sees every day on a dining table. A knife and a . . .'

Holmes broke off and glanced across at Dr Parry and myself, his eyebrows raised in a teasing, quizzical fashion as he waited for us to supply the missing word.

'Fork!' Parry and I chorused together.

'Excellent, gentlemen!' Holmes exclaimed. 'You have come to the same conclusion that I myself made. A fork! Now what kind of fork would you find in a barn? A pitchfork, of course. And once I had realised that, much of the evidence began to make sense. It accounted for the two wounds in Dai Morgan's chest, for example; not two separate stabbings as we thought at first, but a single strike with a double-bladed weapon. It also explained the force with which the blow had been struck, strong enough to knock Dai Morgan off his feet, as well as the downward direction of the thrust. This suggested it was not the result of a close encounter, but of an attack delivered from a distance as from a spear or a javelin. This downward direction also suggested that whoever had thrown the weapon had been standing above the victim and, given the location of the murder, the obvious place was the hayloft. I deduced that fact when I examined the loft on the first day we entered the barn. Footprints were clearly visible in the dust on the floor but there was only one set and they were freshly made. As Dr Parry stated that neither Inspector Rees nor his colleague had climbed into the loft, they therefore had to belong to someone else; a man, judging by their size, and this evidence pointed directly at Owen Madoc, the only other male on the premises that morning apart from Hywel. But according to the statement Rhian Madoc made to the police, at the time of Dai Morgan's death, Owen Madoc was tending to the injured sheep in a field some distance from the farm.

'However, at some point he must have returned to the barn, presumably without her knowledge, to carry out another task, almost certainly to prepare feed for the cows.

'From these deductions, we can build up a scenario of the events that must have taken place in this barn four days ago, including the positions of the two participants in the drama. Madoc was standing in the loft, presumably in the act of pitchforking hay down to the floor of the barn when Dai Morgan enters. A quarrel breaks out between the two of them – the cause of which I will recount later – and in a rage, Madoc hurls the pitchfork down at Dai Morgan who is standing below him, with sufficient force to knock Morgan off his feet and to drive the tines of the fork into his chest, rupturing his heart and causing a massive haemorrhage.

'One has to imagine the rest of the scene – Madoc's terror as he scrambles down the ladder and discovers Morgan is dead, his panic as to what he should do next. There is no point in sending for Dr Parry; Morgan is past human aid. But what of himself? If he admits to the murder, he will hang. The horror of this realisation forces him into a frantic attempt to cover up the deed before anyone discovers the truth. He cannot get rid of the body. Where would he hide it? But he can dispose of the weapon and this may throw the police off the scent. So he tries to prise the pitchfork out of the victim's chest. But even this simple task is difficult to accomplish. The tines are embedded too deeply. So he does what any man would do under similar circumstances. He tries to get a purchase on the fork by putting his foot on the dead man's body.'

'Of course!' I cried. 'The muddy print on the front of Dai Morgan's jacket!'

'Exactly, Watson! And having levered the weapon free, he now has to rid himself of it. There is blood on it and, no doubt, traces of flesh as well. His instinct is to take it away as far as possible from the scene of the crime, so that no one would associate the implement with Dai's death and also to disassociate himself from the murder and the accompanying guilt, on the simple precept of "out of sight, out of mind". So he takes it out of the barn to the stable yard and thrusts it into the dungheap.

'In the event, it was not a wise decision. Had he simply cleaned the blood from the pitchfork and put it back among the other farm implements in the barn, it is much more likely that no one would have associated it with the murder of Dai Morgan and the crime might have been recorded in the list of unsolved cases, attributed perhaps to a passing thief who had entered the barn looking for something worth stealing and was confronted by Dai Morgan, who therefore had to be eliminated.

'What had not occurred to Madoc, an omission that, I think, supports my theory that the murder was a spur-of-the-moment crime, was the likelihood that Hywel Morgan would be accused of his father's death. If Madoc thought about it at all, which I very much doubt, he would have relied on the fact that Hywel had gone to the pig yard, some distance from the barn, to feed the animals, so he was nowhere near the scene of the murder. The other factor in establishing Hywel's innocence was the close relationship between Hywel and his father that everyone knew about and which would also count in clearing him of any suspicion of guilt, Madoc assumed. He was therefore genuinely horrified when Hywel was arrested.

'But in his blind panic he discounted another

relationship that appeared to give Hywel a motive for killing his father, as you, Dr Parry, pointed out when you first met us – that beween Dai Morgan and Carys Williams. Evidently the possibility of marriage between the two was common gossip in the village, a situation which Madoc was probably not aware of. He is unsociable by nature and made a point of not mixing with the local people. The tragic irony is that, when he heard the gossip, Madoc's reaction was almost the same as that which the police attributed to Hywel.'

'In what way?' I asked, bemused.

'As I explained, the assumption of Hywel's guilt was based on the belief that he was afraid that if his father remarried, one of Carys Williams' sons might take precedence over his own claim to the farm, and it was that fear which led to the quarrel between Dai and Hywel Morgan. No one looked at the situation from Owen Madoc's point of view. If Morgan married again, Madoc's position and that of his daughter at Plas Y Coed could be compromised. Their services at the farm might no longer be needed. Carys Williams would take over Rhian's role of housekeeper while one of the Williams boys would replace him as the farm assistant. If that happened, the Madocs could lose their cottage, which was tied to their employment. It is all conjecture, of course, but not entirely baseless. If you remember, Madoc himself had lost his claim to his father's farm because he had an older brother. There may have been another motive as well, although it may never be proved.'

'And what is that?' I asked.

'My theory, like so much else about the case, is also based on conjecture,' Holmes replied with a wry smile. 'But just suppose Rhian Madoc had taken it into her head that Dai Morgan was in love with her and they would eventually marry. She was, after all, a lonely woman who for years had acted as a surrogate wife as Dai Morgan's housekeeper. Like the gossip over Dai and Carys Williams, it would not take much to persuade her that he was in love with her – a smile, a friendly comment which she misinterpreted, a meeting of glances over some domestic chore. She may even have confided her beliefs in her father. If that is indeed what happened, then one must add one more combustible ingredient to this already inflammatory situation.' He turned to Dr Parry. 'Is that interpretation possible?'

'It is indeed,' he agreed gravely. 'But all of that is now in the past. At the moment, Mr Holmes, I am more concerned with Rhian's future. Dai Morgan is dead, her father will presumably be hanged for his murder. What will happen to her and the others caught up in this dreadful tragedy?'

No one ventured a solution and it was not until a year later that we received a letter from Dr Parry giving a partial answer to this dilemma.

Rhian, he wrote, had left Pentre Mawr to join her younger brother in Cardiff where, for a time, she had acted as his housekeeper before marrying a local cobbler. Hywel, too, had married, in his case Bronwen Hughes, a

179

cousin of Carys Williams, and seemed happy and settled at Plas Y Coed with his wife and their newborn son.

As for Owen Madoc, he had pleaded guilty to Dai Morgan's murder at Abergavenny Assizes[5] and had been sentenced to be hanged, but before the sentence could be carried out, he had collapsed and died of a heart attack.

And so, as Holmes expressed it, the final curtain had fallen on our Welsh adventure and, considering the circumstances, it was indeed a most fitting conclusion.

---

[5] Assizes were judicial court sessions held periodically at major administrative towns or cities in England or Wales, in which criminal cases were tried by jury under the jurisdiction of a high court judge. Dr John F. Watson.

THE CASE OF THE
MISSING *BELLE FILLE*

It was a morning in mid November, not long after our return from Devonshire following the conclusion of the Baskerville Case in which Inspector Lestrade had played a not inconsiderable role,[1] when, much to our surprise, who should be shown upstairs to our Baker Street sitting-room than the inspector himself. Usually dapper in appearance, he was looking unaccustomedly

---

[1] During the Hound of the Baskervilles case, Sherlock Holmes telegraphed Inspector Lestrade asking him to help both him and Dr Watson with the investigation, as he was 'the best of the professionals'. Among other instances, the inspector helped them to reconnoitre Merripit House, to rescue Mrs Stapleton and also to search Grimpen Moor for Roger Baskerville, aka Jack Stapleton. Dr John F. Watson.

dishevelled, a condition which my old friend commented on as our guest, at Holmes' invitation, seated himself by the fire.

'I see,' he remarked with a twinkle, 'that you have been doing some digging recently. May I inquire if that is the reason for your calling on us?'

Lestrade looked astonished.

'How the deuce—?' he began.

'"To discover a man's calling, just look at his fingernails, his coat sleeves, his boots and the knees of his trousers",' Holmes murmured in explanation.

I recognised it immediately as a reference to a magazine article by my old friend,[2] but one with which Lestrade was clearly unfamiliar for he stared at Holmes in bewilderment.

'The sleeves of your overcoat, my dear Inspector,' Holmes explained, 'and the knees of your trousers, not to mention your boots, have given the game away. There are smears of London clay on all of them. So where have you been digging recently and why?'

Instead of replying directly, Lestrade reached into his pocket and produced an envelope which he handed to

---

[2] A quotation from a magazine article entitled 'The Book of Life', written by Sherlock Holmes, which he deliberately left open on the breakfast table for Dr John Watson to read and which explained his theory of 'the science of deduction and analysis'. In it, Sherlock Holmes claims he could deduce a man's history and background on first acquaintance by means of observation of his clothes, his hands and so on. *Vide*: *A Study in Scarlet*. Dr John F. Watson.

Holmes. Rising from my chair, I went to stand behind him so that I could see the missive over his shoulder. Long acquaintance with him had taught me the importance of close observation and I saw that the envelope, which was of a cheap quality available at many stationers', was addressed in crude capital letters, almost certainly disguised, to 'THE INSPECTOR IN CHARGE OF MURDER CASES, SCOTLAND YARD'.

Holmes raised a quizzical eyebrow.

'Murder?' he asked coolly, although I noticed that he had lifted his head like a bloodhound testing the air for the scent of a quarry.

'Read the letter, Mr 'Olmes,' Lestrade suggested in a lugubrious tone.

On Lestrade's instruction, Holmes opened the envelope and extracted from it a brief note on a single sheet of writing paper of the same poor quality as the envelope and written in the same ill-formed capital letters. There were no opening or closing inscriptions and it read: 'Go to the back garden of 17 Elmshurst Avenue in Hampstead and dig under the tree ten paces to the left of the gate and you will find the body of Mlle Lucille Carère, the stepdaughter of Mme Hortense Montpensier who murdered her and buried her body there.'

There was a hard, cold-blooded quality about this matter-of-fact statement that made my own blood run cold.

'So have you recovered the body, Inspector?' Holmes

inquired, laying aside the letter. 'Judging by the state of your clothes, I assume you have.'

'I 'ave, indeed, Mr 'Olmes; about an hour ago. As soon as I got the letter first post this morning, I set off for the address with a sergeant and a constable. We found the grave exactly where it says in the letter. It wasn't difficult to find. Even though it was overgrown with ivy, you could tell the earth had been disturbed. It was looser than the soil around it.'

'And the body?'

'Well, it's not exactly a body; it's more of a skeleton really. I sent for an anatomist from St Clement's, the local hospital, and 'e took a look at it. He reckons it's been down there for at least a year, more likely eighteeen months, so there's not much left of it apart from bones and a few scraps of clothing.'

'Where is the body now?'

'Still in the grave.' Lestrade hesitated and ran his tongue over his bottom lip before continuing, 'I didn't want to move it until you'd 'ad a chance to look at it.'

'Me?' Holmes inquired sharply, although I noticed he sat up immediately in his chair ready for action.

Lestrade looked uncomfortable and shuffled his feet on the carpet.

'Well, the point is, Mr 'Olmes, all the people in the 'ousehold are French and I don't speak the lingo except for a few words like "sieveooplay" and "wee-wee", which won't get me very far in a murder inquiry, will it?'

'How many people?' Holmes interjected.

'There's four altogether: Mme Montpensier 'oo owns the house, and her lady-companion, Mlle Benoit. Then there's a married couple, M and Mme Daudet. I understand from the wife, 'oo's the housekeeper and 'oo speaks a bit of English, that she's Mme Montpensier's cousin. The 'usband's a sort of jack of all trades; 'e's the butler-cum-'andyman-cum-anything else you care to name. I got the impression they're the poor relations. 'E doesn't speak any English at all. And that's the point, Mr 'Olmes. Now, I know you speak French like a native[3] and I wondered if you'd be willing to come along and 'elp out with the investigation . . .'

'Of course, as long as Mme Montpensier agrees,' Holmes replied with an indifferent air, although, knowing him as well as I do, I could tell by the set of his shoulders that he was eager to take up the challenge.

'I think she will. She's not a young woman and the finding of the body 'as set 'er back on 'er 'eels, if you get my meaning. As far as I could make out, she's denying any knowledge . . .'

'Leave all that to my interview with her, Lestrade.'

'Then you'll come?' the inspector asked, his face brightening.

---

[3] Sherlock Holmes could speak French well enough to pass himself off as a French workman in the case of the disappearance in Lausanne of Lady Carfax. His maternal grandmother was the sister of Vernet, the French artist, a relationship which is referred to in 'The Adventure of the Greek Interpreter'. Dr John F. Watson.

'I would not miss it for the world. Apart from anything else, there is the matter of the names.'

'Names?' Lestrade repeated. 'Well, like I said, they're all French . . .'

'Of course they are. But I was not referring to that.' Lestrade and I exchanged a bewildered glance, wondering what he meant but there was no time for further explanation. Holmes was saying, 'Now, Watson, coats, boots and sticks and we are ready to go!'

'I came in a four-wheeler,' Lestrade was saying as we bustled about in preparation for the journey, 'and, trusting you'd take up the case, I've taken the liberty of asking the cabby to wait by the door.'

'Excellent!' Holmes declared, seizing up his hat and making for the stairs.

Moments later the three of us were in the cab and rattling off down Baker Street on our way to Hampstead.

At Holmes' request, Lestrade refrained from mentioning the case during the journey. As my old friend explained, he would prefer to come to his own conclusions once he had seen the evidence for himself, an opinion Lestrade apparently agreed with; at least, he made no reference to the inquiry until the cab drew up in a quiet, tree-lined road when he announced, ''Ere we are, gentlemen! Number 17 Elm'urst Avenue, the scene of the crime!'

It was a large, ugly house of dark-red brick, with a heavy slate roof that put me in mind of a leaden-coloured dish-cover clamped down over the building beneath, as if to keep its occupants in close confinement. The ivy which hung in swags from the wall and errant tendrils of which were creeping across the windows added to the general air of melancholy entombment.

A tall iron gate gave access to a black and white tiled path leading to the front door, but to my surprise, Inspector Lestrade made no attempt to approach this entrance but struck off to the right in the direction of an alleyway that ran along the side of the house towards its rear, before turning sharply to the left a few yards from where a uniformed constable was standing guard outside a wooden door set in a high hedge.

On seeing us approach, the constable saluted and, pushing open the door, ushered us inside the garden that lay beyond. It was large and full of overgrown trees and bushes, most of which had shed their leaves, their interlaced bare branches forming a natural lattice which partly obscured the view. Even so, it was possible to catch a glimpse through this barrier of the grave. It lay to the right, a pile of disturbed fallen leaves and freshly dug earth marking its position. A sergeant stood guard over the scene while a constable waited nearby resting on his shovel, his face flushed with exertion, his jacket hanging nearby on a convenient branch. On our approach, they straightened up, the sergeant stepping forward to salute, ready and eager to give his official account, if requested.

'Where's Doctor Chitty?' Lestrade demanded.

''E left about twenty minutes ago, sir; said 'e'd got a patient to see at St Clement's,' the sergeant replied.

'But 'e said to tell you that 'e'd send you a more detailed report later by messenger. In the meantime, I was to tell you that the body's that of a young woman in 'er twenties, by the look of 'er; approximately five feet four inches in height; slight build; dark-haired; no obvious signs of 'ow she might 'ave met 'er end – no fractured skull, for example, or broken neck.'

As he spoke, the sergeant shuffled sideways in the dead leaves to give us a clear view of a shallow grave, no more than four feet deep, and the skeleton it contained. It was neatly laid out on its back, legs straight, arms by its sides as if it were drawn up to attention, the skull turned a little to the left and fixed in that ghastly rictus of death which no matter how often I had seen it during my medical career, in particular in Afghanistan,[4] always aroused in me the chilling thought that death was nothing more than a macabre joke played on mankind by some malign power to demonstrate our ultimate insignificance.

Holmes, who had moved forward to the very edge of the grave, was staring down at its contents with keen attention and I, too, tried to shift my gaze from the grinning skull to a more general view of the body and its surroundings. It had evidently been wrapped in a makeshift shroud, probably a blanket, for scraps of

---

[4] Dr Watson had served as a medical officer with the Berkshire regiment in Afghanistan. Wounded at the Battle of Maiwand in July 1880, he was invalided out of the army and retired on a pension in England. Dr John F. Watson.

brown woollen cloth still clung to some of the bones together with remnants of a fabric of a finer texture that may originally have been a dress. It was blue in colour with the faint suggestion of a pattern in a paler blue. But it was Holmes' sharper observation that pointed out an anomaly that I had not noticed.

'Were there no shoes with the body?' he inquired sharply.

Lestrade, who from his expression was also clearly unaware of their absence, started forward.

'Not that I know of, Mr 'Olmes. What about you, Benson? Did you find any?'

The sergeant shook his head.

'No, sir.'

'And what is that?' Holmes continued, raising his stick to point at a clod of earth that lay a little to the left of the body and that, as far as I could see, was no different to the other lumps of clay that lay strewn about in the bottom of the grave.

Lestrade stared and then, with a jerk of his thumb, summoned the constable with the shovel to join us.

''Ere, you; Palmer, isn't it? See that lump of dirt down there? Bring it up to me,' adding, as the man stepped carefully down into the shallow pit, 'and mind where you put your feet!'

The clod in question, having been retrieved, was handed first to Lestrade who, after a cursory examination of it, passed it on to Holmes with a shrug.

Knowing my old friend would not have chosen that

particular lump of earth without good reason, I watched closely as he took it between his fingers and with great care broke it open, revealing what it contained.

It was, we discovered, when Holmes crumbled away the soil that enclosed it and displayed it on his open palm, a silver, heart-shaped locket attached to a fine-linked chain, also of silver, but both so caked with clay and so tarnished that it was a wonder anyone had observed it lying there at the bottom of the grave.

'How on earth did you notice it?' I asked.

'Surely it should be "in earth" my dear fellow?' he remarked with a chuckle. 'And to stretch the epithet to even more extravagant lengths, the solution is equally down to earth! I merely noticed a glint of metal in the soil. Now, what is its significance, do you suppose, to the body?'

'It belonged to 'er, of course,' Lestrade replied, without any hesitation, jerking his thumb towards the skeleton.

'That is indeed possible,' Holmes concurred. 'But why should whoever buried her take care to place her locket in her grave but not her shoes?'

There was a silence in which Lestrade puffed out his cheeks and exchanged a glance with me, as much as to say, 'It's your turn to speak up.' Well aware of Holmes' tendency to lure the overconfident into making a fool of themselves by jumping to a too hasty conclusion, I refused to rise to the bait and remained silent. Holmes seemed disappointed by this lack of response and, making the most of the advantage of having the upper hand, turned to the inspector and inquired sweetly, 'I trust you will allow me, my dear Lestrade, to take the locket and chain home with me? There are one or two tests I should like to make on them. But rest assured, they will be returned to you undamaged.'

'I think I may permit that in the cause of justice, Mr 'Olmes,' Lestrade replied with a magnanimous air, adding a hasty proviso, 'provided I have *your* permission to call on you later this evening to find out what conclusions you've come to re the objects in question.'

'Of course,' Holmes agreed with equal graciousness and, with a small, secret smile, he placed the locket and chain in one of the little envelopes he carried about with him for such a purpose before putting it away in his pocketbook. 'And now,' he continued more briskly, 'I think it is time we interviewed Mme Hortense Montpensier about her stepdaughter Mlle Carère.' As we set off towards the gate, he added, 'Odd that, Inspector, do you not agree?'

'Odd? What's odd?' Lestrade demanded, hurrying to catch up with him.

'The names, Lestrade,' Holmes replied.

'Names? What about them?' Lestrade demanded. 'They're bound to be odd. They're French, aren't they?'

It was the second time Holmes had specifically referred to them but I was no closer to understanding the relevance of his remark; nor was Lestrade, judging by his expression, who seemed satisfied by his own facile explanation. But, as we set off down the path towards the front of the house, I continued to puzzle over Holmes' insistence on drawing our attention to them.

I was no nearer finding a solution as we approached the front door to number 17 Elmshurst Avenue. I therefore dismissed the matter to the back of my mind for later consideration as Lestrade lifted the heavy iron knocker and let it fall with a thud loud enough to wake the dead.

The door was opened by a man dressed in black, who might quite easily have taken the role of a mute at a funeral. M Daudet, which I assumed was his identity, was a tall, heavy-shouldered man, bent forward at the hips as if he found his height a handicap – a posture that thrust his face towards us and made us too conscious of his features: the long nose, the pendulous cheeks and the thick black eyebrows that jutted out like thatching and below which his eyes peered out warily like those of an animal trapped in a thorn bush. He seemed to know the inspector, presumably from that earlier occasion when Lestrade had first called at the house following the arrival of the letter, for he acknowledged him with a nod and, opening the door wider, ushered us into the hall.

Curious though I was to see the interior of the house, there was little time to look about me and, apart from registering a general impression of dark wallpaper hung with even darker oil paintings, and a staircase that ascended on the right to an upper landing totally lost in shadows, there was no opportunity to examine it any further before we fell in behind M Daudet and followed him down the passage to a door on which he knocked.

Having received the order '*Entrez!*', he opened the door and, announcing our names in a strong French accent – '*Inspecteur Lestrade, Monsieur 'Olmes, Docteur Watson, madame!*' – he stood aside to let us enter.

The room beyond was large but, like the hall, was full of shadows and oddly muffled, as if the air had been sucked out of it by the thick velvet drapes at the windows and the crowded furniture that stood cheek by jowl in every available space. There was not a surface that was not packed with objects, from pictures on the walls to vases on the tables and knick-knacks on the shelves, all in sombre shades. The only colourful feature was the fire that burnt red and gold in a large black marble fireplace, beside which sat the small figure of an elderly lady in an invalid chair, Mme Montpensier, I assumed, dressed in widow's weeds and muffled up like the room in rugs and shawls, despite the heat from the flames. Ramrod stiff, her hands clasped tightly in her lap, she wore an expression of extreme distaste at the invasion of her drawing-room by three total strangers.

Behind her stood another younger figure, also in black, whom I took to be her lady-companion, Mlle Benoit, and who, with her severe air and bunch of keys hanging at her belt, gave the impression of a female gaoler.

Lestrade stepped forward and embarrassed us all with a faltering attempt to explain in French the reason for the presence of the three us in her drawing-room that might, under other circumstances, have been amusing but which Mme Montpensier listened to with tight-lipped disapproval.

As soon as Lestrade had stumbled to a halt, Holmes advanced, cool and urbane, and addressed her in what I assumed was fluent French, judging by the expressions of relief and admiration that lit up the faces of Mme Montpensier and Mlle Benoit.

When Holmes had finished his soliloquy, Mme Montpensier gave some instruction to her companion, who hurriedly drew up chairs for the three of us into a semicircle by the fire and, with a gracious '*Asseyez-vous, s'il vous plaît, messieurs*', invited us to sit down.

There followed a rapid dialogue between Holmes and Mme Montpensier in French that I, with only my schoolboy knowledge of the language, was not able to follow apart from the gist of it. In this manner, I gathered that Mme Montpensier gave Holmes permission to investigate the case. Once that formality had been decided, there followed a question-and-answer session from which I deduced that Holmes had managed to establish a great deal of information, judging by the number of times the name of Mlle Carère occurred. At one point, I heard the word '*photographe*' and guessed that my old friend had asked to see a likeness of Mlle Carère for, at Mme Montpensier's instruction, her lady-companion rose to her feet and left the room, returning shortly afterwards with a black leather-bound volume with gilt-edged pages that Mme Montpensier opened at a particular section.

Lestrade and I crowded behind Holmes' chair and were able to see the page in question over his shoulder. It contained a sepia photograph in an oval frame of a handsome, dark-haired young woman with a resolute chin and very straight, determined brows, who gazed back at us with calm self-confidence. Seeing this image of her was a strange experience, for I could not associate her direct gaze and firmly modelled lips with the soil-encrusted skull I had seen in the grave with its empty eye sockets and gaping jaws.

After he had closed the album and returned it to Mlle Benoit, there followed a discussion between Mme Montpensier and my old friend that I deduced concerned the locket found with the body for, addressing her directly, he sketched a heart-shaped object in the air with his index finger that was apparently an adequate enough description for her to identify the piece of jewellery for she inclined her head in agreement. As she did so, I noticed that, for the first time, she showed signs of distress. Her lips trembled and her eyes became moist with what looked suspiciously like tears.

As this was taking place, it crossed my mind to wonder why Holmes should go to such lengths when he could quite easily have produced the locket in question from the little envelope he was carrying in his pocketbook, but ascribed this evasion to his innate secrecy.

Meanwhile, Mme Montpensier had recovered from her brief moment of distress and had resumed her usual dignified manner that she maintained during the rest of the interview. It concluded, it seemed, with a request from Holmes for permission to examine Mlle Carère's room. This she granted with no obvious reluctance and Mlle Benoit was despatched once more to fetch the housekeeper, Mme Daudet, returning with her shortly afterwards and resuming her place behind Mme Montpensier's chair. Meanwhile, Mme Daudet remained standing just inside the door.

It was difficult to form any opinion of the housekeeper. Like the other two women of the household she was dressed in black, but was so insignificant that the moment after I took my eyes off her features I would not have been able to describe them except with only the minimum of detail. She was middle-aged, of medium height and build; in fact, everything about her was so middle and medium and ordinary that she seemed to possess nothing outstanding or individual about her appearance, the only exception being her eyes, which were very dark and had a wary, watchful quality about them, but even this characteristic had been subdued by the years of training in controlling all emotions or reactions. With her flat, round cheeks and little beak of a nose, she put me in mind of a caged owl I had once seen. It had sat silent and motionless on its perch and its eyes had that same guarded intensity, revealing nothing, neither fear, nor submission, nor even hatred of its captors.

She listened impassively to Mme Montpensier's instructions before leading us in silence from the room and up the stairs to the shadowy landing, where she opened a door, standing aside to let us enter.

Like the rest of the house it was overfurnished but, even so, it had a freshness and air of virginity about it which was appealing. The bed with its elaborately carved mahogany headboard was lightened by a simple, white crocheted cover and the pictures on the walls in narrow gilt frames were watercolours of flowers or scenery. Although the curtains at the windows were of the same dark velvet and heavy lace of those downstairs, these were looped back to reveal a view of the trees in the garden, but not of the grave, and I was absurdly pleased by this, thinking that the handsome young woman with the firm chin and direct gaze whose photograph I had seen only a short time before had been spared the prospect during her life of looking out over her final resting place, even though she would not have been aware of this.

With a quick glance at Mme Daudet for her nod of permission, Holmes crossed to the large mahogany wardrobe which occupied almost the whole wall and, opening it, disclosed its empty interior. The drawers of the chest and dressing table revealed the same absence of any contents. Not even a handkerchief nor a hair ribbon remained to show that Mlle Carère had once occupied the chamber and I felt a sudden sense of overwhelming grief for the young woman whose life had ended so meanly in that shallow grave under the trees.

Holmes meanwhile, untouched by any such emotion, had paused to glance at one of the watercolour paintings hanging on the wall beside the bed and, turning to Mme Daudet, asked a question in French which I took to be 'Who painted this?'

Her answer was comprehensible even to me.

Lifting her shoulders, she said dismissively, '*Je ne sais pas.*'

Holmes made no response. He appeared to have become, like her, quite indifferent to the matter and, with that, we returned downstairs to take our leave of Mme Montpensier.

Once outside the house, Lestrade set off again for the garden, announcing that he wanted to make a last examination of the grave and its surroundings before arranging for the skeleton to be taken to the mortuary at St Clement's, adding that he would call on us later in the evening. Holmes nodded in agreement and together he and I made our way to Finchley Road, where we took a cab back to our lodgings.

The conversation during this journey was desultory. I could understand Holmes' reluctance to give me a report on the interview with Mme Montpensier in advance of his meeting later that evening with Lestrade, when he would have to repeat the same information. But I sensed that, in addition to this restraint, my old friend was deeply troubled by some aspects of the case and that he preferred to be silent while he turned these over in his mind.

I, too, mulled over the inquiry. What relevance, if any, I asked myself, was the absence of any shoes in the grave? And why was he interested in the identity of the person who had painted the watercolour hanging by Mlle Carère's bed? For despite his apparent indifference to the matter, I knew him well enough to realise he would not have asked the question unless it had some bearing on the investigation.

As we rattled our way down Finchley Road, I tried to remember what had been the subject of the painting but could recall nothing more than a bridge crossing a river and, in the background, a cityscape of tall, many-windowed buildings.

However, uppermost in my mind was Holmes' twice-repeated reference to the importance of the names. That, I felt, had great relevance but, despite racking my brains, the answer to that particular riddle continued to evade me.

As soon as we returned to Baker Street and installed ourselves in the sitting-room, Holmes set about examining the locket and chain with great assiduity, sending the boy in buttons to fetch a whole collection of articles for this purpose, including a clean towel which he spread over his workbench, a bowl of warm water and some cotton swabs. To these, he added from his own stock of equipment a small, soft-bristled brush, a scalpel, two Petri dishes and his jeweller's eyeglass.

Once these were laid out in readiness, he produced the little envelope from his pocketbook and carefully emptied the locket and chain on to the towel.

I quietly moved my chair closer to his so that I could observe his actions, for I found this aspect of his work particularly fascinating – comparable, in my opinion at least, to the meticulous precision of a surgeon preparing to operate on a patient.

First, the locket and chain were brushed over to remove any remaining fragments of dry soil clinging to the metal before both were carefully swabbed with a piece of the cotton cloth, wrung out in the warm water. That done, the chain was set aside while Holmes, using his jeweller's eyeglass, examined the back and front surfaces of the locket. Whatever he found seemed to afford him great satisfaction, for I heard him give a little grunt, partly of gratification and partly of amusement – quite why I had no idea, for I could not imagine what he had found humorous in the reverse side of the little silver object. But he said nothing and I did not like to ask.

Next, he picked up the scalpel and, with great delicacy, slipped the blade between the two halves of the locket, sliding it to and fro until at last the tiny hinge gave way and, opening the sections back, Holmes revealed its interior.

'Come here, Watson,' said he, 'and tell me what you make of this.'

Leaning forward, I peered into the two segments but could see nothing of any significance, apart from some tiny shards of thin glass, some scraps of discoloured paper and a pair of thin silver frames, heart-shaped like the locket that I assumed had once held two photographs in place, the remnants of which were presumably the fragments of paper.

I described all of this to Holmes who listened gravely and nodded his head in agreement as I itemised each component of my observations.

'Well done, my dear fellow!' he exclaimed when I had finished, much to my secret pleasure. 'In my opinion, your deduction is quite correct. The locket did indeed contain two photographs. But see if you can take your analysis a step further.'

'In what direction, Holmes?' I inquired. I could see no other feature of the object that needed any further explanation.

'Well, to begin with, the broken glass and the mutilated photographs. How did that damage occur?'

'But there's nothing unusual in either of them, is there? After all, the locket has been lying in the ground for over a year. It was bound to be affected by the damp and the weight of the soil.'

'My dear Watson, reasonable though your argument

is, it still does not explain how the glass came to be broken into such small pieces and the photographs reduced almost to pulp.'

'I do not follow you,' I began, bewildered by his reply.

'Then allow me to assist you. Look at the glass. How has it been broken?'

'It has been smashed, Holmes!' I protested. 'What more can I say?'

'Oh, a great deal more. Exactly how was it smashed?'

'How?' I cried. 'Well, something may have fallen on it and fractured it.'

'Such as?'

'For goodness' sake, Holmes!' I protested, beginning to feel more and more harassed by this catechism. 'A stone, perhaps, or someone could have trodden on it.'

'Oh, come, Watson! Use your eyes, my dear fellow!' He picked up the locket and held it out, face upwards in the palm of his hand. 'Is there any damage to the outer surface?'

'No, Holmes,' I agreed humbly, at last grasping the purpose behind this inquisition.

'Or on the back?' he persisted, turning it over.

'No, none.'

'So what can we deduce from these simple observations?' He must have caught sight of my expression, for he continued in a much softer tone, 'I think we may safely assume that the locket was not fastened round the dead woman's neck when she was buried as we might have concluded. The little clasp holding the two ends of the chain together is closed. The locket itself is also closed. But the glass covering the two photographs that it no doubt contained was not just broken, but was smashed into small pieces; deliberately, I believe. Take my magnifying glass, Watson, and examine the edges of the pieces. I think you will see that they are not merely broken but crushed, as if they have been hit with some hard object, such as a hammer. Do you not agree?'

'Yes,' I said simply.

'And the photographs?'

Copying Holmes' technique, I picked up the magnifying glass and, training it on the small scraps of paper, was amazed at the result.

'Good heavens, Holmes! They also look as if they have been deliberately torn and the edges pulverised with something heavy!'

'The same hammer?' Holmes suggested.

'Most probably,' I agreed.

I had recovered from my exasperation over Holmes' cross-examination and had begun to appreciate, even to enjoy, the method by which he was leading me, step by step, to a new and totally unexpected conclusion.

'So we can now revise our interpretation of how the locket found its way into the grave, can we not? It was not put round the victim's neck but was placed in the ground quite separate from the body. But before that was done, someone went to the trouble of opening the locket and removing the glass and the photographs before crushing all of them with a heavy implement such as a hammer, the motive for this presumably being to prevent the photographs from being identified. The glass over the photographs had also to be destroyed; had it remained intact it would have looked suspicious. After this was done, the fragments of glass and paper were placed inside the locket, which was then closed. However, two questions arise from this interpretation of the evidence of the locket. Can you suggest what they might be, Watson?'

'Well,' said I, with no great confidence, 'while you were speaking, it did cross my mind to wonder why whoever carried out the damage bothered to take the photographs out of the locket in the first place. Why did not he—'

'Or she,' Holmes pointed out.

'Or she,' I concurred before continuing, 'simply smash the locket with the photographs still in it?'

'Excellent, my dear fellow!' Holmes exclaimed. 'You have asked the very question which I myself would have posed. Why indeed?'

Pleased though I was with Holmes' complimentary remarks, I was aware that I had shot my bolt and could not for the life of me puzzle out the riddle any further.

Holmes came to my rescue in a kindly manner which was intended to be face-saving.

'As you were no doubt going to add before I so rudely interrupted you, had he – or she – done so, then the locket would have been so damaged that a positive identification of it might not have been possible and it was vital that the two, the body and the locket, were incontrovertibly associated one with the other. However, our perpetrator failed to follow up this line of thought to its logical conclusion. One must always remember that deduction is not merely a matter of a succession of individual concepts, however brilliant each one may seem. Like the chain of the locket under present consideration, it is a whole series of perceptions, each one linked to the other until the sequence is completed and the only rational conclusion is achieved.

'On that basis, we may perceive the flaw in our antagonist's logic. He, or she – we must not be biased in our choice of gender – was so anxious that the locket itself should remain easily identifiable that this person forgot one important distinguishing mark which, had the locket been badly damaged, might have been destroyed.'

'What mark is that, Holmes?' I asked, puzzled once more by this unexpected twist to the investigation.

'The mark which every piece of silver has to carry by law.'

'Of course! A hallmark!'

'Exactly. Now take this, my dear fellow,' he continued, handing me his jeweller's eyeglass, 'and look for the hallmark on this particular piece of silver.'

It was not easy to find but, after a careful scrutiny, I discovered it on the rim of the left-hand interior section, just above where one of the photographs would have been placed.

Holmes, who had lit his pipe, was leaning back in his chair, eyes half closed, as he watched the smoke gently spiral upwards towards the ceiling. He seemed to be in a world of his own, far from the demands of the investigation but alert enough to be aware of any changes, however slight, in my own demeanour, for no sooner had I stiffened slightly in the excitement of finding the hallmark than, removing the pipe from his mouth, he said, 'Well done, Watson! Now, if you would be kind enough to describe it to me, I should be much obliged.'

Even with the eyeglass, it was not easy to distinguish the tiny symbols and letters and I began slowly to focus on them one by one and to describe them for Holmes' benefit.

'Well, there is an animal's head, rather like a cat's . . .'

'A leopard's?' Holmes suggested.

'Yes, it could be. After that is a capital "A", followed by what looks like a tiny lion with its tail and one paw raised . . .'

'*En passant?*'

'If you say so, Holmes. Then there is a woman's head in profile . . .'

'Queen Victoria's by any chance?'

'Indeed yes, Holmes! Now you mention it, I can just make out a crown.'

'Ah!' Holmes replied, a simple enough exclamation but into which he managed to inject a whole complexity of reactions from delight to satisfaction, the latter having a ring of triumph about it.

'Just as I thought,' he began but got no further, for there was a knock on the door and Mrs Hudson stepped into the room to inform us that there was a visitor for us downstairs – much to our surprise, for the good lady rarely came up to our sitting-room to announce a client, sending Billy, the boy in buttons, in her stead.

'She's a foreign person,' Mrs Hudson concluded, as if this fact explained and excused her unusual conduct.

'Thank you, Mrs Hudson,' Holmes said gravely. 'You may show her up.'

As Mrs Hudson left the room to carry out this instruction, Holmes glanced across at me, raising his eyebrows and his shoulders in a Gallic gesture of ignorance, similar to that which Mme Daudet had made when he asked the name of the artist who had painted the watercolour in Mlle Carère's bedroom. At the same time, he drew the edge of the towel covering the table over the locket to hide it from sight.

It was Mme Daudet herself who, moments later, was ushered into the room by Billy, Mrs Hudson having gone downstairs to resume her normal role of housekeeper.

Despite Holmes' invitation for her to take a chair by the fire, she remained obstinately by the door, back erect, lips compressed, hands clutching a shabby black reticule in front of her as if it were a shield to ward off an enemy attack. It was obvious that whatever she had to say had been carefully rehearsed, for, before Holmes could ask her what had brought her to Baker Street, she broke into a torrent of French so rapid that I could distinguish no individual words apart from the names Mme Montpensier and Mlle Carère that were repeated several times. However, nothing else gave me any inkling of the purpose of her visit.

Holmes heard her out, occasionally inclining his head as if to indicate that he had understood what she was saying. But his response was strangely neutral, expressing neither concurrence nor disagreement, although he thanked her gravely when she had finished and shook hands with her before showing her out of the room.

No sooner had the door closed behind her than he crossed quickly to the window and, drawing aside the curtain, watched her leave the house.

'What an extraordinary affair!' I exclaimed. 'What on earth did she want?'

'Later, Watson,' he replied. 'Events are moving too quickly for even a brief summary. And anyway a second visitor is on his way to see us.'

'Who?' I demanded as the front doorbell pealed to announce this new arrival.

'None other than our old friend Lestrade,' Holmes replied and began to chuckle. Letting the curtain fall back into place, he turned to me, struggling to keep a straight face. 'Watson,' he continued, 'if ever you hear me complain about the tediousness of life and its lack of action and diversity, just repeat the name "Mme Daudet" to me, there's a good fellow.'

Before I had time to reply, Lestrade was ushered into

the room wearing an expression that I can only describe as shifty. He seemed to be acting a part, and not playing it very well either, as if, like Mme Daudet's speech, it were over-rehearsed. The eagerness with which he shook hands with Holmes was certainly artificial; and so was his show of innocent curiosity when he jerked his thumb towards the door and asked: 'What was she doing 'ere, Mr 'Olmes?' Holmes, who was well aware of Lestrade's deviousness, assumed an air of puzzled naivety himself.

'To whom are you referring, Inspector?'

'The French 'ousekeeper – what's 'er name? – Madam Doodah.'

I saw the corners of Holmes' mouth quiver upwards and I knew that, unless I found the means to divert him, and quickly, too, he would burst out laughing and Lestrade would be deeply offended.

'Oh, Mme Daudet!' I intervened. 'Such a curious lady. And so difficult to talk to, as she speaks no English.'

'But what she had to say in French was most illuminating,' Holmes remarked in his normal tone of voice, thank goodness, and he invited Lestrade to join us in the comfortable half-circle of chairs in front of the fire and to accompany us in a glass of Holmes' choice single-malt whisky which Lestrade, who was off duty, as he was at pains to point out, accepted with alacrity.

'Illuminating? In what way?' Lestrade asked with ill-disguised eagerness.

'Oh, on various aspects of the case,' Holmes replied airily. 'She called unexpectedly as a direct consequence of my interview this afternoon with Mme Montpensier, anxious to find out what was said, or not said, during our tête-â-tête, which, with your permission, Lestrade, I will give you my account of first, before moving on to the matter of Mme Daudet's visit.'

'Of course, 'Olmes,' Lestrade agreed, by now thoroughly mellowed, his feet stretched out towards the fire and the glass of whisky cradled in his hands.

'I questioned her most closely over her relationship with her stepdaughter and she gave me a full, or what seemed a full, account of their association which I will summarise. But we have to go back some few years to an earlier stage of their lives, to the time, in fact, of M Montpensier himself.

'This gentleman was a well-to-do banker, a bachelor of some fifty years when he married the then Mme Carère, a widow who had inherited a considerable fortune on the death of her first husband and the father of her only child, a daughter Lucille, whose mysterious disappearance is the *raison d'être* of our present inquiry. The two gentlemen were colleagues, both being directors of the Banque Continentale, M Carère of the main branch in Paris, M Montpensier of the London branch in Lombard Street. They were both on friendly terms, but from what Mme Montpensier told me during our interview this morning, Mme Carère and her daughter were not particularly intimate with M Montpensier. He was a confirmed bachelor, very set in his ways. However, on the death of M Carère, M Montpensier became very attentive to his widow, helping her with matters connected with her late husband's will, a relationship that had inevitable consequences. They fell in love and two years later they married. Mme Carère, now Mme Montpensier, and her daughter came to live in London in the house in Hampstead. The daughter was then about eleven years old.

'Unfortunately, the relationship between M Montpensier and his stepdaughter was fraught from the very beginning. Mlle Carère, who had been close to her father, very much resented M Montpensier usurping her dead father's place, a situation which was exacerbated six years later when her mother died. To make matters worse, M Montpensier married again, to the lady who now bears his name and resides in the same Hampstead house.

'To the stepdaughter, this was yet another betrayal of her parents; to M Montpensier, it no doubt seemed a practical solution to a family situation which was becoming more complex and troublesome as Mlle Carère grew older.

'As you probably guessed from her photograph, Watson,' he continued, turning briefly to me, 'she was a stubborn young lady with a mind of her own and her animosity towards her stepfather grew with every passing day, until he was at his wits' end to know what to do with her. Finally, in desperation, he came to a decision that was foolhardy in the extreme. Having no children of his own and having been a dyed-in-the-wool bachelor for most of his life, he decided that what his stepdaughter needed was a mother, and in his bumbling, masculine way he set about looking for one. He could not have made a worse choice if he had tried. She was one of the late Mme Montpensier's family members, a second cousin, a spinster of strong-minded principles and a will of iron whom he judged would be acceptable to his stepdaughter, as they were distantly related, and therefore the best person to keep the recalcitrant Lucille Carère on the straight-and-narrow path of filial meekness and obedience.'

'Oh, I say, Holmes!' I interjected, appalled at the situation but not without a tremor of *Schadenfreude* at the same time, a reaction which Holmes evidently shared for he cocked a wry glance in my direction. 'But surely,' I continued, 'Mme Montpensier did not confess all this openly to you?'

'Not in so many words, of course, but in such a manner that I was able to read between the lines. The discovery of the body in the garden no doubt came as a dreadful shock to her and may have weakened her defences, although, when I spoke to her this morning, she did her rigid best not to let it show. By the way, it was because of this marriage that the Daudets were introduced into the household. Mme Daudet is related to the second Mme Montpensier. Perhaps, like an embattled army general, Mme Montpensier was looking for reinforcements whom she believed she could trust.'

'And the locket, Holmes? What did she have to say about that?'

'Ah, the locket!' Holmes replied in a musing manner. 'She recognised it from my description and was positive it belonged to Mlle Carère. It was evidently given to her for her tenth birthday by her father, who had it designed specially for her by a jeweller in Paris, and it contained photographs of her parents. It was the last present he gave her before he died and consequently she was very fond of it and wore it all the time. She may, of course, have done so deliberately in order to vex her stepmother, by reminding her that, as far as she, Lucille, was concerned, she was an interloper in their family circle.'

There was something about his demeanour which prompted me to ask, 'So, given the evidence of the locket, the body must have been that of Mlle Carère?'

Before Holmes could reply, Lestrade had intervened excitedly, 'Of course it is! There has never been any doubt of that in my mind. But what I want to know is, did Mme what's-'er-name say anything about her stepdaughter's disappearance? 'Ad there been a quarrel between the two of them?'

'Leading to an act of violence in which Mme Montpensier murdered her? Is that what you are thinking, Inspector?'

Taken aback by Holmes' directness, Lestrade shuffled his feet on the carpet.

'Well, she did agree quite candidly that the two of

them were not on very good terms,' Holmes conceded. 'She even admitted there had been arguments between them on occasions. As to a violent quarrel, it was Mme Daudet, who called here just before you arrived, Lestrade, who gave a most detailed and revealing account of an incident that happened about eighteen months ago. It was an early evening in June. Mme Montpensier was in the drawing-room with her companion Mlle Benoit, Mlle Carère was upstairs in her bedroom, while the Daudets were in the basement kitchen, washing up the supper things, when a messenger delivered a letter which Mlle Benoit took from the boy and handed to Mme Montpensier. Having glanced at the name on the envelope, Mme Montpensier put it into her pocket. Minutes later, Mlle Carère came downstairs and demanded to see the letter. She had evidently been expecting a message and had heard the front doorbell ring and Mlle Benoit answer it, so had assumed, quite correctly, that a letter had been taken in.

'Perhaps her manner was too high-handed or Mme Montpensier was too dismissive; we shall never know the cause, but Mme Montpensier refused to give her stepdaughter the letter unless she agreed to open it and read it out loud in her presence. There ensued a violent confrontation, so vocal as to be overheard downstairs in the kitchen, with Mlle Carère accusing her stepmother of intercepting her letters and Mme Montpensier replying that, as long as Mlle Carère remained in her house, she was responsible for her moral behaviour.'

'Moral behaviour!' I repeated. 'Oh, Holmes, what an awful thing to say!'

'Especially to a young lady of twenty-two years of age who had achieved her majority and had legal control of a considerable sum of money inherited from her parents. You may imagine the effect it had on Mlle Carère, especially as only a few days earlier she had been forced by her stepmother to abandon the drawing lessons she was taking at the Art Training School in Kensington.'[5]

'When did you hear this, Holmes?' I inquired, much surprised by the information.

'Only this afternoon, from Mme Daudet, who strongly disapproved of Mlle Carère's desire to learn to draw. She mentioned it as an example of the young lady's recalcitrant manner and inappropriate behaviour. Mme Daudet claimed the young lady had no talent and the whole affair was a waste of money, quite ignoring the fact that Mlle Carère had paid for the lessons herself. She was clearly reflecting Mme Montpensier's attitude to the situation. It was, Mme Montpensier stated, quite improper for a young, unmarried lady to mix with artists, infamous for their loose morals, quite

---

[5] The National Art Training School was situated in South Kensington. As well as preparing students who wished to teach art, it also held classes for members of the general public in drawing, painting and modelling, as well as other artistic accomplishments. The fees were five pounds a month for five whole days and the entrance fee was ten shillings. Male and female students were taught separately. Dr John F. Watson.

ignoring the fact that arrangements had been made for male and female pupils to be taught separately. Mme Montpensier even took it upon herself to write to the governors demanding that her stepdaughter's name be removed from the list of students.'

'How very high-handed of her!' I exclaimed, quite shocked by this information. 'Mlle Carère must have been very annoyed.'

'Annoyed! She was furious, and the final straw was Mme Montpensier's attempt to keep back the letter delivered by hand. It was that which lit the fuse to the angry argument I have already described. The next morning, Mlle Carère had disappeared.'

'Disappeared?' Lestrade interjected.

'Exactly how?' I added.

'Ah, that is the mystery, gentlemen. Mlle Benoit discovered she was missing when the young lady failed to arrive downstairs for breakfast on the morning following the argument. On further examination of her bedroom, it was discovered that her bed had not been slept in and that her jewellery and some of her clothes, together with a valise were missing. The rest of her possessions were later collected up on Mme Montpensier's instructions and deposited in a trunk in the attic.

'Further searches by the Daudets revealed that, although the front door was locked, the bolts had been unfastened and it was assumed she had left the house by this means. However, there was no farewell letter to explain her actions, nor any forwarding address by which she might be contacted. In fact, nothing has been heard of her since.'

'Was she reported missing?'

Again, it was Lestrade who posed the question, although it was more in the nature of a statement rather than in inquiry.

'Not officially. Mlle Carère's absence was of course noted by neighbours, who were used to seeing the young lady coming and going in the area. She was young and very striking in appearance. However, nobody cared to ask Mme Montpensier directly what had happened to her. No one could speak French well enough to express their concern but, apart from the language problem, Mme Montpensier had a formidable reputation. But evidently there was gossip, some of it loud enough to reach the ears of the local constabulary, to the effect that Mlle Carère had been murdered by her stepmother for her not inconsiderable fortune and her body disposed of in the garden.

'It was a plausible story. No one who had had any dealings with Mme Montpensier liked her. She was very abrupt and autocratic in her attitude to the local tradesmen and made no effort to befriend the neighbours. Consequently, she was generally disliked. But what told against her the most was the fact that she was French and, moreover, a stepmother, which was sufficient proof for quite a number of people of her innate wickedness. Finally, the gossip reached such a pitch that the police despatched an inspector to the house to make inquiries, but he was sent away by Mme Montpensier with his tail between his legs or, as Mme Montpensier herself might have expressed it: *avec sa queue entre ses jambes*.

'Although nothing more was said openly regarding Mlle Carère's whereabouts, a question mark continued to hang over her fate.'

'Did she herself not contact Mme Montpensier to let her know where she was living and to set her mind at rest?' I asked.

'Not a word,' Holmes replied. 'It was as if the young woman had vanished into thin air.'

'So her stepmother could have murdered 'er and buried 'er body in the garden,' Lestrade remarked with a satisfied air, as if the mystery had been finally solved and there was nothing more to be said about it.

'Oh, come, Lestrade!' I protested. 'Is it as simple as that? Mme Montpensier is an elderly lady. Are you suggesting that she not only killed her stepdaughter, but managed to carry the body out of the house to the grave she had dug in the garden?'

Holmes sat back in his chair, smiling quietly to himself as Lestrade hastened to put forward his own explanation.

'She could 'ave 'ad an accomplice,' he remarked.

'Who?' I demanded. For some reason, I felt the whole discussion was unfair and, on that basis alone, I was eager to defend Mme Montpensier.

'That other French woman.'

'You mean the lady-companion, Mlle Benoit?'

'Yes, that's the one!' Lestrade exclaimed, looking pleased with himself.

I was about to refute this suggestion on the grounds that there was no evidence to support such a theory when Holmes, who had been refilling his pipe and tamping down the tobacco as we spoke, broke off from this task to comment in a voice which brooked no argument, 'Oh, no, Lestrade; you are quite wrong, my dear fellow. Mme Montpensier is innocent of the death of her stepdaughter. That fact is proved beyond doubt.'

If the situation had not been so serious, the effect on Lestrade would have been comical. His mouth fell open in a ridiculous gape of astonishment, and when he eventually recovered enough to speak, he could barely enunciate the words.

'Innocent?' he stuttered. 'B-but I 'ave been asked to submit a report to my superior confirming 'er guilt and laying out my reasons for saying so.'

'Then I suggest that you delay sending it for at least a week until I have gathered together the evidence to prove Mme Montpensier's innocence.'

'What evidence?' Lestrade demanded belligerently. 'I saw no evidence.'

'Neither did I, Holmes,' I interposed, a little reluctantly at finding myself for once on Lestrade's side.

'Some of it was not there, so it was quite understandable you failed to see it,' Holmes remarked, smiling and puffing away contentedly at his pipe.

His behaviour was intended to be infuriating

and Lestrade rose to the bait. Getting to his feet, the inspector stalked over to the door where he paused to declare, 'I can't be doin' with your methods, Mr 'Olmes. If the evidence isn't there, then as far as I'm concerned, it don't exist. That's all I've got to say.' Drawing himself up to his full height, he remarked, not without a certain dignity, 'So, I wish you goodnight, gentlemen!'

And with that, he left the room.

'Oh, Holmes!' I protested as we heard Lestrade's footsteps loudly descending the stairs. 'You have offended him deeply. I really do think you ought to apologise.'

'All in good time, my dear fellow,' Holmes replied, gently blowing smoke at the ceiling. 'When I have gathered together the last pieces of the evidence, I shall be suitably contrite and the good inspector shall have his just rewards.'

Holmes left the house the following morning soon after breakfast to search out these remaining pieces of evidence, but what they were or where he proposed looking for them he refused to tell me on the grounds that it would spoil his *coup de théâtre,* which he was planning to spring on both Lestrade and myself later in the week.

And with that I had to be content, although, as the days went by, I found I was becoming more and more exasperated by his expression of smug satisfaction when he returned from these various fact-finding missions.

By Friday, however, his researches had evidently been completed, because at six o'clock I was instructed to take myself off and not to return until exactly half past seven. Evidently, Lestrade had received the same orders for, as I approached the house at the appointed time, the front door key in my hand, who should alight from a hansom cab but the inspector, looking as surprised at my presence as I was at his.

'What's all this about?' he demanded suspiciously. 'I've been told by Mr 'Olmes to call 'ere on the dot of 'alf past seven. Do you know why?'

'I think it is to do with the dénouement of the case,' I replied.

'Dénouement? You mean the solution?'

'Yes, I think it is his intention to tell us exactly what happened.'

'Well, I blinkin' well 'ope so,' came Lestrade's rejoinder as he followed me into the house and up the stairs.

The *coup* began as soon as I opened the door. Our workaday sitting-room had been transformed into a *salle à manger* fit for the most exclusive gentlemen's club. It was illuminated by a bright fire burning on the hearth and by a dozen or so candles arranged along the mantelshelf, the bookshelves and on the table itself, which was laid with a white damask cloth, wine glasses and an opened bottle of wine that stood in an ice bucket, as well as enough cutlery for several courses, the precise contents of which were temporarily concealed under domed silver dish-covers to preserve their heat.

No sooner had the door closed behind us than the inner one to Holmes' bedroom opened[6] and Holmes himself entered, dressed like a head waiter, with a napkin over his arm. His manner was suitably solemn but, as he invited us to sit down, he could no longer maintain the role and a broad smile lit up his features.

'Now, gentlemen,' said he, 'if you are ready, I shall serve you with a choice little supper, sent for specially from the Mouton Rouge which I trust will titillate your taste buds, if you will forgive the excess of alliteration. But, before we begin, I entreat you to make no mention of the present case until we have finished. Do I have your word?'

As Lestrade and I murmured our concurrence, Holmes, with all the panache of a stage magician, lifted the dish-covers with a flourish to reveal what lay under them and the meal began.

It was indeed a choice supper. It began with sole meunière followed by pheasant *à la Normande* served with a julienne of celery and potatoes, and lastly, *poires belle-Hélène* and a Brie at the very peak of perfection. The courses were accompanied by well-chilled bottles of *Château Saint Jean des Graves*, a very drinkable dry white Bordeaux.

When the meal was over and the dishes had been

---

[6] Sherlock Holmes' bedroom was at the back of the house on the first floor (American second floor) and opened directly off the sitting-room. Dr John F. Watson.

cleared from the table, Holmes passed round coffee, brandy and cigars to add the final touches and, when we were all served, produced a white envelope from his inner pocket which he solemnly placed before him. Its appearance together with the little tap he gave to his brandy glass with his coffee spoon announced that the serious business of the evening was about to commence.

'Gentlemen,' he began, rising to his feet, 'I take great pleasure in declaring that the mystery of the missing *belle fille*, or Mme Montpensier's stepdaughter, Mlle Carère, has been solved and we may now all rest easy in our beds.'

This statement was received with a mixture of emotions – astonishment tempered by relief on my part and, on Lestrade's, ill-disguised suspicion.

'If that is so, Mr 'Olmes,' he replied, 'then tell us 'oo the murderer is and put us out of our misery.'

'There was no murder,' he declared, a response which caused as much sensation as his opening remark.

'No murder!' Lestrade repeated, half rising from his chair. 'Then 'oo wrote the letter and 'oose is the body buried in the grave?'

'All in good time, Lestrade. If only you can contain your curiosity for a moment, I shall come to the letter shortly. As for the body, it was not that of Mlle Carère but of a young woman by the name of Lizzie Ward, who had died of pneumonia eighteen months earlier. To use the epithet that we so-called members of the respectable classes would use to protect ourselves from the less salubrious aspects of life today, she was an "unfortunate"; in short, a prostitute who had collapsed in the Whitechapel area and was taken to the London Hospital,[7] where she died. A few days later her body was claimed by a man and a woman who came to the mortuary looking for their missing daughter. They were a respectable-looking, middle-aged couple dressed in black, but what made the mortuary attendant remember them in particular was the fact that, although the woman could speak a little English, they conversed between themselves in French.'

'The Daudets!' I exclaimed.

'Undoubtedly,' Holmes replied.

Lestrade looked unconvinced.

'But if they were looking for their daughter, why did they go to the London 'ospital? Didn't they report 'er missing to the police first?' he protested.

'My dear Inspector,' Holmes said, with the long-suffering air of a schoolmaster trying to explain Euclid's theorem to an innumerate pupil, 'there was no daughter. What they were looking for was a body which roughly corresponded to Mlle Carère in age, height and so on.'

Understanding lit up Lestrade's countenance like a slow dawn coming up over a horizon.

'Oh, I see!' he exclaimed. 'So the body we found in

---

[7] The London Hospital was situated in the Mile End Road, Whitechapel, a poor working-class district, and mainly served patients living in the East End. Dr John F. Watson.

the grave wasn't M'zelle Career's after all but this other woman's?'

'Quite,' Holmes said crisply. 'I had my doubts about its true identity the moment I saw it. The absence of shoes first roused my suspicions—'

'But why were there no shoes?' I interjected. 'Judging by the remnants of clothing found in the grave, the dead woman was wearing a dress, not nightclothes. So was she barefooted when she died?'

'Almost certainly yes. But that is not the point, Watson. There was a specific reason for making sure there were no shoes in the grave. You both saw the skeleton. Did either of you notice anything particular about the joint to the big toe of the right foot?' When both of us shook our heads, Holmes continued, 'It was slightly deformed. A swelling had begun to form, probably a bunion, due no doubt to ill-fitting shoes. This deformity would have been evident in the right shoe, where the leather would have been distorted by the swelling. I think we may safely assume there was no such deformity on Mlle Carère's right foot and that the Daudets were aware of this.

'However, they were very anxious to make sure there was evidence to prove that the skeleton was that of Mlle Carère and they went to considerable trouble to supply it. I am referring, of course, to the silver locket which was found with the body. On the face of it, it was a clever ploy. As we already know, the locket was a birthday present to Mlle Carère from her father and she was known to wear it constantly. Therefore, the presence of a locket answering the description of Mlle Carère's in the grave would, they thought, confirm that the body was that of Mlle Carère. The problem was finding a locket to match the original. Unfortunately, the substitute they placed there only strengthened my suspicions that the body was not hers.'

''Ow was that?' Lestrade asked.

Reaching into his pocket, Holmes produced the little envelope containing the silver locket, which he carefully tipped out on to a napkin on the table.

'It is a long story, I am afraid, which I will tell as succinctly as possible. The Daudets were familiar with the locket and knew it contained two likenesses of Mlle Carère's parents that they would have to substitute with two other photographs.'

''Oo of?' Lestrade demanded.

'That is not important, Inspector. They could have been of anybody. But there had to be evidence that the locket had contained two photographs. The obvious answer to this dilemma was to so badly damage the substitutes that they could no longer be recognised. So someone, probably M Daudet, defaced them and their settings, but in doing so, he failed to submit the locket itself to the same treatment, as it was imperative that it remained recognisable, and it was this that roused my suspicions. There was something else he also failed to remove, probably because they were so small they were not easily seen. These were the hallmarks on the locket itself. They comprised a leopard's head, profiles of a lion and the Queen's head and, most importantly, the capital letter "M" in Gothic style, all of which prove it was made of English silver, assayed in London and manufactured between the years 1887 and 1888, not in Paris in 1866 when Mlle Carère would have been a young girl.' Catching sight of Lestrade's doubtful expression, he continued, pushing the locket and the jeweller's eyeglass across the table, 'Would you like to examine them for yourself?'

Lestrade waved them away.

'I'm not much good with them things,' he said, indicating the lens, 'so I'll take your word for it. But what puzzles me about the 'ole business is why they did it in the first place.'

'Ah, motive! A good point, Inspector!' Holmes declared. 'It was avarice, in my opinion the deadliest of the seven deadly sins and the motive behind a great deal of criminal behaviour. If you remember, Mme Daudet was a cousin to Mme Montpensier, a poor relation and apparently her only living one. No doubt Mme Montpensier had remembered her in her will but, if I have read the situation correctly, the legacy was probably a small one, reflecting the lady's low social standing. Now, if Mme Montpensier was unfortunate enough to be hanged for her stepdaughter's murder, her estate – and quite a considerable one, I would imagine – would pass to her next of kin, in short, to Mme Daudet.'

'I can understand that,' I interjected. 'What I am

puzzled by is the reason why Mme Daudet called on us the other evening.'

Holmes shrugged his shoulders.

'I am not absolutely sure myself. Women are such irrational creatures, likely to act on the smallest of whims, that I sometimes doubt if they themselves understand their own motives.[8] She is a very cunning woman but not very intelligent. I think she was merely testing the water, so to speak, and using the opportunity to sow a few seeds of suspicion against Mme Montpensier. If you remember, Watson, she gave the impression that she supported the theory of Mlle Carère's disappearance while at the same time throwing doubt on its veracity. I am convinced that, despite her own limited intellect, she was the brains behind the scheme. Daudet was a mere tool in her hands. It was he, of course, who dug the grave and buried Lizzie Ward's body in it, after conveying it from the London Hospital to Hampstead.'

Lestrade, who had been listening to Holmes' account with increasing impatience, broke in at this point.

'That's all very well, but 'ow did 'e manage it, Mr 'Olmes? You tell me that. I can't go back to the Yard

---

[8] Sherlock Holmes could at times be very scathing about women. In 'The Adventure of the Illustrious Client', he declares that a woman's heart and mind are 'insoluble puzzles to the male' and in 'The Adventure of the Second Stain' he is even more critical, stating that 'their most trivial action may mean volumes, or their most extraordinary conduct may depend upon a hairpin or a curling-tongs'. Dr John F. Watson.

with some 'alf-baked theory. I need to have everything cut and dried.'

'Then, Inspector, cut and dried it shall be. I made a few inquiries of the cabbies in the vicinity of the London Hospital and came across a Sidney Wells, whose memory – assisted, I must admit, with the judicious stimulus of half a crown and a few brown ales – recalled an occasion about eighteen months ago when a couple, who answered the description of the Daudets, summoned his growler[9] and asked to be taken to Hampstead, together with their young niece who had fainted. She was wrapped up closely in a blanket, which no doubt the Daudets took with them for this very purpose, and was supported by the man and his wife. As requested, he dropped them off in a street, the name of which he could not recall, and the last sighting he had was the pair of them half-carrying the young woman down a narrow alleyway that ran alongside a large house. I think we can safely assume it led to the garden behind Mme Montpensier's residence where a grave already awaited its occupant.'

At this point he stopped and looked keenly from Lestrade to myself.

'Well, gentlemen,' he said. 'Are there any more questions?'

Questions? The inspector and I exchanged puzzled glances. What on earth was Holmes referring to?

---

[9] A 'growler' was the popular name for a four-wheeled cab which seated four passengers. Dr John F. Watson.

'The victim, gentlemen,' my old friend reminded us gently.

'The woman, Lizzie what's-'er-name?' Lestrade suggested.

'No, no, no!' Holmes protested. 'I am referring to the other young lady, Mlle Carère.'

'Oh, Holmes!' I exclaimed, greatly mortified to think that Lestrade and I should have forgotten to consider the fate of that young woman about whom the inquiry had first arisen. 'What happened to her?'

'She is safe and well and living in New York with her husband,' Holmes announced coolly.

''Usband?'

'In New York?'

''Ow did you find that out?'

'Who is he?'

Laughing, Holmes held up a hand to stem the flow.

'One at a time, gentlemen, if you please!' he protested. 'Allow me to answer your questions in a proper sequence. Her husband is Henri Chevalier, an artist, whom she met at the Kensington School of Art where he was teaching drawing. How did I find out his name? Easily enough. From his signature at the bottom of that watercolour which was hanging in her bedroom in the Hampstead house. It was, by the way, a view of New York seen from the banks of the River Hudson, which provided me with the American connection.

'As for finding out where she was, I sent a cable to my old friend Wilson Hargreaves of the New York

Police Bureau[10] and he most kindly discovered her whereabouts and the details of her marriage. It seems she met Chevalier at the art school, where they fell in love. It was a genuine *coup de foudre*, as the French would say, and they were planning to marry in New York after Henri Chevalier's contract at the school expired. In fact, the letter which Mme Montpensier so high-handedly withheld was from Chevalier, giving Mme Carère details of the sailing times of ships from Liverpool to New York. Under the circumstances, they decided to hurry forward their plans, rather than allow Mlle Carère to stay a moment longer under Mme Montpensier's roof. So they married in London and booked their passage immediately.

'By the way, Mlle Carère, or Mme Chevalier as she was by then, did write to Mme Montpensier explaining the circumstances, a letter which I strongly suspect Mme Daudet intercepted and destroyed. I have received a cable from Mme Chevalier stating that, if need be, she will send a statement, witnessed by an attorney, should there be any legal repercussions.'

'But what would the Daudets be charged with?' I asked. 'Not murder?'

'Indeed no. Lizzie Ward died of natural causes and no actual fraud had been committed—'

---

[10] Wilson Hargreaves was an officer in the New York police force. He and Sherlock Holmes regularly exchanged information about criminals and their activities in their respective cities. *Vide*: 'The Adventure of the Dancing Men'. Dr John F. Watson.

To my surprise, it was Lestrade who spoke up with a confidence I had not expected of him.

'According to civil law, there is an indictable offence, passed, if I remember right, in 1788, to do with preventing a dead body from 'aving a Christian burial; average sentence about two years.'

'Well done, Lestrade!' Holmes exclaimed with genuine admiration and, refilling our glasses, lifted his, adding, as he rose to his feet, 'I think a toast is called for! To our excellent Inspector Lestrade!'

'Hear! Hear!' I exclaimed loudly in agreement.

As for Lestrade himself, I have rarely seen a man beam so broadly or blush so deeply as our old friend and colleague, the inspector, on that evening.

However, in our pleasure at the successful outcome to the inquiry and the good news of Mlle Carère's survival and subsequent happy marriage, we had forgotten one other person whose fate we had failed to give a second thought to: that of Mme Montpensier. Much to my surprise, it was Holmes who reminded us; Holmes, whom in the past I have criticised for his lack of human warmth towards other people, especially women!

Nevertheless, he went to the trouble of contacting an old acquaintance of his in France through whom he later learned that Mme Montpensier had returned to Paris with Mlle Benoit as her companion where, using her considerable fortune left to her by her late husband, she had leased a large and comfortable apartment in the Champs-Élysées. There the two ladies shared a very pleasant life, going to the theatre and the opera or shopping in the Rue Rivoli.

I wish them both good luck.

As for Holmes, I realise I was too quick in jumping to the wrong conclusion. I should have given him the benefit of the doubt and for that I apologise most heartily.

THE CASE OF THE
WATCHFUL WAITER

Although I admit I can at times be careless over certain facts regarding my accounts of Holmes' cases, in particular their dating, the day that this case began is firmly fixed in my mind as if burnt on to it in figures of fire.

It was the second Wednesday of April 1896 and the time was about half past nine in the morning. Holmes and I had finished breakfast and, once Mrs Hudson had cleared the table, we removed ourselves to the two armchairs on either side of the hearth where a small fire was burning, the weather being a little chilly, to read the newspapers at our leisure as was our custom.

Holmes seemed restless that morning and, laying his newspaper aside, had risen to his feet to prowl about the room like a cat that cannot settle, pausing at regular intervals to glance out of the windows. He could not be waiting for the morning post. That had been delivered before breakfast and he had read it over his bacon and eggs. There had been only a few letters which, after he had perused them, he had pushed to one side as if disappointed by their contents. In fact, the past ten days had been a particularly unproductive time for him. No one had written or called asking for his help with an investigation and consequently he was at a loose end, a very disturbing state of affairs to find himself in. Without the stimulus of an investigation to occupy his mind, he tended to become bored and might easily revert to that other unorthodox form of stimulation from which I had been trying to wean him for some time. Although I thought I had succeeded, with Holmes' mercurial temperament it was impossible to be positive about anything. Depending on his mood, he could be maddeningly unpredictable at times.

With this thought in mind, I watched his movements with covert attention as he paced about the room, turning his head for what must have been the tenth time towards the windows.

'Holmes—' I began, but got no further than that.

'I know what you are going to say, Watson,' he stated in a dismissive tone, 'but there is a purpose to my walking about in this fashion and also in my apparent obsession with the view from the windows. It is to make sure of the appearance of the young man who is watching the house so that, should the need arise, I can give the police a precise description of him.'

'Watching the house?' I repeated. 'Are you sure?'

'Of course I am, my dear fellow! I would not make such a claim unless I were certain of the facts.'

'Perhaps he is a client or one of your many admirers who has found out your address and is hoping to catch a glimpse of you.'

'I think not,' he retorted. 'Clients or, come to that, admirers, do not keep vigil for a whole day nor go to the trouble of altering their appearance from time to time.'

'In what way?' I exclaimed, quite taken aback by this piece of information.

'By discreetly changing his headgear, for example, or occasionally even his hair.'

'Changing his hair!' I repeated disbelievingly, starting up in my chair so that I might go closer to the window to catch a clearer view of this extraordinary individual. But Holmes waved me back with a peremptory gesture.

'Stay where you are!' he ordered. 'Although the lace curtains are thick enough to hide a general view of the interior of the room, sudden movements can be seen through them and, if you approach too close to the glass, my peeping Tom will almost certainly be aware that he, too, is being watched and this might frighten him off. If you must catch a glimpse of him, I suggest you stand well back and concentrate on the curtain to your left. About halfway down, there is a small tear in the fabric through which you can get a better view. But take care not to stay there too long. He may not be able to see you in detail but he would certainly know if you were moving about or not.'

Following Holmes' instructions, I carefully stepped to the left and, realigning my feet, found the tiny rent in the curtain, no longer than a man's little finger, through which I was able to catch a glimpse of the street outside, unobstructed by the gauzy pattern of leaves and flowers that was woven into the lace.

Even so, the view was restricted and I saw only the hazy shape of a young man who gave the impression of a black-haired youth, slight of build, who was wearing dark clothes. I could not make out any details of his features but his stance suggested tension and an ominous pertinacity, although, had I been asked to explain this last impression, I would have been hard put to do so.

Behind my back, Holmes was saying, 'I see you have found the little slit in the lace. I made that myself on purpose after our visitor first started watching the house last week. It makes my own observation of him so much easier.'

'You mean he has been here before?' I cried, turning round to look at him in some alarm.

'Yes; last Wednesday.'

'But why?'

'There lies the mystery,' Holmes replied. 'Now do come and sit down, my dear fellow. If you remain like that at the window you will not only get a crick in your neck but the man, whoever he is, may notice that you have been lurking there for some time and get suspicious. I do not want him to be frightened off until I have had the opportunity to discover who he is and what business has brought him here.'

As I resumed my seat by the fire, Holmes continued, 'As I explained, I first noticed him last week purely by chance. I took him to be a reluctant client, nervous of approaching the house, but I soon realised I was wrong, for he remained there for at least three hours, pacing up and down and occasionally crossing over the street and resuming his vigil a few doors down. It was when he changed his wig that I became really intrigued and decided to let the situation develop to see what would happen.

'After an hour, he set off down the street to number 217, where he disappeared briefly behind that large privet hedge by the gate, and when he reappeared he had fair hair and a tweed cap and what appeared to be a pair of eyeglasses. Later that afternoon, he reverted to his dark hair, although he had, in the meantime, abandoned the tweed cap and replaced it with a beret such as French workmen wear. He also seemed to have grown a small moustache, but as it was so difficult to distinguish details through the lace, I decided to cut that small eyehole after it began to get dark and he gave up the vigil.'

I listened to Holmes' account in astonished silence until he had finished, when I broke in to exclaim, 'But who is he, Holmes?'

'I have no idea,' he admitted with a shrug.

'And what does he want here?'

'I do not know that either.'

'So you are completely in the dark?'

'Not entirely,' Holmes replied. 'Let us say more in the dusk. There are several facts about him which may be deduced.'

'Such as?' I asked, much bemused as I failed to see how Holmes, for all his detective skills, could have come to any positive conclusions from a few meagre details such as the man was young and was of medium height and build.

'Well, there is the fact that the only other occasion he was watching the house was also a Wednesday.'

'So?'

'Oh, come, Watson! Do try not to be so obtuse!' he chided me impatiently. 'I think we may safely assume that the young man has some occupation that keeps him busy all week except Wednesdays. Now what does that suggest?'

'That he does not have to work on that day, of course,' I replied, thinking that perhaps Holmes' deductive talents were not as complex as I had sometimes imagined.

'Exactly so,' he concurred. 'Now let us take that assumption a step further. He has so far not appeared at the weekends, an important omission as most employees are free at the weekend, if not on a Saturday then almost certainly on a Sunday, with certain exceptions such as . . . ?'

And here he paused to cock an interrogative eyebrow in my direction. It was then I realised that I had stepped into a little trap that he had carefully laid for his own amusement. I tried to bluff it out.

'Well,' I began, racking my brains, 'there are several possibilities.'

'Such as?'

'Oh, Holmes!' I protested. 'I am not in the mood for such games. But if you insist; perhaps he has a lady friend whom he visits on a Sunday.'

'Well done, my dear fellow! You have come up with an excellent answer that even I had not considered. A lady friend! Well, he is young, I concede, so it is a distinct possibility but it gives rise to too many other questions, such as: Does he spend the whole of Sunday in her company? And if so, what about the evenings, when one would assume he is also free to go courting? No, Watson, ingenious though your theory may be, there must be a simpler explanation that does away with the need of the dubious delights of courting several young ladies. Whatever his employment is, he is free all day on a Wednesday until the evening. Now, that could suggest a shop assistant who might have a half-day on Wednesday. But a *whole* day? Consequently, we must think of some other occupation: that of the catering trade, for example. If so, then he may work in a restaurant or a hotel. He could therefore be a chef, or a pageboy . . .'

'Or a waiter?' I suggested.

I do not know what put that word into my head, but as I uttered it, I saw Holmes' expression light up and he clapped his hands together.

'Excellent, Watson! Congratulations! Of course he must be a waiter. What does he do on a Wednesday but wait outside our house? Never has a man been so suitably employed. In future, we shall call him the Watchful Waiter. Do not you agree?'

'If you wish so, Holmes,' I replied, rather brusquely for, to be frank, I was becoming a little tired of his flippant attitude. As far as I was concerned, there was nothing amusing about a young man, waiter or not, keeping vigil outside our house for hours on end. To me, it had a sinister quality about it and, had I been in charge of the situation, I would have marched up to the man in the street and demanded to know what was the meaning of his behaviour, rather than spend my time peering at him through a hole in a curtain.

To give Holmes his due, he was aware of my exasperation and, seating himself once more by the fire, he adopted a much more conciliatory tone.

'Now, Watson,' said he. 'What do you think we should do about him? I should like to have your opinion.'

Flattered though I was by this direct appeal, I declined to be mollified by it and I expressed outright my preference for accosting the man face to face.

'You are right, of course, my dear fellow,' Holmes replied, 'but excellent though your advice is, I shall not take it for the simple reason that I think there is some complex motive behind the young man's actions. Do not ask me why because I cannot give you a rational explanation, except to say that, like Macbeth, my thumbs are giving me warning signals. You remember the quotation: "By the pricking of my thumbs, Something wicked this way comes"?[1] Well, *my* thumbs are pricking and it disturbs me greatly.'

At this I sat up and regarded him seriously.

'How do you account for that, Holmes?'

'I cannot, Watson. It is a purely instinctive reaction that has no logic behind it. All I can give you in the way of an explanation is my feeling that I have met the Waiter before and that he represents danger. But I cannot for the life of me remember where or when I encountered him.'

'What do you propose doing about it?'

'For the time being nothing at all. I shall stay in the house reading the *Morning Chronicle* and writing letters. I might even sort and file some of my papers, which no doubt will please you, Watson. You often remark on

---

[1] In *Macbeth* Act IV, Scene 1, the second witch makes this comment just before Macbeth enters. Dr John F. Watson.

their abundance and how they encroach on our sitting-room.[2] If the Waiter keeps to his usual routine, he will abandon his vigil at about six o'clock this evening. So, all being well, I shall start taking action tomorrow.'

'In what way?'

'To begin with, by sending a telegram.'

'But could you not do that later this evening after he has gone?'

'I do not wish to do so, although I am sure your suggestion was kindly meant, Watson. However, this man is an unknown quantity. I have no idea which way he will jump; neither do you, and I would not wish to place you, or myself, come to that, in any danger.'

'But—' I began.

'But me no buts,' Holmes replied, wagging an admonitory finger in my direction, only partly in jest.

So I held my peace and Holmes and I spent the rest of the day quietly at home, he sorting through the accumulation of papers, which he put away tidily in the box he kept in his bedroom,[3] I in a more desultory manner reading through the lists of stocks and shares in *The Times* and deciding which ones I might invest

---

[2] In the adventure of 'The Musgrave Ritual', Dr Watson refers to Sherlock Holmes' 'horror of destroying documents' and how they tended to turn up in unlikely places, even in the butter dish. Dr John F. Watson.

[3] There are several references to Sherlock Holmes' bedroom, which was apparently the back room that opened directly off the sitting-room. It was where he kept his papers in 'a large tin box'. Dr John F. Watson.

in should Holmes release my cheque book from its captivity in his desk drawer.[4]

The following morning, Holmes set about whatever plan he had in mind for outwitting the Waiter, having first made a preliminary reconnoitre through the slit in the curtain to make sure that, as he had anticipated, the coast was indeed clear, although, with his innate delight in secrecy, he omitted to tell me where he was going or to what purpose.

His destination could not have been far away, for he returned in less than half an hour, rubbing his hands together with obvious satisfaction.

'That is stage one of my plan completed,' he announced. 'If all goes well, the second part should be completed later this morning. By the way,' he added, as if changing the subject, 'are you free at lunchtime? You have no prior engagement with your friend Thurston?'

'No; I am free,' I replied, wondering where all this was leading up to.

'Good! Then we shall lunch together at Marcini's[5] at twelve noon.'

---

[4] In 'The Adventure of the Dancing Men', Sherlock Holmes deduces that Dr Watson might have bought shares in South African property if he had not locked his cheque book in his desk as a precaution against him spending too much money. Dr John F. Watson.

[5] Marcini's was a restaurant in London that, judging by its name, served Italian food. Holmes and Watson dined there after the conclusion of the Hound of the Baskervilles inquiry. Dr John F. Watson.

And with that, he retired to his bedroom, where I heard him playing a brisk little Scottish air on his violin, a sure sign that he was in a cheerful mood.

However, he said nothing more about the coming arrangement, such as whether or not it had anything to do with the Watchful Waiter, as he had come to speak of him, and when I asked him in the hansom on the way to the restaurant, he merely smiled in an infuriatingly secretive manner and turned the conversation to the gossip in the popular newspapers about the scandal of the Lord Mayor's recent claim for expenses, including the purchase of a new set of solid-silver buckles for his dress shoes.

However, his manner remained somewhat unpredictable for, when we had arrived at Marcini's and were shown to our table, he insisted on my taking the chair facing the door while he took the one that had its back to it.

This careful arranging of our places at the table warned me that Holmes had more in mind than a simple luncheon for the two of us. Even so, I was not prepared for what happened next.

It was not long after we had seated ourselves that I noticed Holmes smile and half rise to his feet as if to welcome someone who had just that moment entered, and I instinctively turned my head to see who this new arrival might be.

To my utter astonishment, the person who was approaching our table was Holmes himself! For a moment, I was too shocked to say anything and could only stand there, my mouth wide open, until I recovered my senses and realised the man was not Holmes after all but someone who looked remarkably like him. He was the same height and build and had the same lean countenance and hawk-like nose, as well as the same sharp line to his jaw, but there the similarities ended. Although very nearly a doppelgänger, the man lacked Holmes' look of alert intelligence. His clothes were not Holmes' style either. He wore a long, loose coat slung over his shoulders like a cloak and a soft, wide-brimmed black hat that gave him a foppish, theatrical appearance.

As he joined us at the table, Holmes made the introductions and, on hearing the man's name, I had to suppress a small smile. Sheridan Irving, indeed! There was hardly any need for Holmes to add in way of explanation, 'He is an old theatrical acquaintance of mine, Watson, who from time to time has been extremely useful to me.'

'As a double,' Irving added with a little airy gesture of his hand as if dismissing the compliment.

'And very good he is at it, too,' Holmes added with genuine appreciation.

'Which, no doubt, is why you have invited me to luncheon today,' Irving commented without any sign of resentment.

'Indeed it is. But we shall come to that later, Irving, together with the matter of your fee. In the meantime, let us enjoy our luncheon. Business can come with the coffee,' Holmes replied, beckoning over a waiter.

It was an entertaining meal. Irving was an agreeable companion and over the *tagliatelle con prosciutto* he kept us amused with a fund of anecdotes about the theatre. It was not until coffee was served that a more serious mood replaced the laughter and repartee.

'Now, to business,' Holmes said briskly, putting his elbows on the table and leaning towards his guest. 'I have been pestered for the last two Wednesdays by a stranger who lurks about outside my house and whose identity I am anxious to discover. With your permission, Irving, I propose using you as a lure. So, as he usually arrives soon after breakfast, I suggest you move into our lodgings next Wednesday early in the morning, say at eight o'clock, if that is convenient to you, and that later in the morning, dressed in my clothes, you leave the house—'

'Alone?' Irving broke in to ask. 'I'm afraid when it comes to accepting an assignment, I must be informed of all the details, otherwise one can become involved in heaven knows what kind of embarrassing situations which, I confess, naming no names, has happened to me in the past.'

Holmes glanced quickly towards me.

'If Dr Watson agrees, I was going to suggest that he accompanies you. Is that all right, my dear fellow?' he added, addressing me directly.

The proposal was a surprise to me but I raised no objection, for I could understand his reticence about his plan. Had I known in advance that Sheridan Irving would join us at luncheon, I would not have been so taken aback by his likeness to my old friend and it was this similarity that Holmes had wanted to test. If I were hoodwinked, then the Waiter would accept the subterfuge, especially if I were seen in the company of the bogus Holmes. As he apparently had been watching the house, then he would have been aware of my presence there and also of my friendship with the man whom he was keeping under surveillance.

'Yes, of course, Holmes,' I replied without hesitation.

'And what about you, Irving?' Holmes asked, turning to his guest.

Irving was less positive, partly, I thought, out of a genuine curiosity to know more about the assignment Holmes was proposing, but largely, I suspected, out of a desire to wring the greatest dramatic effect from the situation by not appearing too eager to agree.

'You did say you do not know who this man is?' he asked, with a doubtful pursing of his lips.

'No, I do not.'

'Nor why he has been watching your house?'

'None whatsoever. He could, of course, be a potential client who is nervous about approaching me.'

Sheridan Irving looked unconvinced by this suggestion and I realised that, despite the cloak and the ridiculous name, not to mention the hat, he was a great deal more astute than I had given him credit for.

'Or,' he pointed out, lowering his voice and glancing conspiratorially to the left and right as if expecting our conversation was being monitored by foreign agents, 'he could be an old enemy of yours who is seeking revenge.'

'Oh, I think not,' Holmes replied with a shrug. 'He is a mere youth who I cannot imagine is harbouring murder in his heart.'

'In that case, then,' Irving said, making a great show of coming to a decision, 'I shall be delighted to accept your invitation. Next Wednesday, you said? And at eight o'clock in the morning? It is an early start but, as an ac*tor*,' stressing the final syllable of the word, 'I am used to keeping unconventional hours.'

Rising to his feet, he draped his coat cloak-like over his shoulders, placed his hat on his head and, with a quick glance at the nearest mirror, adjusted it to a more becoming angle before holding out his hand to each of us in turn.

'*Au revoir, mes amis,*' he declared. 'To next Wednesday at eight o'clock!'

And with a swish of his cloak, he made his exit.

I could hardly wait until the restaurant door had closed behind him before I turned to my old friend.

'Really, Holmes—!' I began. But he was ready for me.

'I know what you are going to say, Watson, and I thoroughly agree with you. I am behaving quite irresponsibly in inviting Irving to take part in my little deception.'

'But it is not a little deception!' I protested. 'You have already admitted that the situation could be dangerous . . .'

'Oh, you mean the business of the pricking of the thumbs?'

'Yes, the pricking of the thumbs!' I repeated quite hotly. 'And yet you propose involving Sheridan Irving in what could be a dangerous undertaking without warning him or giving him any choice in the matter!'

'I realise that, Watson,' Holmes replied gravely. 'But please let us discuss this in a less public place. We are drawing attention to ourselves.'

Glancing quickly about me, I was dismayed to discover that two or three customers at nearby tables had turned their heads in our direction, clearly aware that some dispute was taking place between us. It was an embarrassing moment which Holmes neatly defused by murmuring to me *sotto voce*, 'If you would call a cab, my dear fellow, I will pay the bill.'

The journey back to Baker Street was conducted in silence which might have continued even longer, for Holmes took up his position in front of the window with the torn curtain, where he stood silently staring down into the street, as if assuming his old role of keeping watch on the Waiter, even though he knew it was Thursday and therefore the man was unlikely to appear. His arms were tightly folded across his chest and the rigidity of his shoulders warned me that he was deeply engaged in some private deliberation that, knowing him in this mood, I dared not interrupt.

Then suddenly, without a word being spoken by either of us, he gave a cry and spun round on his heels.

'Of course!' he exclaimed, striking himself on the forehead with the open palm of his hand. 'Fool! Fool! Fool! Irving was right!'

'Right about what, Holmes?' I cried, alarmed by this sudden outburst. 'Are you ill?'

'No, I have never felt better in my life. Come here, Watson. I want your opinion.'

Greatly mystified, I joined him at the window.

'Now, look down at the street and tell me what you can see.'

I peered out.

'Well, nothing much really, Holmes,' I replied.

'Look again!' he urged me. 'Who is walking down the street?'

'Why, it is only a messenger boy who is apparently delivering a telegram or some similar missive to the house next door.'

'And?'

He had fixed on me such a hard, bright look that I began to wonder if he had not temporarily lost his reason.

'And what, Holmes? I do not understand,' I replied, by now totally bewildered.

'What did I say yesterday about the Waiter?'

'You made several comments, including one about feeling you had met him somewhere before.'

'Oh, well done, Watson! You are indeed a star! That is exactly what I meant. I now know who he reminded me of. So let us see how perspicacious *you* are, my dear fellow. I see a messenger boy and, like a bolt from the blue, I immediately call to mind who the Waiter reminds me of. Does that help?'

'Not really, Holmes,' I confessed.

'Then allow me to give you a few more clues. Think of mountains and a waterfall.'

'A waterfall!' I exclaimed. 'You are surely not referring to . . . ?'

But I could not bring myself to name the place. My recollection of it was still too raw in my memory and it was Holmes who spoke the words I hesitated to articulate.

'Yes, the Reichenbach Falls,' he said, quite calmly in almost a matter-of-fact tone of voice.

I still could not collect my thoughts, nor see the connection between the events that had taken place on that dreadful day in May 1891, five years earlier, in the Bernese Oberland in Switzerland, when I had been convinced that Holmes had died at the hands of his arch-enemy Moriarty. For a dreadful moment an image of the place flashed before my eyes as, it is said, scenes from the life of a drowning man rush headlong through his mind at the point of death. I saw quite clearly the narrow path, the dark rocks glittering with the spray thrown up from the torrent as it poured over the lip of the ravine, and heard its demented roar as it crashed down in a tumult of foam and seething water into the abyss below. And I experienced again that empty, aching loss I had felt then as I came to what seemed the inevitable conclusion that my friend, my better than a brother, had died in that fearful maelstrom.

I do not think Holmes was aware of my reaction any more than he had been conscious at the time of my feelings as I stood alone on the edge of the Reichenbach Falls, where I believed he had died while he was, in fact, lying hidden on the ledge above me, for he was saying in a brisk, slightly impatient voice, 'Come on, my dear fellow! Surely it is not difficult? The waterfall, the messenger . . .'

'Oh, you mean the boy from the hotel who brought the message from Herr Steiler[6] about the English lady who was dying of consumption, asking me to return to the hotel with him? But surely you do not think the Waiter and the boy are one and the same person?'

'Indeed I do,' Holmes replied, sounding relieved that I had at last grasped the point.

---

[6] Peter Steiler was the landlord of the Englischer Hof at Meiringen, near to the Reichenbach Falls. Holmes and Watson had stayed there overnight before continuing on their journey through the Swiss Alps. Steiler had worked as a waiter at the Grosvenor Hotel in London and consequently spoke excellent English. It was a note ostensibly from him which lured Dr Watson back to the hotel to treat a dying English lady, leaving Sherlock Holmes alone and at the mercy of his arch-enemy, Moriarty. Dr John F. Watson.

'But Holmes—' I began in protest.

'I know what you are going to say,' he broke in. 'If the Waiter is the lad from the Swiss hotel, then he must be a member of Moriarty's criminal gang, one of the few the police failed to round up after Moriarty's death. We know only too well that some of them escaped the net. There was Parker, the garrotter,[7] who laid in wait outside our lodgings in Baker Street for my return. Then there was the affair of the Dutch steamship *Friesland*, which I am convinced was devised by Moriarty as a revenge against me, not to mention Colonel Moran, Moriarty's chief of staff . . .'[8]

'Surely you are not suggesting . . . ?'

---

[7] Garrotters were thieves who attacked their victims by throttling them from behind with a cord or a piece of wire before rifling their pockets. Dr John F. Watson.

[8] Colonel Sebastian Moran was a former Indian Army officer, a big-game hunter and an excellent shot. He had been Moriarty's chief of staff and, after Moriarty's death, took on the task of eliminating Sherlock Holmes. He was an accomplished killer, having murdered the Hon. Ronald Adair and attempted to murder Holmes. He was found not guilty of Adair's murder, largely because there were no witnesses and the bullet he used was soft-nosed and flattened out on impact and therefore could not be identified. He was apparently still alive in 1914 because, although Dr Watson in 'His Last Bow' refers to the 'late lamented Professor Moriarty', when he speaks of Colonel Moran he uses no qualifying adjective to suggest he too is dead. Had he still been alive, he would have been in his late seventies or early eighties. He was certainly still alive in September 1902 because in 'The Adventure of the Illustrious Client', Sherlock Holmes speaks of him as 'the living Colonel Sebastian Moran'. Dr John F. Watson.

'That Moran is still alive? It is not impossible, Watson. We know he is devilishly clever and quite capable of murder. Think of the fate of young Ronald Adair. Although Lestrade arrested him that evening in Camden House and he was brought to trial, he managed to escape the gallows.

'As for the Waiter being the Swiss youth, the dates could correspond. If the lad was seventeen in 1891, the year of my encounter with Moriarty at the Reichenbach Falls, he would now be twenty-two, which accords with the present age of the Waiter who, judging by his appearance, is in his early twenties.

'Now let us take the hypothesis a step further. We know that Moran and the Swiss youth were alive in May 1891, the date of Moriarty's death and the attempt by Moran on my life. I think we may also safely assume that the Swiss youth was a member of Moriarty's organisation from the part he played at the Reichenbach Falls in luring you back to the hotel, leaving me to face Moriarty alone. Agreed, my dear fellow?'

'Yes, Holmes,' I agreed in a low voice, reluctant to be taken back even in memory to that dreadful afternoon in the Bernese Oberland when the Swiss youth came running up the path to the Falls and, like a fool, I did not doubt the letter in his hand was genuine.

I have since castigated myself mercilessly for my gullibility. I should have known it was a trick! Holmes had apparently known this but had said nothing, realising that the time had come for a final confrontation with his arch-enemy. But to me, the message had seemed authentic. The letter bore the address of the hotel, the Englischer Hof, where we had been staying, as well as the signature of Peter Steiler. The contents also had the ring of truth about them. An English lady, in the last stage of consumption, had arrived at the hotel shortly after our departure and had suffered a sudden haemorrhage. Her death seemed imminent. Would I return to the hotel at once? It would be a great consolation to her if she died with an English doctor in attendance.

It was a fiendishly clever appeal. As a doctor how could I refuse, particularly as the patient was a compatriot? So, not without a certain reluctance, I had left Holmes standing there with his back against a rock, arms folded, gazing at the torrent of water as it gushed down into the abyss while the Swiss youth waited nearby, ready to escort me back to the hotel.

What an idiot I had been!

And now, here was Holmes calmly stating that this same youth was none other than the Watchful Waiter who was keeping vigil outside our lodgings, the intention of whom was presumably to complete the mission that Moriarty had set in motion all those years before at the Reichenbach Falls; in other words, the death of Sherlock Holmes.

I found my voice at last.

'Holmes, you must go to the police immediately!' I exclaimed.

He looked at me in utter astonishment.

'My dear fellow, that is the last thing I should do,' he replied.

'But if you do nothing that could very well be the last thing you will do anyway. The man intends to kill you!'

'Of course,' he agreed calmly. 'That is why he is here. I am well aware of that. I also have no doubt that, in the intervening years since we last met him at the Reichenbach Falls, he has been carefully coached by none other than our old antagonist Colonel Moran about how he should set about killing me. Moran is, after all, quite an expert in the black art of murder. Moriarty recognised his skills, which is why he made him his chief of staff and used him for those special assignments which none of the ordinary members of his criminal gang could have undertaken. Remember the death of Mrs Stewart of Lauder in 1887? I am certain Moran was guilty of that crime, although, like the Camden House affair, nothing could be proved. Then there was the time immediately after Moriarty's death when I was lying on that ledge above the Reichenbach Falls and he fired down at me with that special airgun of his.[9] It was a wonder he did not finish me off then, considering he is one of the best shots in the world. Remember? And then more recently there was the

---

[9] Colonel Moran's special airgun was made by von Herder, the blind German mechanic. Dr John F. Watson.

murder of Ronald Adair, whom he shot through the open window—'[10]

'Yes, I *do* remember, Holmes, and that is why you should go to the police.'

'And tell them what?'

'Everything, of course.'

'My dear Watson, we have had this conversation before. Do you not recall it? It was when Moran was at large and I explained at the time that there was little I could do to protect myself. I could not shoot him, or I myself would have been charged with murder. I could not appeal to a magistrate. The law would not have acted on what was mere suspicion. I am in exactly the same position now with regard to the Waiter.'

'Oh, Holmes!' I cried out, horrified by the hopelessness of it all.

He was at my side in a moment.

Placing a hand on my shoulder, he said, 'But that does not mean we have to give up, Watson. I have learned a great deal from my experiences with that old *shikari*,[11] Moran. Believe me, we will get the better of him. In fact, I have already put a plan into motion which I think will see him behind bars.'

'A plan!' I exclaimed. 'What plan? Does it involve Sheridan Irving?'

---

[10] Moran shot Adair through the open window of his drawing-room, almost certainly from Hyde Park, which was across the road from his house in Park Lane. Dr John F. Watson.

[11] *Shikari* is the Hindi word for 'hunter'. Dr John F. Watson.

Holmes looked uncomfortable, one of the few occasions when I have seen him ill at ease.

'Now, look, Watson—' he began, but for once I overrode him.

'No, *you* look, Holmes. If you are going to involve Irving in any plan regarding the Waiter, I insist he is informed of the exact circumstances. You have made it clear that the Waiter could be seeking revenge on you. And, if I am not mistaken, your plan is to use Irving, who resembles you, as a decoy. Am I correct?'

For a long moment there was silence as he stared off across the room, his expression inscrutable, and I thought, for a dreadful second, that I had gone too far. He was deeply angered by what I had said and, as a consequence, I had damaged our friendship, perhaps beyond repair. But at the same time, I could not in all honesty feel any regret. I had been right to speak out on Irving's account. Had I not done so, I would have let myself down – quite how or why I found it difficult to define.

The silence hung like a threat between us, thickening the air until it became so heavy I could bear the weight of it no longer and I was about to cry out, to say something, anything – quite what I did not know. An apology, perhaps? A word of reconciliation?

It was Holmes, thank God, who took the initiative.

Turning his head, he looked me straight in the face, his expression sombre, and when he spoke, his voice was low-pitched and grave.

'You are correct, Watson. I have no right to involve Irving or, come to that, you, too, my dear friend, in any plan that might put your lives at risk. I was being insufferably arrogant and for that I apologise. The only excuse I can offer is that my resolve, nay, almost my *raison d'être*, is to rid this world of these last scourings of Moriarty's organisation, including Colonel Moran if, as I believe, he is still alive, and this young man, the Waiter, who is the malignant spawn of their conspiracy, before they can infect the rest of society. But in doing so, I must play according to the rules, otherwise I shall descend to their level. I see that now, Watson, and I am grateful to you for pointing this out to me.

'I also realise that I must not only rethink my plan but I must explain my intentions fully to Irving, so that he understands the risk before he agrees to take part in it.'

'Do you think he will?' I asked rather hesitantly, for I could not imagine Irving taking kindly to any plan that put his life in danger.

'We can only hope for the best,' Holmes replied, smiling wryly as he went to the door, adding over his shoulder, 'I may be gone for some time, Watson. There are several other details I must attend to as well as seeking out our erstwhile luncheon companion.'

I wanted to call out 'Good luck!' after him but the door had closed and he had gone before I could utter the words.

He was away for several hours, during which time

I fretted at his absence and mulled over in my mind the question as to whether or not Irving would agree to taking part in Holmes' plan. I decided finally that he would probably reject it. Having met the man, there seemed to be no other outcome. He was not the type to risk himself or his well-being for anyone else.

I was therefore in very low spirits when at last I heard the street door slam shut and Holmes' footsteps coming up the stairs. I listened hard to them, hoping they would give some clue to his state of mind, foolish though that might seem. But they gave nothing away. Neither did his expression, although I scanned his face eagerly as he entered the room.

'Well, Holmes?' I demanded. 'What happened? Did you meet Sheridan Irving? What did he say?'

'My dear fellow, so many questions!' Holmes exclaimed. 'Pray let me sit down first. And, by the way, a cigar and a whisky and soda would not come amiss.'

As I bustled about between the tantalus and the gasogene, Holmes helped himself to a cigar from the coal scuttle[12] and, when both of us were served, we settled down by the hearth.

---

[12] Sherlock Holmes kept his cigars in the coal scuttle and his tobacco in the toe of a Persian slipper. A tantalus is a container for holding decanters of whisky, brandy and other spirits. It could be locked to prevent servants from having access to it. A gasogene was an apparatus for making soda water. It consisted of two glass globes, one of which contained an acid and also an alkali carbonate. When water was passed through it, the chemical reaction aerated the water. Dr John F. Watson.

'Now,' Holmes declared as the smoke from his cigar rose in languid coils above his head, 'as with all stories, I shall start at the beginning. First, Sheridan Irving.'

'Did he agree?' I broke in eagerly.

Holmes burst out laughing.

'Oh, Watson, Watson!' he chided me. 'I know you have taken upon yourself the role of my biographer[13] but even so, pray let me tell my story in my own way. As soon as I left here, I sent a telegram to Irving, asking him to meet me at our usual rendezvous, a small, discreet tavern off Fleet Street. We never meet at his house. I fancy he is a little ashamed of its location.

'Anyway, we met and I explained to him the exact circumstances, including the involvement of the Waiter and the possible danger to anyone who had dealings with him. And to get to the point, my dear fellow, he agreed, much to my astonishment.'

'Agreed?' I echoed, my own astonishment mingled with profound relief that, with Irving taking the part of Holmes, the Waiter might see through the ruse and abandon any plans he had of attacking my old friend.

'Indeed so, Watson. And what is more, he agreed without a moment's hesitation. I think I have seriously underestimated him, for which I apologise deeply to him in his absence. I had no idea he was made of such mettle.

---

[13] In 'The Adventure of the Blanched Soldier', Sherlock Holmes refers to Dr Watson as 'my old friend and biographer'. Dr John F. Watson.

'So, that aspect of the situation being settled, I went through the plan in detail. As already agreed, he is to come here next Wednesday early in the morning, when he will put on one of my suits of clothes and at ten o'clock, by which time the Waiter should have arrived and begun his vigil, you and Irving will set out together from the house. As soon as both of you are a little distance down the street, I shall fall in behind you suitably disguised so that, should the Waiter look back, he will not recognise me.

'I shall, of course, be armed and so shall you. In addition, you and Irving will be wearing a special jacket, two copies of which a tailor in Cripplegate is, at this very moment, fabricating according to my instructions.'

Curiosity got the better of me and I could not help intervening.

'A jacket?' I queried.

'Yes, a jacket, one each for you and Irving. It occurred to me that the Waiter, not being a gentleman, will not play according to the rules. If I am correct, he will not, therefore, confront you face to face but will take the coward's way out and will assault you from behind. But to make sure, I have made arrangements for your backs to be covered just in case. But more of that later.

'First, let us consider what we know of the tactics Moran is likely to employ. If my assumption is correct and he is still alive, he will have tutored the Waiter in using similar methods. Judging by his previous conduct,

Moran prefers to attack from a distance, as his attempts on my life at the Reichenbach Falls and again at Camden House demonstrate. In neither case was the assault made at close quarters. The same applies to the murder of the Honourable Ronald Adair. He too was shot from some distance, in his case from Hyde Park on the opposite side of the road.

'In all instances, the murders, or attempted murders, were committed with a powerful airgun which was virtually silent apart from a whizzing sound when the bullet was ejected.

'To take another example. Parker, also a member of Moriarty's gang, who waited outside our lodgings in Baker Street, was a garrotter who practised another form of silent assassination, although in his case at closer quarters. In thinking over these various incidents, it occurred to me that the Waiter had almost certainly been coached by Moran in similar methods of murder, using a weapon that is easily concealed and, if used competently, can kill a man in seconds. Not a gun – even an air gun makes a noise – nor a garrotte either. The Waiter is slight of build and shorter than the proposed victim who is, of course, myself. Besides, I have trained in martial arts[14] and might fight back before he could finish me off. So what would he be likely to use?

---

[14] Sherlock Holmes had trained in *baritsu*, a Japanese form of self-defence. Dr John F. Watson.

'The obvious answer is a knife. It is silent; it can be carried in a pocket and, if used properly, can be lethal. It also kills at arm's length. So, putting all these facts together, I came to the conclusion that, having followed you and Irving, the Waiter will attack you from the rear. To make sure this happens, I dropped by at Scotland Yard while I was out and called on the services of Stanley Hopkins[15] who will arrange for a constable wearing a postman's uniform to walk a little way in front of you, thus forcing the Waiter to attack you from behind.

'Now for the details of my plan, Watson: the place where the attack will occur, which must be our choice, not the Waiter's. So, my dear fellow, if you fetch your coat and stick, I will show you its exact location.'

The following Wednesday morning every part of Holmes' plan was ready to be put into action. The site for the attack had been inspected and approved of and the various participants were allocated their positions. In the meantime, the main actor in the coming drama, Sheridan Irving, had arrived and had changed into a set of Holmes' clothes under which he was wearing one

---

[15] Stanley Hopkins was a young Scotland Yard detective who accompanied Sherlock Holmes on several of his investigations and whom he thought 'promising'. Sherlock Holmes advised him on some inquiries including the murder of Willoughby Smith ('The Adventure of the Golden Pince-Nez') and the case involving Sir Eustace Brackenstall in the Abbey Grange inquiry. Dr John F. Watson.

of the special jackets that had been made according to Holmes' design and were delivered the previous evening.

It was a curious garment, resembling a short, sleeveless coat, the back of which consisted of a layer of quilted canvas stuffed with horsehair that proved to be stab-proof when tested. It was not uncomfortable, as I discovered when I put mine on, Holmes having insisted I wore it even though it seemed unlikely that the Waiter would attempt to attack both of us. Worn under a loose, unbuttoned top coat, the extra bulk of the jacket was not too conspicuous.

Holmes' own disguise was simple in contrast. It consisted of a pair of workman's overalls, the capacious front pocket of which held his favourite weapon, a weighted riding crop. The whole outfit was topped off with an old peaked cap and a roughly trimmed beard.

Thus dressed for the roles we were to play, the three of us kept watch in the sitting-room at Baker Street, Irving pacing up and down as if waiting in the wings of a theatre to go onstage, I seated by the small fire that Mrs Hudson had lit to take the early morning chill out of the room, Holmes standing well back from the window, his eyes fixed on that tiny slit in the curtain that allowed him a narrow view of the scene outside.

He appeared quite calm but I, who knew him better than any other person, could tell by the set of his shoulders and the angle of his head that every nerve and muscle was alert and stretched tight like the strings of a violin.

It had been arranged that we would set our plan in motion soon after the Waiter's arrival, which was usually at about half past eight, thereby giving him as short a time as possible to settle down to his vigil and feel comfortable in his role. A good quarter of an hour before his estimated arrival, Hopkins' colleague was already in place, disguised as a postman, and was walking casually up and down the pavement, checking house numbers against the envelopes he was holding in his hand but ready, when the time came, to cross over the road and place himself in front of Irving and me, thus forcing the Waiter to fall in behind us. The other police officers assigned to the case had, I assumed, already taken up their agreed places.

The waiting was almost unbearable. Mrs Hudson and the boy in buttons had been instructed to keep strictly to their part of the house and under no circumstances to intrude on the hall or the stairs. The house itself was as quiet as a tomb, the only noise the sound of footsteps and the clatter of horses' hooves and wheels passing by in the street outside; and the inexorable ticking of the clock on the mantelpiece as the minute hand crept closer and closer to the half hour.

I watched it with a dreadful fascination.

Then, just before it reached it, Holmes lifted

his hand, signalling the arrival of the Waiter, and I managed to catch a glimpse of him by half rising from my chair and craning my neck to the right. He was partly hidden by the lace curtain and appeared as little more than a gauzy figure, ghost-like in its vague insubstantiality.

After what seemed like an eternity, the hand of the clock pointed at last to the quarter hour, the time we had decided to put the plan into motion, and, with a glance to the left and right to make sure we were all ready, Holmes nodded and the three of us started for the door, Irving and I first, Holmes waiting for half a minute before following us down the stairs.

As Holmes had instructed us, we walked at a normal pace and, strong though the temptation was, neither of us glanced back to see if the Waiter was following behind, although I imagined I could feel his presence a few paces to the rear, like some evil phantom dogging us at every step we took.

It was Holmes' decision that the chase should not be drawn out but should be quick and decisive, in order to take the Waiter by surprise and to rob him of any opportunity to guess our movements.

According to the plan, we turned right into Fulbeck Way about fifty yards from our lodgings in Baker Street, a quiet byroad with very little traffic and, at that time of the morning, few passers-by. Shortly before we took the turning, the policeman, who was acting the part of the postman, overtook us as arranged and walked on a few paces ahead to prevent the Waiter from making a frontal attack, as he did so opening the leather bag he was carrying over one shoulder and extracting a handful of letters. At the same time, he glanced up at the numbers on the houses as if checking the addresses. Unknown to the Waiter, he was also carrying a nightstick[16] and a pair of handcuffs in the bag.

Seconds later, as rehearsed the day before, Irving and I turned down a narrow passageway leading to an alley that ran at right angles to Fulbeck Way and gave access to the back gardens that lined the street.

This was the most crucial part of the plan and was vital to the successful arrest of the Waiter. Would he suspect a trap? Or would he follow us into the alley where Stanley Hopkins and two of his colleagues were waiting just out of sight?

It was no more than twenty paces to the corner but never before had such a short distance seemed so interminable. And as I walked, I seemed to hear Holmes' last-minute instructions ringing in my ears. Walk and act normally. Do not hurry. Whatever you do, you must *not* look back. And lastly, as a special piece of advice to me when Irving was out of earshot: Do not use your gun unless you are forced to do so. There will be several

---

[16] A nightstick was a weapon carried by a constable on night patrol. It was similar to a truncheon, only longer, and would be suspended from his belt together with his whistle, his rattle and a lantern. Dr John F. Watson.

of us in a confined space and you will run the risk of shooting one of them.

'Besides,' Holmes added, 'I would prefer that the Waiter is taken alive.'

In that short walk along the passageway, Sheridan Irving played his part better than I. Perhaps his training as an actor had taught him how to control any stage fright he might feel, or his self-confidence buoyed him up. True to his nature, he talked the whole time, exclusively about himself and, as far as I could make out, although I hardly took in what he was saying, it was about the time he played the leading role in a production of *Hamlet* in Stroud.

'Ghastly dressing-rooms but you should have heard the applause at the end! Deafening, my dear!'

Instead my attention was fixed on the high brick walls that enclosed the passageway, the ugly monotony of their scabbed, sooty surfaces broken here and there by a stray tendril of ivy that had scrambled over the broken glass that topped them, as if desperate to escape.

I was walking now as an automaton, placing one foot in front of the other, watching as the corner of the alleyway came nearer and waiting for the signal that would set the whole plan into motion.

It came at last: a double blast on a whistle, and suddenly the whole scene erupted into action. Seizing Irving by the arm, I shouldered him into the angle where the alley and passageway met, drawing my gun at the same time. Simultaneously, I saw Stanley Hopkins dart forward in front of me and place himself between us and the figure of the Waiter that came bounding towards us like a panther, clutching something metallic in his hand that caught the light as he raised it to shoulder level.

It was the first time I had seen him without the intervening screen of the lace curtain and I was struck by his youth and the pallor of his face, accentuated by the blackness of his eyes and hair, a flap of which fell across his forehead. But there was some other quality about him that made an even deeper impression on me. It was the madness of his expression and the look of utter hatred such as I had never seen before on a human face, and I instinctively drew back, shocked by the nakedness of the emotion.

The next moment, his face had disappeared under a scrum of bodies amongst which I recognised that of Hopkins and the erstwhile postman, shoulder bag abandoned, who were in the thick of the mêlée. Holmes stood a little to one side, like a referee.

The Waiter fought so fiercely that it took several minutes before he was subdued and led away in handcuffs by two uniformed constables, followed by Stanley Hopkins, who was carrying a sharp knife with a six-inch blade that he had retrieved when the Waiter had dropped it to the ground. It was a deadly-looking weapon which even Stanley Hopkins handled with respect.

At my side, Sheridan Irving expelled a long, drawn-out sigh of relief and admiration.

'That was excellent!' he remarked. 'I haven't seen a fight so well staged for years. Congratulations to your stage manager!'

It had been arranged that Stanley Hopkins would call on us at Baker Street later that evening, once the formalities of charging the Waiter of attempted murder and committing him to the cells had been completed; a lengthy process, it seemed, for it was nearly nine o'clock before he arrived.

Holmes had gone out of his way to make him feel welcome. A cheerful fire was burning on the hearth, coffee had been made and one of Mrs Hudson's excellent fruit cakes was set out on the low table, together with the necessary china and cutlery. I also noticed the decanters in the tantalus were topped up with whisky and brandy, should a more celebratory refreshment be called for.

'Well, gentlemen, that was a most satisfactory day's work!' Hopkins declared, rubbing his hands together as the boy in buttons ushered him into the room. 'The arrest of the Waiter was an enormous feather in our caps, including mine. But, of course, you don't know yet who he is. His real name is Hans Tetzner and he's wanted by the Austrian police on several serious charges, including murder, attempted assassination and suspected treason.'

In his eagerness to pass on this information, he had remained standing by the door, looking flushed with excitement. He was a young inspector – only in his thirties – alert, intelligent and very impressed by Holmes' methods of detection. In his turn, Holmes respected him and had high hopes for his future career in the force. There was an enthusiasm about him that was almost boyish in its fervour and was immediately disarming.

Smiling, Holmes waved him forward to a chair by the fire.

'Coffee?' he suggested. 'Or something stronger?'

'Well,' Hopkins began, his glance straying toward the tantalus as he took his seat, 'I am off duty and it is a bit nippy out tonight, sir.'

'Then whisky all round it shall be,' Holmes declared, nodding to me to do the honours with the glasses and the decanter.

When the three of us were settled, Holmes turned to our guest.

'Now, my good Hopkins, tell us all you know about Hans Tetzner. But before you begin, there is a question I must ask you about a matter that needs settling first. Does a Colonel Sebastian Moran figure at all in your account?'

Hopkins immediately sat up, his glass halfway to his lips.

'Not under that name, Mr Holmes. But my Swiss contact, Erik Werner, did mention a Colonel Victor

Norland. A big man, he said; late Indian army; excellent shot.'

'It must be the same man,' Holmes replied with a satisfied air. 'So the old *shikari* is still alive. I thought he might be. It would be a good day's work to see the pair of them, Tetzner and Moran, in handcuffs together. An excellent bag indeed!'

Hopkins pulled a rueful face.

'Then I'm afraid I shall have to disappoint you, Mr Holmes. According to Herr Werner, the Swiss authorities have lost sight of him. It seems he jumped ship, so to speak, a couple of days ago. But they're looking for him and we are also determined to round him up, together with his little gang.'

'Gang?' Holmes repeated, his eyes brightening.

'Oh, yes, Mr Holmes. There's quite a little nest of them, some of them counts and young army officers.'

'Do you know the names of any of them?' Holmes inquired, leaning forward eagerly.

'Now I come to think of it, Herr Werner did mention two or three names. Let me have a think . . .' Hopkins replied, setting down his empty glass in order to rub his chin with a display of concentration that would have impressed even Irving.

Holmes hastened forward with the decanter to top up the inspector's glass before retiring to his own chair where he sat, elbows on knees, looking across at Hopkins with such avid intensity, as if trying to extract the information from him by sheer willpower. Aware of this fixed scrutiny, Hopkins cleared his throat and took a sip from his replenished glass.

'Well, Mr Holmes,' he said at last, 'there was a Baron von Staffen, an Ernst Hiedler[17] and Gustav somebody-or-other, but I can't remember the rest of his name.'

'Were they all Swiss nationals?'

'No, not all of them. As Herr Werner pointed out, quite a few were German, including that waiter we arrested.'

'Was he indeed?' Holmes murmured in a nonchalant manner, having apparently lost interest in the subject, although, knowing him as well as I do, I realised his interest had been aroused, an assumption that was later to prove correct after Stanley Hopkins had taken his leave.

'You realise how important this matter is, Watson?' he asked as soon as the door closed behind the inspector.

'You mean the Waiter being German and not Swiss?'

'Exactly! But there is more to it than the mere matter of nationality. Hopkins named two other members of the gang associated with the Waiter, alias Hans Tetzner. I wondered if we might know of others who could be included in the list.'

'Others?' I queried, unsure as to whom he was referring.

---

[17] I have not been able to trace Baron von Staffen or Ernst Hiedler and I suggest that they were either unknown to Erik Werner or, like Colonel Moran, they were using false names and identities. Dr John F. Watson.

'Eduardo Lucas?'[18] Holmes suggested, raising a quizzical eyebrow.

'Eduardo Lucas!' I exclaimed. 'But surely you are not referring to the Second Stain case? You yourself stated at the time that the inquiry was a matter of high international politics and that, if the missing letter was published, it could involve this country – and I use your very words – in a "great war that could lead to the loss of thousands of lives".'

'Indeed I did. And I meant every word,' Holmes replied in a sombre voice.

'But Lucas is dead, Holmes!' I protested. 'He was murdered by his French wife!'

'I am well aware of that, my dear fellow. But that does not exclude him from having been a member when he was alive of that "little gang" that Hopkins referred to. We must also consider adding another name to that list – Hugo Oberstein's.'

'You mean . . . !' I cried, aghast at the implication.

---

[18] Eduardo Lucas was an international spy who had blackmailed Lady Hilda Trelawney Hope, wife of the Secretary for European Affairs in Lord Bellinger's government, into stealing a letter from her husband's despatch box which, should it be published, could lead to 'European complications of the utmost moment'. Sherlock Holmes, who was asked to investigate the case, deduced that the thief was Lady Hilda and persuaded her to return the letter to the despatch box. Eduardo Lucas, who was living a double life as Henri Fornaye in Paris with his mentally unbalanced wife, was murdered by her. She had followed him to his address in London and, seeing Lady Hilda enter the house, assumed her husband was being unfaithful and fatally stabbed him. Dr John F. Watson.

'Yes, I am indeed referring to the theft of the Bruce-Partington plans and the subsequent murder of Arthur Cadogan West.[19] As Mycroft himself pointed out[20] at the time, that too could lead to an international crisis. In fact, he took the situation so seriously that he promised me, should I undertake to recover the documents, I would have the whole force of the State behind me. In both cases I could see the hand of a certain European head of state who regards himself as a latter-day Caesar who, together with his chancellor, would seize control not only of our empire but of the high seas as well. If we do not heed the warnings, it will be pointless to urge Britannia to rule the waves as the song says because we shall have lost the game and, while we may not exactly be enslaved, we shall certainly become second-class citizens of the world.

'And that is not the end of it, Watson. There are even more sinister names that I believe should be included in

---

[19] Hugo Oberstein, also an international spy, arranged the theft of the plans of the Bruce-Partington submarine, 'the most jealously guarded of all Government secrets', from the offices of the Woolwich Arsenal, where Arthur Cadogan West worked as a clerk. Because Cadogan West had witnessed the theft, Oberstein murdered him and left his body on the railway lines outside Aldgate underground station, making his death appear as an accident. Sherlock Holmes was asked to investigate the case by Mycroft Holmes, his elder brother. Mycroft, who was apparently an auditor for the Government, was in fact a governmental adviser and was the *éminence grise* behind all its decisions. Dr John F. Watson.

[20] In 'The Adventure of the Norwood Builder'. Dr John F. Watson.

that roll-call of international gangsters and murderers who, if given the opportunity, would certainly rule the world. I am speaking, of course, of Colonel Moran who, as far as we know, is still alive.'

'So you see a connection between the two organisations, Moriarty's criminal gang and these international spies?' I asked, greatly puzzled by Holmes' assertion.

'Indeed I do, Watson, for while they may appear to be quite separate, they both share the same aims: to seize control of any independent countries and to destroy all democratic principles. Both groups are inspired by greed for power and for the loot which power can provide once they have conquered Western Europe. Think of the gold in the banks, the profits made from international trade, not to mention the museums and the art galleries with their priceless paintings and historic treasures that will be theirs for the plundering! The line between ruthless politicians, avaricious businessmen and members of the criminal underworld can be very fine indeed and, at times, can become virtually invisible.

'We can, however, thank God that loathsome spider that sat in the centre of the web has gone. I witnessed his death at the Reichenbach Falls.[21] Those of his

---

[21] The Reichenbach Falls is a series of waterfalls near Meiringen in Switzerland. It was where Sherlock Holmes met his arch-enemy, Professor Moriarty, for a final confrontation in May 1891. Dr John F. Watson.

organisation who remain are mere insects compared to him, although, if roused, they can still sting and, if there are enough of them, they can, like soldier ants, come swarming out of their nests and devour much larger creatures than themselves. Hans Tetzner was one of them. His mission, entrusted to him by Moriarty himself, I believe, was to destroy me should his other plans, such as the one involving the Dutch steamship *Friesland*, fail.

'Tetzner's presence in the plot is the only bright spot on an otherwise dark horizon. It suggests that Moriarty's confederates are either running out of suitable candidates for professional assassins or of the experts to train them in the skills of homicide.'

'Then that is good news, is it not, Holmes?' I asked, trying for his sake as well as mine to take an optimistic view of the situation.

His reply did little to cheer me.

'For the time being, Watson, for the time being. But mark my words, old friend. We must be on constant watch or the soldier ants will attempt to engulf us.'

It was a prediction I was to recall with awestruck amazement at my old friend's prescience when, eighteen years later, on 2nd August 1914, two days before the outbreak of the Great War, we stood together on the terrace of the house at Harwich belonging to von Bork, the Prussian master spy whom Holmes had captured and whom he was later to hand over to Scotland Yard. Standing there in silence we looked east over the moonlit sea to where those soldier ants were already gathering and whose mission, like Moriarty's, that arch-fiend, was to bring about the downfall of us and all that we, and millions like us, held most precious: our liberty and our lives.

Read on for an extract from the previous book
in The Sherlock Holmes Collection,
The Secret Notebooks of Sherlock Holmes . . .

THE CASE OF THE
UPWOOD SCANDAL

It was a bitterly cold November morning, not long after my old friend Sherlock Holmes and I had returned to London from Devonshire following the tragic conclusion of the long and complex Baskerville case,[1] when a visitor, a Mr Godfrey Sinclair, called at our Baker Street lodgings. His arrival was not unexpected, for Holmes had received a telegram from him the previous day

---

[1] The date when Sherlock Holmes undertook the investigation entitled 'The Hound of the Baskervilles' is disputed, but internal evidence suggests the late 1880s. The great Sherlockian expert William S. Baring-Gould has opted for the autumn of 1888. The account of the inquiry was first published in serial form between August 1901 and April 1902. Dr John F. Watson.

requesting an interview, but the reason for his visit was quite unknown, Mr Sinclair having failed to mention the nature of his business. It was therefore with some curiosity that we waited for Billy, the boy in buttons,[2] to show this new client upstairs.

'At least we know one fact about him. He is a man with a proper sense of the value of time. A businessman, would you say, Watson? Certainly not a dilettante,' Holmes remarked when, on the stroke of eleven o'clock, the hour fixed for his appointment, there was a peal on the front-door bell.

However, I noticed when Mr Sinclair was shown into the room, that his appearance was not quite that of a conventional businessman. His clothes were just a little too well-cut and the gold watch-chain looped across the front of his formal waistcoat a touch too decorative for a banker or a lawyer, and I marked him down as having a connection with the theatre, perhaps, or some other occupation in which the fashion of one's coat was of great importance.

---

[2] The first reference to Billy, the pageboy or 'the boy in buttons', surname unknown, is in 'The Adventure of the Yellow Face', ascribed by some commentators to 1882. There are several references to him in the canon. His duties included running errands and showing clients upstairs to the sitting-room. His wages were presumably paid by Sherlock Holmes. He should not be confused with another pageboy, also named Billy, who features in the later adventures at the turn of the century, such as 'The Adventure of the Mazarin Stone' and 'The Problem of Thor Bridge'. Dr John F. Watson.

He also had the bearing of someone used to the public gaze, an impression borne out by an air of social ease and almost professional *bonhomie*. And yet, beneath this social gloss, I fancied I detected a certain caution, as if he preferred to be the observer rather than the observed. Although only in his thirties, he gave in addition the impression of a much older man, experienced in the ways of the world and consequently wary of its practices.

Holmes was also conscious of his client's reserve, for I noticed his own features assumed a bland, non-committal expression as he invited Sinclair to take a seat by the fire.

In accordance with his punctual arrival, Sinclair came straight to the point in a pleasant but competent manner.

'I know you are a busy man, Mr Holmes,' he began, 'and I shall not waste your time with a long explanation of my affairs. To put the matter briefly, I am the owner of the Nonpareil Club in Kensington, a private gambling establishment which is, of course, by its very nature against the law.[3] Two of its members are a Colonel James Upwood and a friend of his, a Mr Eustace Gaunt, who joined the club only recently and about whom I am less familiar. Although several card games are played at

_____
[3] Until the Betting Act of 1960 was passed, all betting in public places was illegal, but gaming clubs such as Crockford's were well established, although they ran the risk of being raided by the police and shut down. Dr John F. Watson.

3

the Nonpareil, including baccarat[4] and poker, Colonel Upwood and Mr Gaunt prefer whist. Both appear to be accomplished at the game and visit the club regularly on a Friday evening at about eleven o'clock for a rubber or two.

'Generally speaking, the stakes are moderate and there is nothing in their play to arouse suspicion. Their gains and losses are more or less balanced. However, on two occasions in the past six months, they have won considerable sums, in one case of over £500, in another of £800. I noticed on these two evenings they were particularly careful in choosing their opponents, although it was subtly done and I doubt if anyone else observed this, certainly not the gentlemen they played against.'

'Who were?' Holmes interjected.

'I would prefer not to name them, if you have no objections, Mr Holmes. Suffice it to say that all four of them were wealthy young men, scions of well-known aristocratic families and inclined to recklessness, who

---

[4] It was because of a game of baccarat that Edward, Prince of Wales, became involved in the Tranby Croft scandal. He and some fellow guests were staying at a country house called Tranby Croft, the home of a rich shipowner, Arthur Wilson, in 1890 when a fellow guest, Sir William Gordon-Cumming, was accused of cheating at the game. He was made to sign a paper promising never to play cards again, which the fellow guests, including the Prince of Wales, also signed. But the scandal leaked out and Gordon-Cummings brought a libel action. The Prince was subpoenaed as a witness. The case was lost but the publicity damaged Edward's reputation. Dr John F. Watson.

had on the evenings in question indulged a little too freely in the club's champagne.

'Their losses probably meant less to them than they would to some other members, but that is not an excuse for cheating at cards, if that is what Colonel Upwood and Mr Gaunt were doing, as I strongly suspect they were. However, I have no proof. That is why I have come to you, Mr Holmes. I would like to know one way or the other for my own peace of mind and for the good name of the Nonpareil. If they are cheats, then my response is quite clear. I shall speak to the gentlemen in question, cancel their membership and warn the other clubs to which they belong of their activities. Are you prepared to take on the case, Mr Holmes?'

Holmes replied with alacrity.

'Certainly, Mr Sinclair! Your card-players are a refreshing change from the usual run-of-the-mill criminals. But I cannot promise immediate results. If the two gentlemen in question are indeed cheating, then they will clearly not indulge themselves every week. You said they play regularly on a Friday evening. Then I suggest my colleague, Dr Watson, and I call at the Nonpareil next Friday at half past ten and the subsequent six Friday evenings at the same time. If nothing suspicious occurs on any of these occasions, then we shall have to review our strategy. By the way, I think it prudent if we assume false identities during the investigation in case our names are familiar to any of your members. Dr

Watson will therefore be Mr Carew and I shall be Mr Robinson.'

'Of course. I quite understand,' Sinclair replied, getting up and shaking hands with both of us before giving Holmes his card. 'Here is my address. I shall expect to see you both next Friday at the time agreed.'

'Well, well!' Holmes declared after Mr Sinclair had left the room and we heard the street door close behind him. 'What do you think of the affair, Watson? Gambling, indeed! A case after your own heart, would you not say, my dear fellow, although, in your case, it should be horses or billiards, not cards?[5] How is your whist-playing, by the way?'

'I play a little,' I replied a little stiffly, for I was somewhat piqued by Holmes' teasing manner.

'Enough to win £400 at a sitting?'

'Hardly, Holmes.'

'Then we must not plunge ourselves too deeply in the game on Friday evening,' Holmes rejoined. 'A rubber or two should suffice, combined with a little stroll about the gaming-room to establish the lie of the land and to acquaint ourselves, if only at a distance, with Messrs Upwood and Gaunt. You know, Watson, or rather Carew, to accustom you to your new *nom de guerre*, I am quite looking forward to the assignment,' Holmes

---

[5] Dr Watson enjoyed betting on horses and confessed that half his army pension was spent at the races. *Vide*: 'The Adventure of Shoscombe Old Place'. There is no evidence that he bet at billiards. Dr John F. Watson.

continued, chuckling and rubbing his hands together. 'It is not often one is paid a fee for indulging oneself at one of London's better-known gambling clubs.'

The Nonpareil, as we discovered when we alighted from our hansom on the following Friday evening a little before ten o'clock, was not quite what I had been expecting. I had envisaged a more flamboyant establishment, its windows ablaze with a myriad of gas lamps and with a uniformed flunkey in knee breeches and a satin waistcoat to escort us inside.

Instead, we found ourselves mounting the steps of one of the tall, elegant houses which lined a quiet side street in South Kensington. The only decoration on its plain façade of brick and stucco was the rather severe iron railings to the first-floor balcony and the basement area. As for the blaze of gas lamps, only a subdued glow escaped round the edges of the tiers of heavily-curtained sash windows, lending the building a soft, shrouded air, like the proscenium in a theatre before the curtain goes up to reveal the stage.

There was no satin-coated footman to welcome us either, only a tall, pale-faced butler, dressed in black, who had the sombre gravity of an undertaker's mute.

As he took our cloaks and silk hats, I had an opportunity to glance about me and was, despite the initial disappointment, impressed by what I saw, although the interior of the Nonpareil no more corresponded to my image of a gaming-house than its exterior.

The foyer was square and plain, floored with black

and white marble tiles and, like the façade of the house, unadorned apart from two enormous gilt-framed looking-glasses, each accompanied by matching marble-topped console tables, which faced one another and created a bewildering profusion of reflections of Holmes and myself standing within a diminishing arcade of other gilt-framed mirrors, glittering under the lights.

When I had recovered from this momentary visual confusion, I saw that a pair of double glass doors led into a drawing-room furnished, like a gentlemen's club, with leather armchairs, ceiling-high bookcases and low tables on which were displayed newspapers and periodicals, meticulously folded. A bar, sparkling with crystal glasses and ranks of bottles, occupied one wall.

Another pair of double doors in the far wall allowed a glimpse of a supper-room beyond, where there was a long buffet table loaded with tureens of soup and huge platters of food, together with piles of plates and silver cutlery. Small round tables, covered with starched white linen, were scattered about at which several gentleman were already seated, making use of the club's hospitality. More were occupying the leather chairs in the drawing-room with brandy or whisky glasses in their hands, while soft-footed waiters padded about carrying silver salvers containing more glasses of wine, champagne or spirits.

The atmosphere was hushed. There were no loud voices, only a subdued murmur of conversations and the tinkling of glass, while the air was fragrant with the warm scent of cigars and wood smoke from the blazing fires, the aroma of leather, rich food and the fresh flowers which decorated both rooms as well as the entrance foyer.

Mr Sinclair must have been watching for our arrival for, hardly had we divested ourselves of our outer garments, than he came forward to greet us.

'Mr Carew! Mr Robinson! I am delighted to welcome you as new members!' he cried, holding out his hand to each of us in turn before escorting us up the staircase to a broad upper landing and from there into a large double salon running the width of the house. This, I assumed, was the gaming-room, the heart of the Nonpareil Club.

Unlike the discreet apartments on the lower floor, this huge chamber was sumptuously furnished and brilliantly lit. Four large chandeliers hung from the coffered ceiling, their radiance enriching the already flamboyant splendour of the gilded leather chairs, the ormulu and silver mounts on the furniture and the towering swags of scarlet and gold brocade which hung at the windows. The walls were painted with scenes from an Olympian banquet at which gods and goddesses, draped in diaphanous robes and crowned with gilded laurel leaves, dined to the music of lyres and flutes.

It was all much too extravagant and elaborate – a deliberate effect, I suspected, designed to create an atmosphere of excitement and hedonistic pleasure in order to encourage the players seated at the baize-covered tables placed about the room to indulge themselves more freely than they might have done in a more decorous setting. Although there were no overt signs of excitation, no raised voices or boisterous behaviour, the atmosphere was vibrant with an almost inaudible ebullience, like the faint humming from a hive of bees or the trembling left in the air after a violin has played its last note.

Mr Sinclair paused with us in the doorway, as if to let us, as new members, grow accustomed to our surroundings, murmuring as he did so, 'Look to your left, gentlemen, at the table nearest the far wall.'

We moved on, Sinclair stopping now and again to introduce us to those members who were not engaged in play, and both Holmes and I took the opportunity to glance covertly towards the table he had indicated.

Colonel Upwood was immediately identifiable by his military bearing. A bulky man, he sat stiff and upright in his chair, his tanned, weather-beaten features suggesting he had served in the East. During my own service in Afghanistan,[6] I had seen many faces similar to his. The flesh becomes dry and lined, like old leather, particularly about the eyes, where the effort of continuously squinting into the bright tropical light forms a myriad of tiny wrinkles in the skin, the inner crevices of which

---

[6] After training at St Bartholomew's Hospital in London and the Army Medical School at Netley, Hampshire, he was posted to India where he joined the 66th Berkshire Regiment on foot as an army surgeon in Afghanistan. He was wounded at the Battle of Maiwand in 1880 and was invalided out of the army with a pension of 11/6 a day, approximately 57 pence. *Vide*: *A Study in Scarlet*. Dr John F. Watson.

remain pale where they have not been exposed to the sun. These tiny lines created the impression of a jovial man, much given to laughter, but the eyes themselves were cold and watchful, while the mouth, under the clipped white moustache, had a grim, humourless twist to it.

His companion, Eustace Gaunt, who faced him across the table, was, by contrast, a thin, weak-chinned man, with reddish-brown hair and moustache. Although generally of a very undistinguished appearance, his most striking feature was his brilliant, dark-brown eyes, which were never still but were constantly darting to and fro. His hands were delicate, like a woman's, and had the same restless quality as the eyes, fluttering over the cards laid out upon the table or moving up to finger his cravat or the white rose in his buttonhole. The rest of him remained curiously immobile, like a dummy on display at a fashionable tailor's.

They made a strange, ill-assorted couple and, as Mr Sinclair drew our attention to them, I saw Holmes give a small start of surprise, followed by a stifled chuckle of amusement.

'Most interesting, Watson!' he murmured in my ear – a reference, I assumed, to their incongruous partnership. But there was no opportunity to follow up his remark, as Sinclair was arranging for partners to join us in a rubber or two of whist.

It was an uneventful evening. Holmes and I won a little and lost a little, our gains almost cancelling out our losses to our final disadvantage of three guineas. However, after the initial excitement of the novelty and sumptuousness of our surroundings had worn off, the occasion became rather prosaic. Because of his phenomenal gift of storing information which he can later recall at will,[7] Holmes was potentially an excellent card-player, for he could remember exactly which cards had been played and which remained in our opponents' hands. But the mental challenge was too trivial to keep him occupied for long and his attention soon strayed from the game, his gaze wandering from time to time in the direction of Colonel Upwood and Mr Gaunt. Neither man, however, seemed aware of his interest.

I, too, am not a dedicated card-player. After the excitement of the race-course, where the physical prowess of both horse and jockey can send the blood tingling through the veins, I found whist too static for my taste. I missed the roar of the crowd and the thunder of hooves on the turf. Even billiards had more allure, for in that sport the players at least have the opportunity to move about the table, while the co-ordination of hand and eye calls for real skill. In comparison, card games seemed quite tame.

It was two o'clock in the morning before Colonel

---

[7] Sherlock Holmes once stated: 'I hold a vast store of out-of-the-way knowledge, without scientific system, but very available for the needs of my work.' *Vide*: 'The Adventure of the Lion's Mane'. Dr John F. Watson.

Upwood and Eustace Gaunt left the club, having won, according to Holmes' calculation – for he had been surreptitiously assessing their play – the modest sum of about twelve guineas, not enough to warrant a charge of cheating.

We waited for half an hour before taking our own leave, so that our departure should not coincide too closely with theirs and perhaps arouse suspicions.

'I suppose,' I remarked when we were inside a hansom, rattling our way through deserted streets towards Baker Street, 'that the whole wretched experience will have to be repeated next Friday.'

'I am afraid so, my dear fellow,' Holmes agreed.

'What a waste of an evening!'

'Not entirely,' he corrected me. 'We have gained some very useful information about Gaunt and Colonel Upwood, including their methods.'

'Have we, Holmes? I saw nothing out of the ordinary about their play. They were apparently not cheating or they would have won more than they did.'

'So it would seem,' Holmes conceded. 'But we must wait upon events, Watson, rather than anticipate them. Like all greedy men, sooner or later they will succumb to the temptation of easy money. Meanwhile, I suggest we bear our souls in patience.'

He said nothing more about the case until the next Friday evening, when we again presented ourselves at the Nonpareil. As we mounted the steps to the front door, he remarked to me casually over his shoulder as he rang the bell, 'Perhaps tonight the game really will be afoot!'

But events were to prove otherwise.

As before, Godfrey Sinclair again introduced us to a pair of partners in the gaming-room and the four of us sat down together at one of the small baize-covered tables to play. On this evening, however, the *ennui* was broken a little by Holmes' insistence that we rose from the table from time to time to stretch our legs by sauntering about the room as other gentlemen were doing, pausing on occasion at other tables to observe the play.

We halted for less than a minute at our suspects' table, no longer than at any of the others, and no one in the room, I am convinced, saw anything suspicious in either our expressions or our bearing. Holmes' face, I observed when I took a sideways glance at him, registered nothing but polite interest. Only someone who knew him as well as I would have been aware of his inner tension. Like a fine watch spring wound up almost to breaking point, he was vibrant with suppressed energy, every nerve alert, every sense concentrated on the two men who sat before us.

As far as I could see, there was nothing unusual about their behaviour. Colonel Upwood sat four-square upon his chair, hardly moving or speaking apart from an occasional jovial comment to the other players about the fall of the cards.

'My monarch has been defeated in battle, I see,' he

remarked as his King of Clubs was trumped. Or, 'Never trust a woman!' when his partner's Jack of Hearts was taken by an opponent's Queen.

As for Eustace Gaunt, I noticed his nervous habit of touching his cravat or his buttonhole, a red carnation on this occasion, was still in evidence. So was the restless movement of his eyes.

The play was not very inspiring and we soon moved on to halt briefly at other tables. As we did so, I noticed that, as soon as we were no longer in the suspects' vicinity, Holmes' nervous tension subsided and he became merely bored, his eyes hooded with lassitude while his lean profile bore the pinched expression of insufferable weariness.

The next two Friday evenings followed much the same pattern. Upwood and his partner neither lost nor won any large sums of money and even they seemed to be growing fatigued with the play, for they left early at half past midnight, to my inexpressible relief.

I half expected the next occasion would be the same and I had to brace myself for the extended tedium of an evening of whist.

Holmes, too, seemed in low spirits, sitting in silence as we rattled in our hansom towards the Nonpareil Club. I felt that, like me, he had begun to despair of ever reaching an end to the inquiry and that it would continue indefinitely as a weekly torment, much like that suffered by the man in the Greek legend who was

15

forced to keep pushing a large stone up a hill, only to have it roll down again.[8]

But as soon as we entered the gaming-salon, I detected an immediate and dramatic change in his demeanour. His head went up, his shoulders went back and he gave a low, triumphant chuckle.

'I think we are about to witness the dénouement of our little investigation, my dear fellow,' he murmured to me under his breath.

I followed his gaze to the table where Eustace Gaunt and Colonel Upwood were already seated in the company of a pair of young men who, judging by their heightened colour and over-loud voices, had indulged themselves too liberally in the bar downstairs.

'The sacrificial lambs are on the altar,' Holmes continued in the same low tone as Colonel Upwood dealt the cards. 'The ritual fleecing of them will begin any moment now.'

We retired to another table and played a rubber of whist with two gentlemen who often acted as our opponents, but neither of us were at our best. Both of us were distracted by the game going on across the room, where soon a small, interested group of fellow members had started to gather. Even our opponents' interest began

---

[8] According to Greek mythology, Sisyphus, king of Corinth, captured and chained up Death, who had to be rescued by the god Ares. As a punishment, he was forced to push a large stone repeatedly up a hill, only to have it roll down again. Dr John F. Watson.

to shift to this new centre of attention until eventually all four of us by mutual consent laid down our cards and, getting to our feet, strolled across the room to join the company, which now numbered about fifteen.

It was clear from the bank notes and sovereigns lying on the table that Colonel Upwood and his partner had already won a considerable sum of money and were likely to win more, for their opponents, the two young gentlemen, although showing signs of unease, seemed determined not to admit defeat but to continue the game.

They were encouraged in this frame of mind by Gaunt and Upwood, whose tactics were subtle. Like two experienced anglers fishing for trout, they kept their victims in play, using the bait of letting them win two or three games in a row, thereby lulling them with a false promise of imminent success. The following game, of course, they lost.

From Holmes' earlier remark about sacrificial lambs, I assumed Gaunt and Upwood were cheating. However, although I watched them with the closest attention, I could not for the life of me see anything in either their manner or their behaviour which could warrant such a charge. There appeared to be no sign of *légerdemain* in the way they dealt the cards. Their hands always remained in full view on top of the green baize and, unless they were accomplished magicians, which I doubted, they were not substituting one card for another.

In all respects, they acted exactly as we had seen

them behave on those other Friday evenings when we had watched their play. As before, Gaunt's nervous mannerisms were in evidence, but no more than usual. Upwood also made the occasional facetious remark, referring to the Queen of Spades as 'the Black Beauty' and to the Diamonds as 'sparklers', an exasperating habit but one which appeared to be quite innocent of deception.

After a few minutes only, Holmes touched me briefly on the arm and murmured, 'I have seen enough, my dear fellow. We may leave.'

'But what have we seen, Holmes?' I demanded as I followed him to the door.

'Proof of their cheating, of course!' Holmes replied dismissively, as if that fact were self-evident.

'But, Holmes . . . !' I began.

There was no opportunity to add any further protest for, just outside the salon door, we met Godfrey Sinclair hurrying across the upper landing, summoned no doubt to the gaming-room by one of his subordinates, his normally urbane manner considerably ruffled.

'Mr Holmes . . . !' he began anxiously, but fared no better than I had.

'Yes, Mr Sinclair, they are indeed cheating,' Holmes informed him in the same brisk manner he had used to me. 'I advise you, however, to do nothing about it at this moment. I have the matter in hand. Call on me on Monday morning at eleven o'clock and I will explain to you exactly how the situation may be resolved.'

And with that he swept off down the stairs at a rapid pace, leaving his client standing at the top, open-mouthed at the decisiveness of Holmes' conclusion.

Knowing Holmes in this assertive mood, I did not mention the matter again and it was not until the following evening that he himself made any reference to it, although in such an oblique manner that at the time I was not aware of its significance.

'Would you care to spend the evening at a music-hall, Watson?' he asked in a negligent manner.

I glanced up from the *Evening Standard*, which I had been reading by the fire.

'A music-hall, Holmes?' I repeated, puzzled by Holmes' sudden interest in this form of entertainment, which I had never known him to favour in the past. An opera, yes; or a concert. But a *music-hall*?

'Well, it would make a pleasant evening out, I suppose,' I replied. 'Which one were you thinking of?'

'I understand the Cambridge[9] has several excellent performers on its programme. Come then, Watson. We shall leave at once.'

Seizing up his coat, hat and stick, he set off down the stairs, leaving me to hasten after him.

We arrived in time for the second half of the evening's

---

[9] I have been unable to trace a Cambridge Music-Hall, except for a small establishment in the East End of London, and I suggest it is a pseudonym for the Oxford Music-Hall in Oxford Street in London, where many famous performers appeared. Dr John F. Watson.

entertainment, which consisted of several acts, none of which I could see might be of particular interest to Holmes. There was an Irish tenor who sang a sentimental song about a young lady called Kathleen, a lady wearing a huge crinoline which opened like a pair of curtains to release a dozen small dogs which then proceeded to jump through hoops and dance on their hind legs; and a lugubrious comic with a huge nose and a check suit who told sad jokes about his wife which the audience seemed to find extremely funny.

The comic was followed by a certain Count Rakoczi, a Transylvanian of Gypsy origin, whom the Chairman[10] announced with a thump of his gavel as 'A Maestro of Mind-Reading and Mental Manipulation!'

I felt Holmes stiffen in his seat beside me and, guessing that it was this particular act which he had come to see, I myself sat up and concentrated on the stage as the curtains parted to reveal a man who, although short of stature, was of striking appearance.

His face and hands were of an unnatural pallor, enhanced by artificial means, I suspected, which contrasted dramatically with his black hair, dashing black mustachios and small pointed beard which gave him a Mephistophelian air. This black and white colour scheme was repeated in his apparel, in his gleaming silk hat and long black cloak which he removed with

---

[10] The Chairman introduced the acts, usually in a comically extravagant manner, and presided generally over the performance. Dr John F. Watson.

a flourish to reveal its white satin lining, as well as his black evening clothes and his shirt front, as blanched and as glistening as a bank of snow.

He passed his hat and cloak to his lady assistant who, in contrast to Count Rakoczi, was more exotically attired in a long robe which appeared to be made entirely out of silk scarves of every colour of the rainbow and which floated about her with each movement she made. Her headdress was fashioned from the same multicoloured silk into an elaborate turban and was sewn all over with large gold sequins which flashed like fiery stars under the gas lights.

As the applause died down, Rakoczi stepped towards the footlights to announce in a strong accent – Transylvanian, I assumed, should there be such a language – that he would identify by telepathic communication alone any object supplied by members of the audience, which his assistant would hold up. He himself would be blindfolded with a mask which he invited the Chairman to inspect.

The mask of black velvet was duly passed to the Chairman, who made a great show of holding it up for the audience to see before fully examining it with meticulous care. Having assured us that it would be impossible for Rakoczi to see anything through it, he then handed it back to the Count who, to a dramatic roll on the drums, pulled it down over his eyes. He then took up his position centre stage where he stood very erect, his arms folded across his chest and his blindfolded face raised towards the upper gallery. While this was happening, his assistant, gallantly aided by the Chairman, who rose to offer her his arm, descended the steps from the stage into the auditorium to a rustle of anticipation from the audience.

She moved up the aisle, stopping here and there to collect an item from individual members of the public which she held up for the rest of the audience to observe, addressing Rakoczi as she did so with various casual remarks in a strong contralto voice which also had a foreign accent, in her case more French than Transylvanian.

'What do I have here, Maestro?' she demanded, holding up a gentleman's gold pocket watch and letting it spin gently at the end of its chain. 'Oh, come!' she protested when he hesitated. 'It is a simple question. We are all waiting for the answer.'

Rakoczi lifted his hands to his face, pressing his fingers theatrically against his temples as if trying to concentrate his thoughts.

'I zee somezing gold,' he said at last. 'Round and shining. It iz hanging from a chain. Iz it a gentleman's vatch?'

'Can you tell me anything more about it?' his assistant persisted as the audience began to murmur its amazement.

'There are initials engraved on it,' Rakoczi continued.

'What initials are they? Let me have your answer!'

Again the fingers were pressed against the temples.

'I zee a *J* and an *F*.'

'Is he correct?' the lady assistant enquired, turning to the owner of the watch, who rose to his feet greatly astonished.

'Indeed he is,' the gentleman announced. 'My name is John Franklin. Those are my initials.'

There was an outburst of applause, which Rakoczi acknowledged with a bow as his assistant moved to another member of the audience.

Altogether, Rakoczi correctly identified five more objects – a signet ring, a black silk scarf, a pair of spectacles, a silver bracelet and, as the *pièce de résistance*, a lady's silk purse embroidered with roses, which he not only described in detail but named the number and the type of coins it contained.

During this mind-reading demonstration, I found my attention being drawn more and more to the Count rather than to his assistant, despite her more obvious charms, although Rakoczi, standing there centre stage in his black and white apparel, was himself a compelling figure. There was, however, something else about him which fascinated me. I felt I had met him somewhere before, quite where or when I could not remember. All the same, there was a disturbingly familiar quality about some of his movements rather than his features or his bearing.

I was still puzzling over this when the performance finished and the lady assistant returned to the stage, where Rakoczi, divested of his velvet mask, took her by the hand and, leading her towards the footlights, bowed with her to thunderous applause from the audience.

Hardly had the heavy curtains been drawn across the stage than Holmes got to his feet.

'Come along, Watson,' he whispered urgently. 'It is time we left.'

Giving me no opportunity to protest that there were two turns still to be performed before the end of the programme, a unicyclist and a famous soubrette well-known for her comic Cockney songs, who was top of the bill,[11] he hurried towards the exit, leaving me with no other option but to stumble after him.

'Where are we going now, Holmes?' I asked as I caught up with him outside the theatre, for it was clear from the purposeful manner in which he strode up the street that he had a specific destination in mind.

'To the stage-door,' he replied briskly.

'But why there?' I asked, much mystified by his answer.

'To interview Count Rakoczi, of course,' he retorted, as if the explanation were obvious.

The stage-door, a dingy entrance poorly lit by a single gas flare, was situated in an alleyway which ran alongside the theatre. Once inside, we found ourselves

---

[11] This is probably a reference to Marie Lloyd, a very popular music-hall artiste who sang comic Cockney songs and performed sketches. Her real name was Matilda Alice Victoria Wood (1870–1922). She first appeared at the Eagle Music-Hall under the stage-name Belle Delmare. Dr John F. Watson.

facing a small, booth-like office with an open hatchway, behind which the doorkeeper, an elderly, bad-tempered looking man smelling strongly of ale, kept guard, who, from his glowering expression, seemed determined to refuse any request we might make. However, a florin soon weakened his resolve and he agreed to deliver one of Holmes' cards, on which he had scribbled a short note, to Count Rakoczi's dressing-room.

Shortly afterwards he returned to conduct us to this room, where we found Rakoczi standing facing the door as we entered, a look of acute anxiety on his face.

He had stripped off his stage persona, not just the evening clothes, which he had substituted for a shabby red dressing-gown, but also the appurtenances of his physical appearance, including the pallid complexion, the curly black mustachios and pointed beard together with the jet-black hair. He stood before us totally transformed from the dashing figure he had presented on the stage to a very ordinary man with reddish hair and a slightly undershot chin.

'Mr Gaunt!' I exclaimed out loud.

Those restless eyes which I had noticed at the Nonpareil Club darted from Holmes to me and then back again to Holmes, while one hand went up in a characteristic gesture to pull nervously at the lapel of his dressing-gown.

'You received my card and read the note, I assume?' Holmes remarked in a pleasant voice which nevertheless held a touch of menace. When Gaunt failed to reply,

Holmes continued. 'I have several courses of action open to me, Mr Gaunt. I could go straight to the police or alternatively I could inform Mr Sinclair or the manager of this theatre of your criminal activities. Any of these choices could lead to your arrest and imprisonment. Alternatively, I could leave you to remedy the situation yourself without my interference.'

Holmes paused and raised his eyebrows but Gaunt still failed to speak, although a slight inclination of his head indicated agreement with my old friend's last suggestion.

'Very well,' Holmes continued in a brisk, business-like manner, 'then this is what you must do. You must go immediately to Colonel Upwood and explain the situation to him. The two of you will then arrange to send to Mr Sinclair at the Nonpareil Club your resignations together with a full list of all the club members whom you have cheated and a precise record of the amounts. With that letter, you will send the money owed, so that Mr Sinclair can return it to your victims.

'Furthermore, you and Colonel Upwood will send me a written guarantee, making sure it is signed with your real name, that neither of you will ever play cards again for money. If either of you break that undertaking, I shall make sure that every gentlemen's club is told of your past misdemeanours, as well as every music-hall manager and Colonel Upwood's commanding officer. As a result, your reputations will be ruined. Do I make myself clear?'

'Yes, yes, indeed you do, Mr Holmes!' cried Gaunt, beating his hands together in so frenzied a manner that I feared he might burst into tears. To my great relief, Holmes nodded in my direction and we left the room before the man succumbed to this final humiliation.

'It was sheer good luck that I realised Gaunt was none other than Count Rakoczi, the self-styled telepathist,' Holmes remarked as we left by the stage-door and stepped out into the narrow alley. 'I saw a poster of him several weeks ago outside the Cambridge Music-Hall and recognised Gaunt as the same man the moment we entered the gaming-room at the Nonpareil. Of course, you realise how he and Upwood arranged the fraud?'

'I think so, Holmes. They used a form of code, did they not, to communicate secretly between themselves?'

'Exactly so, Watson. In the case of the music-hall act, it was certain words or phrases used by Rakoczi's assistant which told him what she was holding – a watch, say, or a purse. Other words indicated colour, number, initials and so on. No telepathy was involved; only a good memory and a convincing stage presence. Of course, the assistant also had to make sure that she chose only those items for which their system already supplied a code word.

'I am convinced that Colonel Upwood saw their performance and realised it could be adapted for cheating at whist, using not just words and phrases but also certain gestures to indicate which cards each of them held in his hand, thereby controlling the play. Gaunt already had several nervous mannerisms which he made a point of using habitually so that no one would think it suspicious when he fingered his collar, for example, or stroked his chin at the card table.

'It was a deception which they could not use too often, otherwise Sinclair and the club members would have suspected them of cheating. So they took pains to choose their victims with care, not experienced card-players but rash young men with plenty of money who might be expected to plunge in too deeply.'

'And always on a Friday,' I pointed out. 'Why was that, Holmes?'

My old friend shrugged.

'Possibly because it was the only evening in the week when Gaunt could persuade the manager of the Cambridge to change his placing on the bill, allowing him to leave a little earlier than usual so that he had time to remove his stage costume and make-up and take a cab to the Nonpareil.'

As he was speaking, he drew me quickly into a doorway, from the shelter of which we could watch unobserved the main entrance as well as the stage-door of the theatre. A few seconds later, we saw Eustace Gaunt, alias Rakoczi, emerge from this side entrance, dressed in street clothes, and walk hurriedly along to the main thoroughfare, where he hailed a hansom.

As it drew away, Holmes remarked with a chuckle, 'I think we may guess Gaunt's destination, my dear fellow.

If I were, like you, a gambling man, I would wager half a sovereign that he is on his way to Colonel Upwood's to lay my ultimatum before him.'

Holmes was, of course, correct, as usual.

The following day, he received two letters, one from Colonel Upwood, the other from Eustace Gaunt who signed himself as Alfred Tonks, presumably his real name. Both men unreservedly accepted the terms which Holmes had laid down.

That same morning, Godfrey Sinclair arrived to thank Holmes for his successful handling of the case and for avoiding the scandal which would have ensued had the affair been made public.

The two men had resigned their membership of the Nonpareil, and Upwood, who presumably was in charge of their finances, had enclosed a list of names of all those they had cheated together with enough bank notes to repay the money their victims had lost.

'A most satisfactory ending, my dear fellow,' Holmes remarked, rubbing his hands together gleefully after Sinclair had left. 'I suppose your faithful readers can expect a written account of the inquiry, suitably embellished in your own inimitable style. What will you call it? "The Adventure of the Colonel's Cardsharping" or "Scandal at the Nonpareil Club"?'

In fact, I decided to call it neither, nor shall I publish an account of the case.

A few days after this exchange, I received an answer to a letter I had written to my old army friend, Colonel

Hayter,[12] asking if he knew anything about a Colonel Upwood, as he had maintained closer contact than I with our former regiments[13] and was better acquainted with army gossip.

He wrote back to tell me that, although he had never met Upwood, he knew a little about his background and his service record, in particular one episode which my old friend thought would interest me, knowing of my own army experiences.

Colonel Upwood had taken part in the relief of Kandahar,[14] the garrison town in Afghanistan to which the British forces, including myself, had retreated after our tragic defeat at the battle of Maiwand on 27th July 1880. The town was besieged by a vastly superior Afghan force led by Ayub Khan, and was relieved twenty-four days later by the heroic action of a British force of 10,000 men, led by Major General Frederick 'Bobs' Robert, which, after a forced march from Kabul

---

[12] Dr Watson first met Colonel Hayter in Afghanistan, where he gave him medical treatment. The two men kept in touch and, on Colonel Hayter's retirement to Reigate, he invited Dr Watson and Sherlock Holmes to stay with him. Dr John F. Watson.

[13] Dr Watson's regiment was the 66th Berkshires. It is not known which regiment was Colonel Hayter's but he may also have served in the Berkshires. *Vide*: 'The Adventure of the Reigate Squire'. Dr John F. Watson.

[14] Kandahar was a strategically important Afghan town situated 155 miles inside the frontier with India, which was captured and garrisoned by a force of 2,500 soldiers, both British and Indian. The siege was raised on 31st August after twenty-four days. Dr John F. Watson.

to Kandahar of 320 miles across the mountains in the scorching summer heat, attacked Ayub Khan's camp, killing thousands of his men and putting the rest to flight. Compared to these losses, our own, thank God, were mercifully light, amounting to only 58 men killed and 192 wounded.

Without the intervention of that gallant force, those of us at Kandahar might have been starved into surrender with consequences which do not bear contemplating.

Among that relieving force was Upwood, then a Major, who was wounded in the left arm during the attack and was consequently, like myself, invalided out of the army with a pension.

One might therefore claim that my life was saved as much by the action of Upwood and his brave comrades as by that of Murray, my orderly, who, after I myself was wounded, threw me across the back of a pack horse and joined the general retreat to Kandahar.

In view of this, I feel it would be disloyal of me to publish this account of Colonel Upwood's subsequent fall from grace at the Nonpareil Club and therefore it will be consigned to my old army despatch box along with other unpublished papers, a fitting resting place, I feel, for this particular manuscript.

If you enjoyed *The Secret Archives of Sherlock Holmes*,
look out for more books by June Thomson . . .

∽

To discover more great fiction and to
place an order visit our website at
www.allisonandbusby.com
or call us on
020 7580 1080

THE SECRET JOURNALS
OF SHERLOCK HOLMES

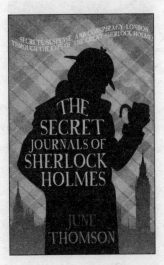

As Dr Watson's secret manuscripts are revealed to the public, a multitude of previously unseen cases come to light. A mysterious box terrifies a shopkeeper . . . Holmes and Watson feel the influence of an old enemy from beyond the grave . . . And a tragedy occurs which Sherlock Holmes will never be able to forgive himself for failing to prevent.

From the smoky streets of London to a countryside mental institution, the renowned detective and his faithful sidekick Watson must use all their cunning to solve this array of mysteries. Murders, madness and diamonds abound as June Thomson continues the Holmes canon with a brilliance and ingenuity that perfectly captures where Conan Doyle left off.

HOLMES AND WATSON

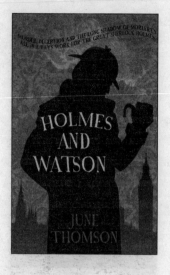

Sherlock Holmes and Dr John Watson, famous for their crime-solving capabilities, are mysterious figures themselves. What is known about their pasts, and the reasons behind their very different personalities? This detailed and enthralling account ponders answers to the many uncertainties and enigmas which surround the pair.

And there are other puzzles to be solved. Who was John Watson's mysterious second wife? And what is the real location of the legendary 221B Baker Street? A thorough investigation commences as Sir Arthur Conan Doyle's most famous creations are placed under the magnifying glass . . .

THE SECRET NOTEBOOKS
OF SHERLOCK HOLMES

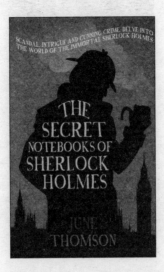

In Sherlock Holmes's London, reputations are fragile and scandal can be ruinous. In order to protect the names of the good (and not-so-good), Dr Watson conceals unpublished manuscripts in an old despatch box, deep in the vaults of a Charing Cross bank . . .

Now, outlasting the memories of those they could have harmed, these mysteries finally come to light. An aluminium crutch betrays the criminal who relies upon it for support . . . An Italian Cardinal lies dead in a muddy yard in Spitalfields . . . Can Holmes and Watson outwit the jewel thief who has the nerve to steal from the King of Scandinavia?